H.L. Swan

COPYRIGHT

This is a work of fiction. Names, characters, businesses, places, events and incidents are either the product of the authors imagination or used in a fictious manner. Any resemblance to actual persons, living or dead, or actual events is purely coincidental.

Copyright © 2020 H.L. Swan

All rights reserved.

Cover Design by Jessica Scott

ISBN-13: 9798638161019

Dedication

My Emden Family, this one's for you.

"I'd never given much thought to how I would die. But dying in the place of someone I love seems like a good way to go."

- Stephanie Meyer, Twilight

Prologue

Two Weeks Later

Sitting on the edge of an unfamiliar bed, Emilia rolls the white golden ring between her index finger and thumb, admiring it. Unshed tears sting her eyes, and she turns her head away.

The weight of the world crashing down on her is unbearable. For she is broken. The ring serves as a reminder of what she lost.

Leo attempts to drag her out from within herself. Despite the resistance she throws at him, he remains persistent.

Abandoning the glass, she grabs the bottle of wine and takes a long pull, relishing the burn of the bitter liquid as it drowns her sorrows.

Destruction will follow me. Just leave me be and let me chase my favorite ghost in circles.

Leo watches on with a worried expression before guiding her out onto the balcony that overlooks the Tyrrhenian Sea.

One

I've been sitting in this endless darkness for an undetermined amount of time. My tears have long since run dry. I stiffen when I hear the clacking of the medal padlock being messed with.

This is it. They found me.

Light filters in as the door opens.

I narrow my eyes, trying to see through the harsh morning light.

"Ms. Emilia?"

Howard's voice is small, so different than usual.

"I'm here." My voice is shaky.

He lifts me out, my body stiff from being confined in such a small space, and carries me across the rooftop. His movements are slow.

I bite my lips in worry, wondering how

he's still alive. From the looks of his bullet-riddled jacket and blood-soaked shirt, we are running out of time. His bulletproof vest is hard against my palms as I try to wiggle out of his grip. He needs medical attention immediately.

I notice a man by his side. He's close to my age, tall, dark and serious. He offers his help, but Howard declines.

My eyes frantically seek out Aiden.

There is blood everywhere.

In a gut-wrenching cry, I yell, "Where's he?"

"He's gone, Ms. Emilia. His body was taken away before I got you out."

Howard covers my mouth with a blood-stained hand, muffling my cry of despair.

I peel myself from his grip, focusing on a small red box on the ground.

"Howard, stop."

He nods, kneeling with a grunt.

I grab the box, holding it tight against my chest as Howard makes his way to the stairs. I examine it with a gasp. It was once white; Aiden's blood had stained it.

I sob against Howard's chest.

"Shh, it's okay," He murmurs through wet coughs.

"Howard, you're hurt. Put me down."

He shakes his head. "You're broken, Ms. Emilia, I can see it in your eyes."

I huff. "And you're shot!"

He ignores me.

"If you insist on me not walking, hand me to him." I gesture to the unfamiliar man walking alongside us.

Loyal to a fault, Howard declines. I hide my face in his chest as he carries me through the bullet riddled apartment, unable to look at the damage.

The stranger opens the car door and I slide into the backseat, focusing on Howard, because if I think about Aiden…I won't make it much longer. He lays his head in my lap. I apply pressure to his wounds, trying to stop him from bleeding out, but he grows paler still.

"Leo, take us to the cabin. Doc is there. If anything happens to me, do not deter from the plans." Howard directs his words to the stranger up front.

Leo nods and pulls out onto the road.

Howard looks up at me, his eyes somber.

"Don't die on me, please." I beg, my tears falling onto his salt and pepper hair.

He smiles. "You're like a daughter to me."

I flash him a weak smile, trying to muster up words. I check his pulse when his eyes flutter. I sigh when I feel a faint heartbeat. He's too close to death.

I direct my attention in front. "Look at me." My tone dead serious. "Go to the hospital."

Leo looks at me through the rear view mirror, his heavily accented voice echoing through the suburban. "I'm sorry, miss. But you heard him."

"I will jump out of this car if you don't stop," I threaten.

His lips lift slightly. "I have orders."

"Are you my guard?" I desperately need him to listen. He nods hesitantly. "Then I order you to go to a hospital. He's going to die if you don't!"

He continues to drive, ignoring me.

"My boyfriend was killed last night. I will not fucking lose anyone else!" I shout at Leo, my emotions clear as day.

Pinching the bridge of his nose, Leo stares into my eyes before panning down to a still Howard and nods.

Leo flings the back door open once we pull into the hospital. "Stay," He orders.

I shake my head.

With a huff of annoyance, he yanks off the black cap he just put on and plops it on top of my head, shoving it down as far as it will go to hide my face.

I haven't really thought of what to do once we got here, but I can't just leave Howard here alone. "Where do we go? The front door?"

Leo lifts Howard into a nearby wheelchair and heads off. His body is slumped, and his skin cold to the touch.

"We're going in the back. I have a friend who's a doctor here. We'll get him taken care of."

I struggle to keep up with Leo's long legs as we make our way through the back door and into the hallway. It didn't take long before we found the person that we were looking for.

I watch as Leo's friend looks Howard over before tightening his lips. He gestures for us into a room before quickly making his way around the space and gathering supplies.

"Put pressure on the wounds," He instructs me.

Leo shakes his head. "I don't want her seeing any of this." He gestures to an adjacent room. "Go wait in there."

My eyes pan around the small surgical room. I shake my head, refusing to leave Howard's side.

"Stubborn," Leo mutters under his breath.

Time slows as I watch him check each bullet wound, wincing in sympathy for Howard as he painstakingly digs around each hole.

He claps his gloved hands together, expression somber. "Good news is all the bullet holes are clear and sealed. Bad news is now we wait. I can't promise that he will make it. He lost too much blood."

I blink, realizing I don't know his name. "I'm Emilia, and you are?"

"Francis."

I nod. "Dr. Francis, I need you to do whatever you need to do. Please, just save him."

His mouth opens, ready to deliver more bad news.

But I'm not having any of it.

"She won't give up," Leo chimes in, a smile playing on his lips, clearly amused.

"I won't."

"He needs a blood transfusion. I'm going to run a test to find out his blood type. His situation is not looking good. I just need you to prepare for that."

I perk up, excited to be able to help in some way. "Doesn't matter. I'm universal. Use me."

Leo steps up next to me. His lean frame obstructs my view as he leans over Howard's body. "Run the test. See if I'm a match."

I push him back with much difficulty. "No, use me." I state with finality in my voice.

Leo throws his hands up, exasperated. "How has he protected you all this time?" He mutters.

We decide on a direct transfusion due to the lack of time, though the procedure took longer than I thought.

I squeak as the doctor inserts the sharp

needle into my arm, connecting me to Howard. Leo makes me eat crackers and ginger ale throughout.

I sit and wait next to Leo when it's his turn. I try to draw in his calm strength, thankful that he listened to me.

Howard will be fine now.
Thank God.
I sigh in relief.

Thick fog fills the air as we stand on the bare hilltop near the cabin in the dark of night.

We'd arrived at the safe house only a few hours ago. Leo and I had stayed overnight at the hospital as Howard recovered. He is doing better but he's still weak.

Ashley clutches my hand as I weep with her.

The funeral is short. The only people in attendance are me, Ashley, Ricky, a bandaged Howard, and two bodyguards. Leo is one of them, but I don't know the other.

I lay a single yellow rose on the closed wooden casket. Howard is by my side, a hand on my shoulder.

"Why couldn't I see him one last time?" I sniff, wiping at my tear-soaked cheeks.

Howard pats the closed casket, his voice rough, distant. "You wouldn't want to have seen him like this, Ms. Emilia."

I block out the stories of Aiden, not ready to reminiscence nor am I ready to smile at fond memories.

I'm fucking pissed.

The guards lower the casket into the damp earth, and we bury the love of my life.

Two

I look around the still unfamiliar room, taking in the comforting décor and rich floor to ceiling wood planks. Yet I still feel cold, my heart aching more each day.

We've been in the safehouse for a week. It's luxurious in true Aiden fashion, large enough to fit all of us.

I leave my designated room for only a few reasons.

To spend time with Ash; we either cry together, or I play with her hair. It's something we've always done. I braid hers, and she braids mine. Only now, we don't speak. We're never far apart.

I also visit Aiden's grave. Leo comes with me. He objected the first time he caught me sneaking out, until he realized I wouldn't give up.

Now, he stands guard at a respectful distance while I mourn. I like it when he smokes, the rich oaky smell is comforting.

The only other time I leave is to get coffee in the morning. I drink it all day long. The nightmares are too fresh and real to sleep. I always fix a cup for Leo. I don't know why, perhaps to show my gratitude for listening to me about Howard.

I call my mom every few days, who thinks Ashley and I are at a summer retreat for a month.

We still don't know who came after Aiden.

It can't be the Matarazzo brothers. They're dead. Besides, Ashley told them my name was Claire, so they wouldn't know who my mom is to begin with.

Nothing seems real anymore, as though I'm living someone else's life. My thoughts are constantly circling around my tired mind, and I can't escape.

I trace my finger across the A and E engraving on the white gold ring, written in cursive and showered in diamonds. Engraved on the inner rim is the day we first met. I clutch it to my chest with a sob.

I had something important to tell Aiden that night, but it seems so miniscule now. I got a full ride at Portland State. I know how much he wanted me to follow my passion and I wanted to surprise him with the good news.

But I don't know if I'm going anymore.

I have no desire to do the things I love anymore.

Because the one I love most isn't here.

Leo walks into the room, his expression stoic. "I need you to get up. There's something you need to see."

I've learned a few things about Leo from our nightly walks. He's twenty-three, born in Greece, and moved here five years ago for some sort of training. He doesn't talk much, but I pry to take my mind off of Aiden on our walks back from the gravesite.

"I'm fine."

This is the fifth time he's tried to get me out of my room today.

Leo's gray eyes are amused. "You can walk, or I'll carry you." He shrugs. "Your choice."

I roll my eyes and stalk past him.

He guides me to the leather couches in the spacious living room. Floor to ceiling windows showcase the lush scenery outside.

I've wondered how many times Aiden came here. I miss him so much.

Leo nods to Howard, before leaning in to whisper in my ear, "Be strong, okay?" With that said, he retreats to the kitchen.

With a grunt, Howard puts in a DVD and gestures for me to sit. I get under the blanket with Ash, who has Ricky on her other side. She holds my hand as we wait.

"You okay?"

She gives me a weak smile.

I feel awful for not being stronger, but we all grieve at our own pace, so I know she doesn't blame me.

"I guess…" She sighs, scooting closer to me. Through all the heartbreak, the one thing I can count on is Ash. We've clung to each other so much during this time.

Just then, the flat screen clicks on.

All I see is Aiden.

A sound so raw and sad escapes me.

Ashley cries into Ricky's chest.

Howard turns the TV off and comes over with a glass of water, placing a hand on my shoulder. "Ms. Emilia, I'm sorry. But Aiden made this tape for the three of you after he…got shot the first time." He looks over at Ashley. "Please tell me when you're ready to watch."

Ash nods silently.

I grab her hand.

How hard it must be for her to lose her brother. Ricky, his friend. Me, my heart.

We take a moment to breathe. Ashley finally musters up the courage to turn on the video and the grainy picture grows clearer.

Aiden sits at his desk. It's nighttime outside. He's in his suit, his hair a disheveled mess and his cufflinks undone. He looks perfect, but he looks…sad.

Hearing that velvet voice of his almost spins me out of control, but I stay calm, holding on to every word. It's almost unbearable having his warm voice envelop me.

"In the event of my downfall, I made this video. If this tape is being played, it's because I've been killed or had an accident." He runs a hand through his hair. "If you're watching this, I'm sorry."

Leaning back against his chair, he continues. "I leave my business to Ricky, my money to Ashley and Emilia. Howard, I don't know if you're okay. You're so loyal I'm afraid you're gone too. If you're not, and I hope you're safe, please watch over the girls. You've been like a father to us all."

Aiden nods, his eyes directed forward. "Ricky, you've been a loyal friend." He grits his teeth, his eyes softening. "Ash, I'm sorry I haven't always been there for you, but I hope you forgive me."

Ash smiles through her tears. "There's nothing to forgive. I love you," She mutters under a shaky breath.

"Emilia, I…" He stops talking and bows his head. "I need you to live, baby." He lifts his head and looks directly at the camera through thick lashes, as though looking into my soul. "I...I love you."

Then, the screen goes black.

I retreat to my lonely room and grab Aiden's computer out of the box of things Howard had brought. Ashley wanted to rest, so I'm on my own tonight. I'm thankful Ricky is okay with sharing her so much, we need each other now more than ever.

Besides his T-shirt that I wear to sleep, I haven't touched anything. Afraid that if I did, it would make his loss more real. But tonight, I need to see him. To get that anguished look of despair out of my mind.

I guess the passcode right on my first try. It's my full name.

I click through the folders of pictures with tear-filled eyes, the gradual timeline showing him enjoying life as our time together passed. I remember taking pictures of him the first time we met, his smile would be flat and serious. He was only ever playful behind closed doors, but he grew into someone happier.

I skim through his folders, half of them business memos and the other half full of photos and videos of me. One in particular catches my eye. It's a software program called 'Mine'.

EMILIA

My eyes widen after clicking on it. It opened a map, showcasing months of my activity. I smile. I had an inkling suspicion that the locket necklace had a tracker on it. Aiden's the type of man who wanted to wrap me up and keep me safe. I didn't mind it one bit.

I wish I had my necklace, I miss twirling it between my fingers. It was in his pocket that night. Howard said they couldn't find it when they took his body away.

I refresh the location.

Then, I stomp out of the room towards Howard's door with furious strides, clutching the closed laptop in my hands. I bang on the door hard enough that my knuckles grow sore.

Howard opens the door with a sleepy look, running a hand through his salt and pepper hair. "What's go–"

I cut him off by storming into the room and flip the light on. "Where is his body?" I bark.

His face grows tight. "I told you. We took it, and we buried him." He speaks slowly, as though I'm a child.

I roll my eyes. "We buried a box, didn't we?"

With a grunt, Howard drops down on the edge of his bed in defeat, clutching his bandaged shoulder. "His instructions were clear, Ms. Emilia."

I calm my voice to get him to see me as

someone other than a little girl he's trying to protect. "Please, Howard. Call me Emilia or Em. Ms sounds too formal." I give him a weak smile as I sit next to him.

He smiles. "Emilia, Aiden's instructions were very clear. If anything were to happen to him, I wasn't to give you hope."

"Tell me the truth please." I firm my voice, my eyes pleading.

"We never found his body."

A smile creeps onto my face. The feeling of my lips turning upward feels foreign. "Oh my God."

He holds a hand up. "It doesn't matter, Emilia. That's the issue. He didn't want us looking for him." He gives me a considerate look, gauging my emotions. "It's likely they took his body as a trophy or to hide evidence. There was so much blood." He lowers his head.

"So you just stop? You give up on him?" I scoff, looking at Howard in a different light.

He smiles at the ground. "Of course not. I already have men looking for him."

"But…whoever took him may have already done something. They wouldn't keep him for long. That's if he was even alive when they took him. Aiden said if something like this were to ever happen, I was to bury a box meant for him so you wouldn't spend your life searching. That was the protocol."

"Why would he put me through all of this if there's a chance?"

Howard places his hand over his mouth. "He didn't do it to be mean, Emilia." He pauses to catch his breath. "He did it because he doesn't want you chasing the ghost of a dead man."

I refuse to believe him. "I know where he is."

Howard's eyes dart to mine, his brow lifting.

I lift the computer screen and click on the tracker app with triumph. "Italy."

Three

Aiden

I'm dying.

The brine of saltwater is overpowered by the pungent stench of mold seeping in through the small barred hole of the metal door.

I've been in this dark and damp concrete basement for weeks, chained like an animal. The thick chains are rough against my blood-stained skin. The iron shackles they'd restrained me in have dug deep into my skin. If I were to somehow survive, I'd be scarred for life.

I've done everything in my power to escape. If I got back to Emilia, we could run away. But she's safe while I'm locked away. That's all I can ask for.

I don't know the men who took me.

I know the Matarazzo's are dead, so it wasn't them.

Who else did I piss off?

Fuck.

I hope Ricky and Howard followed my orders to take Emilia and Ashley to the safe house and keep them under lock and key for a while if anything were to ever happen to me. I can't imagine how they feel right now. I knew if anything like this ever happened, I'd be a dead man. I didn't want Emma chasing a ghost. I wanted her to move on, thinking I was dead and buried.

It won't be long until that's true. I can't fathom what it's like for her to be attending my funeral.

The metal door creaks open, snapping me from my daydreams as a sliver of artificial light seeps through.

A man walks in and slides a bowl of food across the concrete. "Eat," He orders, as though I'm a dog.

"Fuck you," I growl, kicking the bowl away with a grunt. Cursing the shackles for my limited mobility.

Why don't they just kill me? Why hold me here and give me no explanation?

No one has come to speak with me, nor

threaten me. It's as though they're waiting for something. But man, have they tortured me. What kind of man beats another man while he's chained up and defenseless?

I fucking hate having no control.

I wish they'd get it over with and kill me. I'm not afraid of death.

What's with the wait?

They've gotten smarter.

I was only in handcuffs before, but now I'm chained to the ground. After killing two of their guards with my bare hands when I escaped their restraints, they decided this was the best way to hold me. And it's working.

My only solace is that I know Ash and Ricky are safe with my Emilia.

I can die knowing I protected them.

I've never worried about another human other than myself until she danced into my life. From the moment I first saw her, she completely captivated my attention and heart. I've always told her she was mine. Even in my death, she will always be mine.

I wish I was good enough for Heaven. I know that's where she'll be many, many years from now. After she's had a long full life.

After she moves on and meets another man.

Fuck.

Has his children.

Oh, God.

And forgets me.

I hope Emilia Achelois Banks knows how much I adore her.

Four

Emilia

I tap my feet against the hardwood floor impatiently.

"I'm leaving tonight."

Howard looks at me with an amused expression and laughs. He stands and grabs a fresh shirt. "I forbid you from going. I will."

I place my hands on my hips. "You've been shot. You need to rest. You aren't going."

He ponders for a moment before nodding. "I'll send Leo."

"Leo doesn't even know Aiden." I lean in. "Is he even capable of rescuing him? I mean he's cool, but I don't know if he can handle something so important."

Howard laughs. "I wouldn't hire just

anyone to watch over you girls. Leo is a trained assassin. He's young, yes, but he's someone no one will want to mess with and he has a lot of connections. Don't ward him off so easily just because he falls for your charms."

I scoff playfully, my mood elevated. "What is that supposed to mean?"

"I know you talked him into going to the hospital when I ordered him not to." He stares at me pointedly.

I roll my eyes. "You would have died," I remind him with a blank face.

He shrugs. "I also know he takes you to his grave every night."

I throw my head back at his accusing tone. "But this is important. Are you sure he can do this?"

He smiles, happiness brightening his eyes. "He can easily kill twenty men with his bare hands. His only downfall is his incapability to say no to a pretty girl." Howard grows somber. "Emilia, you can't get your hopes up. It's been weeks. The tracker necklace could've been given away to anyone. Aiden could already be gone."

Rolling my eyes playfully, I ignore him. "Just to be sure. I'll go with Leo." I smile.

Howard throws his hands up, grunting in pain from the sudden movement. He grabs my hand. "Emilia, you can't. You must trust me. We don't know what's happening. Tomorrow, I'll find out more intel. But for now, go to sleep."

I nod my head and head to bed, laying there for an hour before sliding out to find Leo.

He can be easily persuaded.

I deftly stalk through the dimly lit cabin, trying to be light on my feet since the entire place is made of creaking wood. I'm dressed in black leggings and a black tank top to blend with my dark surroundings.

I cheer internally when I find Leo leaning against the porch rail, smoking a cigarette. The sight is so achingly similar to Aiden, I have to look away.

"You're not very sneaky."

I look up to see Leo only a few feet away now.

How did I not hear him move?

"I need your help."

He flicks his cigarette. "I know, I know. Aiden has a tracker on him. You want me to take you to Italy. Not gonna happen, Em."

I raise my brow.

He takes another puff. "I'm aware of your brave attempt to save him. Howard told me everything. He won't allow it. And neither will I."

I laugh. *Damn you, Howard.* "You can't tell me what to do."

He leans against the rail, looking bored.

"We're not going anywhere."

"Fine, I'll just go without you," I snipe back.

Leo is in front of me in a flash, his gray eyes glinting in the moonlight. "I already said I won't allow it. My sole job is to keep you safe. Here, safe. Italy, not safe. Understand?"

I bat my lashes. "Please," I beg, knowing full well I won't be able to save Aiden on my own.

He huffs.

I can tell he's caving.

"No."

But there's no conviction behind his words.

I've learned a few of his habits over the worst couple weeks of my life.

But the most important thing I've learned, because of Howard, is Leo can't tell me no.

I try to hide my Cheshire grin as Leo pulls out a large piece of paper to create a map from the tracker on the computer.

For the first time in weeks, I feel warmth.

"What are you going to tell Ash?" He whispers.

"Nothing." I bite my lip. "I know how broken she is. If I tell her what I'm doing, she'll want to come too. I can't risk her getting hurt."

Leo moves, placing himself close to me.

I tilt my head up to see his eyes staring into mine.

His carefree demeanor turns to a scowl. "Em, please, I beg of you. Stay with her. Stay here. Where you'll be safe."

I look around the room before moving away from his protective gaze. Only Aiden can look at me that way.

I give him a weak smile, changing the subject. "Let's get this done. We leave tonight."

He pinches the bridge of his nose with a sigh, a gesture that is so achingly similar to Aiden it makes my brain go foggy.

We begin planning our travels, mapping out every single detail.

"I've written a note for Howard. He won't risk telling Ashley or anyone where we are, out of fear of getting her hopes up, and it will be too late for him to stop us."

Leo rubs a large hand over his face. "You're going to get me killed."

After a long flight, we finally arrive where I need to be.

Campania, part of southern Italy.

I'm coming, Aiden.

Five

Aiden

A singular golden pendulum light swings overhead as three men storm into the room, pointing guns at my face while gesturing for me to stand.

"I'm chained, you stupid fucks!" I spit out.

"Up," One states in a heavily accented English.

I bite back a smile at their stupidity. I hold up my restrained hands and gesture to my ankles. They look among themselves, pushing one another until one finally arrives in front of me.

Bloodied, tied, and murderous, I lurch forward with all my strength.

Then, the butt of a rifle comes down on my head, knocking me out cold.

I wake up in a moving coffin.

The ground is soft. I feel the itchy material against my back and legs. The carpet of a trunk.

Why am I only in boxers?

The car lurches to a stop and the trunk pops open where I'm once again met by the butt of a rifle.

The new room comes into view as my eyes drift back into focus. It's much brighter, and nicer. I'm in a basement of some sorts. People are scurrying past the open door, butlers and maids with bottles of wine, ignoring me.

I'm leaned against a cold stone wall. My ankles and wrist are bound by heavy chains, instead of shackles. I can breathe a little more easily, though my wrists are bloodied still.

A man comes into view. His greasy smile matching his greasy hair. "Aiden," He drawls my name out slowly, sizing me up.

"Where are my clothes?" Anger coats my voice.

He shrugs, continuing his walk through the small room. He looks comfortable…arrogant.

"Why you so special?" He asks, his English a little off.

"I don't know. Tell me who fucking wants me, and then I'll enlighten you," I spit out.

"Feisty, even in chains."

"Take off the chains and we can see about that," I test him.

"Name's Marco," He says haughtily. "You'll know soon enough who wants you."

I lean my head against the cool wall, not bothering to respond. My wounds feel good against the cool hard stone.

"Why did they move me?" I ask, my voice uninterested.

"Those men…they fear you. Boss will be coming in tomorrow for party. He deal with you over weekend." He flicks his wrist nonchalantly.

"Pussies," I spit.

He leans down, coming to eye level with me. "Speaking of pussy, I have question." He smiles, his breath heavy. "You have girl back in America?"

My heart sinks into my stomach. "No," I answer flatly.

"Oh, come on, striking young man like you. Successful, powerful. No girl back home?"

"Only ones I fuck," I lie, trying to keep calm.

He shakes his finger with a laugh. "Too bad. After you dead, it be a fucking treat to get my men and I to run a train on your young American girl next to your corpse."

An instinct reaction.

My skull dives into his. I watch in satisfaction as he staggers back, his head hitting the hard-stone floor before blood begins to pool around him.

Whoopsies.

A new man walks in. Bald, short, sweaty. At the sight of the dead man on the floor, he runs his stubby ringed fingers over his face.

I shoot him a bloody smile, feeling as maniacal as I look.

He drags a metal chair across the stone flooring.

Smart.

"Giuseppe," He points to himself and nods, before sitting down. He holds up three fingers. "Three. You've killed three of my men."

His English is better, but his accent is thick. This is the most anyone has spoken to me since I was taken from the rooftop.

"And I was chained every single time." I shrug, wincing from the pain of my wounds and the ache in my head. "Maybe you need better men." I laugh.

"Two days." He brings a hand to his throat, a smile on his face. Then he slides a finger across his neck. "You be dead."

Six

Emilia

We stand in front of the concrete warehouse the locket last pinged at. My heart pounds as we creep closer. I'm dressed in black, same as Leo, to blend with the shadows. We slide around the side of the building, Leo keeping me behind him.

We arrived in the afternoon and I was itching to come straight here when we stepped off Aiden's private jet. I can't wait to be on our way home after we rescue Aiden, but Leo explained we needed to wait for nightfall.

The uneven walkway makes it hard to navigate in the dark, but Leo guides us. His movements are fluid and swift as he eases through the quiet streets of Italy silently.

We hear some shuffling just as we're about to round a corner, and Leo quickly pulls me back and out of sight. I flatten myself against the stone wall and hold my breath as I hear the sound of doors closing.

"Don't move," Leo warns, his gun out and ready just in case.

The car drives away, and we stay put.

Leo turns to me, his shoulders relaxing slightly. "If shit goes down, I need you to use this and run." He hands me a gun.

I stifle a laugh, trying to hide my true feelings, fear. "I don't know how to use this."

That's a lie. My father was an officer. He taught me how to. But I don't want to have to use it.

He tucks the gun in the waistband of my leggings. "Point. Shoot."

His face falls. "I know you're happy right now, but this is no joke swe…Em." He gives me a weak smile. "Anything could be in that room. He may already be gone. You know that, right?"

I nod for his sake.

Aiden's going to be in that room. I just know it, and no one can tell me otherwise. I wait impatiently, dancing lightly on the balls of my feet.

Minutes pass slowly before Leo finally

squeezes my arm and pulls me into a tight hug.

Then we are off.

My feet inch forward as we enter the large warehouse. It's empty.

A heavy metal door guides us to a stairwell. The smell of brine invades my senses as we descend the stairs into a basement. The further we go down, the more I gag on the stench of mold and damp earth. It's nauseating.

Is this where my heart has been?

Leo holds a small flashlight and his gun in one hand, his other firmly latched around my wrist, pulling me forward. It feels like a military mission as we slink through the deserted warehouse.

"This way," Leo whispers, following the coordinates on his watch.

I roll my eyes.

We'd spent the insanely long plane ride going over the map and our plans, and all along he has coordinates. At least he's thorough.

I slow as we reach a closed metal door with a small box of iron bars.

"I don't think anyone is here," I whisper. I haven't heard the slightest sounds of life. "Maybe everyone's asleep?"

Leo nudges his chin forward, indicating we're at the room the locket last pinged.

I rip myself from his grip and barrel towards the door, swinging it open and tripping inside. Leo is behind me in seconds, his flashlight revealing an empty room.

I shake my head, my voice small. "Where is he, Leo?"

The flashlight pans around the room and my eyes follow, landing on a heap of something in the corner of the room. I run to it, my hands diving through the items. My heart steadily sinks at the realization that these are Aiden's things.

His clothes. Oh my God. His clothes.

I bring them to my face. They are coated in his blood. My locket necklace still sits in his pocket, and I clench it in my shaking hand.

I peer up at Leo with wide eyes. "Why did they remove his clothes?"

His face contorts as he opens his mouth to speak before looking away and stopping himself.

I crawl over to a pile of heavy chains on my hands and knees. Only then do I realize the ground is caked in dried blood.

Leo lifts me against my wishes.

"Leave me here," I beg.

He shakes his head, pulling me closer. "We have to go."

I bury my head into Leo's chest, sobbing.

"I'm so sorry," He pats my hair, his voice soft. "Let's go." He searches my face.

I shake my head.

"Let's go, Em." He begs.

I don't respond. I simply stare at him, broken.

Leo picks me up, wrapping his arms around me.

"We were too late," I cry into the damp room, darkness taking over my vision.

Leo's flashlight bobs as we move further and further away from where Aiden died.

For good this time.

Leo guides me inside the rental house with small, careful strides.

I remember admiring the layout when we first arrived. Bright colors draped the interior and a deck overlooked the beautiful Tyrrhenian sea. But now, all I see is darkness and death.

How much more can a heart take?

I turn to look for the source of the running water, and see Leo running his hand underneath the pouring faucet, checking the temperature.

"In."

I look down at myself, only just noticing the dirt and muck mixed with dried blood from the torture chamber Aiden was in. I burst into tears once more.

Leo makes his way to me, holding me up as he walks us towards the shower. He doesn't try to remove my clothes, but simply steps in with me. He brings a cloth to my face and wipes away the tears and dirt.

I try to stand still, my trembling body reminds me of how high my hopes were just a short time ago, and how quickly it was all taken away… again.

Leo leans me against the wall before exiting the shower, taking off his wet clothes and wrapping himself in a towel quickly. I look away, not wanting to see another man naked even though *he* is no longer here anymore.

I step out of the shower once Leo leaves, giving me some privacy. The floor is a soaking mess by the time I finally wrap a towel around myself and walk into the room. I hastily grab some items from my luggage and throw on Aiden's T-shirt and a pair of sleep shorts.

With my locket in one hand and my promise ring in the other, I sit on the edge of the bed. I twiddle the gold ring in between my fingers, wondering how we got here.

Dressed in a pair of black basketball shorts, Leo slides a small table in front of me, his movements are slow and careful. He uncorks a bottle of wine and pours me a small glass.

"Here. Drink a little. It will help." He offers me a weak smile.

I refuse the glass and grab the bottle, relishing the bitter liquid.

Leo rips it from my hands, causing wine to spill on the tile floor, and guides me out onto the balcony.

I stare out at the black Tyrrhenian Sea, admiring how it goes on forever. I walk to the edge of the balcony and look down, wondering how long it'll take for me to hit the bottom.

"I don't know how to let you go," I whisper into the night.

Dark thoughts flood my mind, and my surroundings fade away.

Just then, a lighter clicks, followed by the drag of a cigarette.

My tear-soaked eyes meet Leo's and he makes his way to me in one long stride, his body blocking me from the edge.

Did he read my dark thoughts?

The smoke lingers in the salty air as he exhales. The comforting scent reminds me of Aiden.

I breathe in deeply. "Can I have a hit?"

He studies me a moment, ready to say no before stopping himself. Pulling out his pack, he places one in between my lips before lighting it.

I inhale and promptly choke. I must still have a sliver of my soul left because this elicits a chuckle from me.

"More wine," I declare before turning to head back inside.

Leo grabs my arm, stopping me. His expression is sharp under the moonlight. "Don't drink to forget, Em. Drink to calm yourself. You're stronger than you think. You've been through this before." He reminds me.

He's right. I know he's heard Ashley and I talking about the loss of my father. I smile, slightly.

I grab another glass and fill it up for him. "Here." I step back out onto the porch.

After a few glasses, my words grow loose, and a tear rolls down my cheek.

"He gets shot."

I take a sip.

"He lives."

I smile.

"But then we go on our rooftop…" I pace around the small porch, my voice growing frantic. Remembering the haunted memory of that night. "He gets kidnapped, though I thought he was dead the whole time."

I take a swig from the bottle as Leo watches me intently.

"I fucking buried him. You were there." I point sluggishly at Leo, my words slurring. "He's alive!" I burst into tears.

Then I collapse to the ground. "Oh, but wait. He's dead again!"

I drop the empty bottle on the floor, glass shatters around me.

Leo wraps me up in his strong arms and carries me inside. The warm air wraps around us. I look at him through a drunken haze. His gray eyes look darker underneath the warm light.

I avert my eyes, the moment too intimate. It's too much. But…I want to be selfish. I need comfort, even if just for one night.

"Bed?" Leo's voice is calm and soothing.

I nod. "I need to be held." I admit sluggishly.

He smiles, but it doesn't reach his eyes. "I'll be whatever you need me to be," He assures.

He takes off his shirt, revealing golden skin and a lean frame free of tattoos. So different from Aiden. He climbs into the bed.

"I'm going to lay on the couch." I suddenly feel nauseous.

He chuckles, low and gritty. "Come on, babe…Em. I'll go."

I shake my head when he moves to get up. Against my better judgement, I climb in next to him. I lay my head on his chest, ignoring the pang of guilt that plagues my body when I breathe in his half familiar scent. The smell of smoke, I know. But the other half is different, more earthy.

I inhale deeply. I know it isn't fair to Leo, but I imagine Aiden's tattooed arms wrapped around me, pretending we are on a vacation together in southern Italy.

Then, I drift to sleep in another man's embrace.

I wake to a flood of light pouring in through the open balcony doors, the smell of saltwater fills my nostrils.

Leo is nowhere in sight.

I look around through squinted eyes and a pounding headache. The room spins slightly. With a jolt, I race to the bathroom where an unopened bottle of Motrin and a glass of water sit next to the sink along with a handwritten note beside it.

I'll be back with food shortly. I'm sorry you were so upset last night. That was never my intention, bringing you here. Take the medicine, I'm sure your head's killing you. I had to get my own coffee, thanks a lot. Haha. - Leo.

I put the note back down and pinch the bridge of my nose. Then, I stop myself and step into the shower. As warm water cascades down my hair and back, tears fall from my eyes from guilt. Nothing happened between us, but lying in another man's arms still felt wrong. Even if Aiden is…really gone this time.

I get changed into comfortable clothing. I'm not sure when we're leaving but I want to get out of Italy as soon as possible.

I open the bathroom door and see a cart.

Leo sips on his coffee before handing me mine. I bring the mug to my lips, letting the frothy liquid warm me up.

"Have whatever you like." He smiles, gesturing to the array of food on the tray.

My eyes skim over the desserts. Any other time, this would be an absolute dream of mine to have authentic Italian pastries.

But all they make me think of is Aiden.

Everything makes me think of Aiden.

I bypass the colorful items and grab some eggs and toast along with a glass of orange juice before heading for the balcony.

Leo follows me, his movements matching mine.

Slow. Careful. Calm.

Why is he watching me so intently?

"When are we leaving?" My voice is still sore from all the crying.

He lifts his brow, a half smile creeping onto his face.

God, he has to stop being so happy all the time.

"Wanting to leave so soon?"

I roll my eyes. "I have to get out of here, Leo."

"You don't want to look anymore?"

I shake my head. *Where is he going with this?*

"Where's that girl I've grown to know who won't give up?" He looks at me pointedly.

"There was nothing there," I remind him. *Nothing.*

"Actually, I was gone this morning because I wanted to try one more thing. I need you to trust me, okay?"

I wave him off. "Leo, I can't do it anymore. Everyone's right. I can't keep going through this." I sigh, fighting back my tears once more. "It's breaking me. I can only be strong for so long. He's alive, he's dead, he's alive, he's dead. People forget I'm only eighteen. I'm chasing a ghost."

Leo ignores me, his stride confident as he paces the small patio.

With a flick of his wrist, he announces, "We're going to a party." A devilish smirk adorns his sharp features.

This elicits a chuckle from me. "You can't be serious."

"Yes, I am. Just do exactly as I say. I don't want to put you in this situation, but you need to find him." His expression is distant, his voice low. "I'd go alone but you'd refuse." He rolls his eyes.

I playfully swat his arm.

His expression turns serious as he takes my hand in his and inhales deeply. "Em, I'm serious. You have to follow my orders."

I only follow one man's orders is what I want to say.

But I don't.

Not anymore.

"I don't know," I admit, my broken heart refusing to beat again. I don't think I can handle it. I really don't. Last night was the hardest moment of my life. The darkest.

"No one was there last night because there's an event going on, Em. It's a party for the Campania Mafia's allies. I don't know why the warehouse was empty, but if he is alive…" He frowns, "And I'm not trying to get your hopes up. But if he's alive, this will be the place he'll be at."

I eye him with suspicion.

"I don't know why they'll take a prisoner to a party, or if they even have him." His gaze remains distant, reluctant to be telling me all of this.

I'm thankful he trusts me enough to confide in me and give me the truth. Everyone always shelters me, but Leo doesn't.

I nod slowly, my heart giving a tentative jump.

His gray eyes dance in the morning sun.

"We're going into the lion's den."

Seven

I place the perfectly curled blonde wig over my brown hair and shake it out. Letting the long blonde curls cascade down my back, I look at my reflection, barely recognizing the girl in front of me. I sweep a crimson red lipstick over my lips, heavy dark make-up adorning my eyes, before heading out to the living room.

Dressed in a pitch-black suit, his hair styled to perfection, Leo's gray eyes scan my body before shaking his head in disapproval.

I roll my eyes. "What?"

I decided to wear my yellow dress just in case Aiden is really in there. He loves seeing me in it. I had spent hours scrubbing his and Howard's blood from the delicate material after that night.

Leo places a hand on his chin. "What happened to listening to everything I say?"

I look around the room, blatantly ignoring him.

"The gown I laid on the bed?" He prompts.

"It's too much."

He gestures to the bedroom. "You're the wife of an Italian mobster tonight, darling. Nothing is too much." He smiles.

With a huff, I plod to the bedroom. I finger the thin fabric of the black gown, slightly thankful for the muted color.

I cringe after pulling it on. Aiden will probably have a heart attack if he sees me in this... if he sees me in this. My cleavage is the main attraction. I sigh, uncomfortable in a dress meant for someone ten years older. I'm not used to such flashy jewelry or expensive gowns.

But that's the point. I'm not eighteen-year-old Emilia Banks, on a mission to save the love of my life, right now. Tonight, I'm Mrs. Madeline Greco, an American woman who married into the Sicilian mafia.

I stumble in my heels as I make my way back out.

With an approving smile, Leo places a large diamond encrusted necklace around my neck. The weight against my already tight chest is surprisingly painful.

"One more thing." He pulls a garter out of his pocket. "Put this around your thigh."

Once it's securely on my thigh, he hands me a gun. I shake my head once, but he gestures to it again. With a sigh, I slide it inside the holster before smoothing my floor length dress. The cold metal chills my skin.

Leo loops my arm through his and we make our way through the dark streets of Campania to grab a cab.

He leans into me with a whisper, "Remember, tonight, you're the wife of Luca Greco." He removes a massive ring from his pocket with a Cheshire grin.

I laugh nervously while sliding it on my naked finger, having left Aiden's promise ring in the room. It's too precious to lose.

"Follow my lead and don't speak. We have an advantage here. I'm obviously not Italian, but I have a few ties within the Sicilian Mafia, who are their allies. It doesn't hurt that I speak their language and blend in." Leo winks at me.

His casual demeanor calms me the tiniest bit. But truly, on the inside…I'm screaming for help.

"I'm nervous."

He places a reassuring hand on the small of my back. "Don't be. I've got you. Always."

Leo escorts me inside the beautifully

decorated mansion. White roses line the bar top tables while soft, classical music fills the marble entryway.

A smiling waiter greets us with a tray of stemmed glasses, red and white wine in different shades. I opt for one of the whites, hoping it will be calmer on my nervous stomach than a rich sweet red.

Leo leans over as the waiter moves away. "Sip it. I need you alert. If anything goes down, you leave me here. Understand?"

I give a subtle nod, taking small sips to calm my nerves.

"I won't let anything happen," He adds with a cocky smirk.

I hook my arm through Leo's, leaning against him as I teeter on my heels. Glancing at the other women in attendance, dolled up to the nines, I'm thankful I wore them.

We try our best to blend in. A few people stop us to shake Leo's hand and speak with him in Italian. He smiles, they laugh, and then we move on. It feels like a networking event where allied mafias meet to keep their bonds strong.

"Where would he be?" I whisper once we are finally alone for a brief moment.

My eyes fall on a table of finger foods and I drift over, needing something besides wine in my stomach. Leo, ever the gentleman, fixes a small plate for me. I note the way his eyes are constantly wandering around the room. I nibble on the assortment of food before grabbing another glass of wine.

A smiling lady, with her auburn locks twisted elegantly and her uniform ironed to perfection, approaches us.

"Ti piace il vino?" She directs her question at me.

I sip my wine as I wait for Leo to answer.

"Lei lo adora. Viene fatto qui?"

The lady nods with a smile, her features growing animated as she speaks with Leo. Grabbing my long-stemmed glass, she tops it off with more liquid.

I know I shouldn't be drinking so much but it keeps me from having to speak. I watch as she gestures down a hall before walking away.

A small smile plays on Leo's lips. "We're going to the cellar." He gestures towards a door at the end of the long hallway.

"Why?" I ask in hushed tones as we descend the stairs.

He pats my arm. "Well, my darling wife, because the waitress saw how much you were enjoying the wine. There's a vineyard behind the mansion. The hosts love sharing their homemade wines and often hold tastings in the cellar."

That must be where Aiden is.

I hold my breath as we make our way down the intricate and rough stone steps. If I weren't so terrified, I'd be in awe of the ornate interior. I tighten my grip on Leo's hand as he escorts us further down.

There's a fork ahead.

A small sign reads "Degustazioni Di Vino", with a scrolled arrow pointing left.

We go right instead, passing through an open archway, and down a small corridor. My eyes search each room we pass. A faint golden glow to my left catches my attention.

My eyes widen at the figure in the room and my heart jolts alive.

Aiden.
He's here.
He's right there.

My joints turn weak in relief as I suck in a breath.

He's hurt. Caked in blood, it seems like he's lost weight.

What have they done to him? Why is he only wearing boxers?

My heart aches at the sight of such a powerful man so…restrained.

It's a jarring sight.

An open archway leads to stone trimmings and warm lighting and then there's Aiden, unclothed and bloody, tied to a wooden pillar.

A greasy head peaks around the corner. It's a short man, almost bald save a few stray hairs on top of his head, with thick jewelry.

I don't miss his busted lip.

He smiles wide. "Ciao, penso che ti sei perso." *Hello, I think you've gotten lost.*

Leo's cool demeanor is a sharp contrast to my racing heart.

"Eravamo diretti alla cantina. Un cameriere mi ha parlato dei tuoi vini della casa e ci piacerebbe provare." *We were headed for the wine cellar. A waiter told me about your house wines, and we would love to try them.*

"Oh, si. Hai appena chiuso la sala sbagliata, vai da questa parte." *Oh, yes. You turned down the wrong hall. Go this way.* He gestures back where we came from before extending a hand. "Giuseppe Russo."

"Luca Greco."

I extend my hand, trying not to flinch as he kisses the back of it. I stay silent, unsure of what to do.

Giuseppe turns to Leo, politely dropping my hand. "Vedo che hai la tua ragazza con te." *I see you have your girlfriend with you.*

"No, no questa è mia moglie." *No, this is my wife.*

Leo takes my shaking hand in his, grounding me.

I watch as Aiden twitches at our voices

before his head lifts and his eyes widen slightly. I hesitantly tear my gaze away, focusing on the man in front of me. I never thought I would see Aiden again, and he's so close that I fight with myself to reach for him.

Giuseppe eyes me with suspicion. "La ragazza non parla?" *Does the girl not speak?*

"È americana, mi è stata regalata da suo padre. Alla fine imparerà la lingua." *She's American, she was given to me as a gift from her father. She will learn the language soon.*

The man claps his hands together. "An American," He says in a heavily accented English.

I hold back a sigh of relief at being able to understand them.

"Hello."

I notice Aiden jerk slightly at the sound of my wavering voice out of the corner of my eye.

"I'm Madeline Greco." I smile, trying to sound formal, as though I belong in this extravagant world with such a fancy name.

I'm glad to be ignored as the men take their time discussing their respected Italian cities while I subtly observe Aiden, tracking his injuries. Leo impresses me with how naturally he lies. Though what floors me is how his usual accent is now much like Giuseppe's.

I'm snapped out of my trance when Giuseppe claps his hands.

"You two head to the wine cellar. You

don't want a pretty girl around a prisoner." He jerks a stubby finger at Aiden.

I guess it's a common sight to see at a mafia's party.

"Of course not. Come, darling." Leo kisses my temple.

I temper my instinct to flinch, my eyes widening when Aiden bares his teeth silently, his eyes holding a possessive glint. He peels his eyes away and looks at the ground, his shackled hands balled into fist.

With a shake of his head, he looks up at me through batted lashes. Creating a perfect moment during an impossible situation. I can't help the whimper that escapes me from the intensity of his gaze or the words he mouths to me. 'I love you.' I can feel the power behind his silent promise.

Leo turns to walk away before stopping. With a cool demeanor, he waves a finger up and down. "Interesting choice to have a prisoner attend a party."

There's a pulse of silence before they burst out into deep laughter.

I'm trying not to pass out, worried that question would raise red flags. Instead, it excites Giuseppe and he grows animated as he speaks about Aiden like a zoo animal.

I bite back the bile rising in my throat.

Giuseppe looks at me, his greasy smile

tight. "Excuse him not being clothed. This one is dangerous." He turns to Leo. "Killed three of our men while chained. We didn't want him covered in our men's blood. Didn't see the point in giving him new clothes." He winks.

Leo raises his brow with a whistle. "Three men? Why keep him alive?"

The question almost brings me to my knees, and I grip Leo's hand hard.

"This one won't be here much longer, once Boss gets here tonight." He walks over and yanks Aiden's head up by his hair, making a slitting motion with his golden ringed finger.

Aiden spits. "Fuck you."

To my horror, Giuseppe lifts his black boot and kicks him hard in the ribs. Aiden doesn't move nor make a sound. He simply looks ahead, gazing deep into my eyes.

An unfamiliar keen escapes my chest, and Leo grips my hand tighter, his thumb rubbing circles on my skin in a calming gesture.

Giuseppe waddles towards me on his short legs and places a sweaty hand on my arm. "I apologize, Mrs. Greco. I shouldn't be discussing such vulgar things in front of a lady. I got carried away, thinking of revenge. Forgive me."

I plaster on a fake smile before motioning to Leo for us to go. I would've fallen to the ground in terror if not for Leo holding me up. He's alive, but not for long.

Sensing my terror, he pulls my hair away from my face and lays it over my back. Saying our goodbyes, we make our way to the wine cellar in case anyone checks on us.

The wooden door to the cellar creaks open and I straighten, leaning into Leo as though we're having an intimate moment. I gratefully sip on the glass of liquid the butler hands me, slightly disappointed when the alcohol no longer has any effect on me.

Watching as more people file into the room, I bring my lips to Leo's ear. "We have to get him out of here."

He nods, his eyes searching my face. "I have a plan. Just be natural. You're doing so well."

I laugh softly at the lie.

I have to have hope. No matter how much terror I feel, I need to trust Leo.

For Aiden.

Aiden

She's here.
She's right there.

If it weren't for me being chained and on my knees, the sight of her in here would bring me to them.

How did she find me?

Who the fuck is this guy with her? Why is he holding her?

Why the fuck is she blonde? And who picked out that dress?

What the fuck is going on?

The sound of her voice makes my body twitch. What a heavenly fucking sound, though full of terror. I wish I could comfort her, but I'm chained like a fucking coward, unable to protect her.

I peel my eyes away, not wanting anyone to see me admiring her beauty. I've retraced her facial structure a million times in my mind. I had thought I would only see her again in my dreams.

My eyes drift back to her, and I tune the men out.

Agonizing moments pass before Giuseppe grabs me, mimicking the slitting of my throat. It takes everything in me to not break free from these chains and hold Emilia when a pained sound escapes her.

But wait…

This guy, Luca…his thumb caresses her skin.

My mind blanks when he kisses her temple.

Who the fuck is this guy with her? Why is he holding her?

Why the fuck is she blonde? And who picked out that dress?

What the fuck is going on?

Emilia

Leo casually looks at his watch. "It's time," He states.

I nod, making my way towards a waitress with Leo in tow as we squeeze through the crowd of drunk dancing women. We've been at this party for hours; it's well past two in the morning. Everyone is wasted.

My heart pounds as we make our way to her. I hope no one can tell.

She smiles and greets us as Leo slings an arm around my shoulder.

I giggle, acting drunk as I lean into Leo.

"Ci siamo trovati benissimo, andrebbe bene se portassimo a casa una bottiglia del tuo vino con noi? Mia moglie lo adora." *We had a wonderful time. Would it be okay if we took a bottle of your wine home with us? My wife loves it.*

She nods happily, gesturing for us to follow her downstairs.

We've been paying special attention to the basement door. No one has gone down in over an hour, but with how proud of their wine they are, we knew they wouldn't mind letting us down one last time to take a bottle home.

I grow increasingly nervous with each step, afraid that everything will be ripped away from me once again.

I step to the side once we enter the empty wine cellar. The dim light illuminates the dusty bottles and stonework. I peer out as the door closes, making sure no one followed us.

"Now," I whisper.

With a nod, Leo silently places a rag over the woman's mouth. She struggles briefly before collapsing in his arms. I watch as he gently lays her on the floor, thankful she doesn't make a peep.

"Stay here," Leo orders.

I shake my head, too terrified to be alone.

Rolling his eyes, he grabs my hand and we creep down the stone corridor as quiet as mice, a dim light illuminating our way. He places a finger over his lips as we near the arch.

I nod.

He attaches a silencer to his gun before peeking around the edge.

The whizz of the bullet is followed by a thud of something hitting the ground.

I rush inside the room as soon as Leo relaxes his stance, diving in front of Aiden, desperate to tend to his injuries.

His emerald eyes bore into mine, strong and calm, and I calm.

"Emilia, sweetheart, look at me okay? Don't look around." Aiden orders gently, his voice hoarse. His tone holds a tinge of panic, something I'm not used to.

My heart warms and aches at his immediate concern for me despite his situation.

I hear movement behind me, and Aiden snaps his finger before I turn my head. Thankfully, it was just Leo getting a set of keys.

Aiden trains his eyes on Leo, his expression murderous. "Bring her somewhere safe, then come back for me."

Leo ignores him, examining the keys.

I look him over, shaking my head furiously. "I'm not leaving without you."

Aiden sighs. "Fuck, I missed you so much, baby." A low growl emanates from his chest when his restraints stop him from moving to me.

I push his hair from his face, caressing it to calm his and my emotions.

Long seconds pass before the lock finally clicks open, releasing Aiden's hands from the chains.

My heart starts beating again in that blissful moment as he cups my cheeks, his expression of disbelief as his jade eyes scan my body. Silently, he pulls away and pushes himself off the ground.

I peer up, admiring his tall frame.

He yanks on the jeans Leo throws at him, before wrapping a hand around my waist and the other around my face, shielding my eyes. He guides me out of the room before removing the shield.

"This way." Leo gestures down the hallway.

With a hand on my back, Aiden guides me down the dark corridor.

Just then, a man rounds a corner, his surprised expression making me dig my nails into Aiden's arm.

Aiden steps in front of me to shield me, as Leo knocks the man out with the butt of his gun. He grunts, cursing under his breath as he reaches back to check on me. Then, he bends over, his breathing unusual. He places one hand on my stomach and the other on my leg, ready to lift me.

"What the fuck is this?" Aiden exclaims as his hand slides up my dress, pulling the gun from the holster. His eyes narrow.

I shrug, not knowing how to explain.

Aiden turns to Leo. "Why in the fuck does she have a gun?"

Leo opens his mouth to speak, but Aiden stops him with a growl, taking the gun for himself before gesturing for us to continue.

Now isn't the time for this.

I swallow as we make our way to another set of doors.

Leo looks between them, conflicted.

Aiden grunts, pushing him aside.

Luckily, he chose right.

His hand clamps firmly around mine as we make our way through the vineyard. The vines scratch my legs while my heels dig into the dirt, making it hard for me to match their long strides.

Noticing my struggle, Aiden lifts me over his shoulder and breaks out into a run.

"Put me down," I whisper my demand, worried about his injuries. I've seen what they've done to him and I can hear the hisses of pain escaping his lips.

"Not a chance."

He holds me firmly as we make our way through a dense forest at a steady pace, only setting me down when we reach the quiet sleeping city.

We walk for long minutes in complete silence until we reach a dark alley, where we stop for a moment to breathe.

I blink at what happens next.

Why is Aiden letting go of my hand?
And why does he have Leo pinned against the wall?

"Who are you? I assume your name isn't really Luca," Aiden snarls.

Is he mad at me?

Aiden pins him harder when Leo looks at me.

"My name is Leo."

Noticing the deep cuts in Aiden's wrist, I run my finger over them lightly. "I need to help you," I cut in.

His eyes cut to me, then back to Leo, burning with fury. "Why in the fuck are you with my girl?"

"Howard hired me."

I touch his arm, biting my lip when he flinches slightly from the pain.

His eyes cut back to Leo and after a moment of thought, he releases him. "I'll deal with you later."

Why is he being so hostile with Leo?

As we make our way down the streets hand in hand, I peer back continuously, paranoid that the mafia will find us once more.

Aiden turns my head forward, pulling me

along. "You're safe, baby girl. I've got you."

I sigh at the familiar words.

Yet with each step I take, a fog builds in my mind. Everything feels like a dream, out of focus. My chest feels tight. I don't understand what is happening. Chills rack my body. I'm not cold, yet my teeth chatter. I'm terrified of Aiden being hurt or taken away again, but I'm also relieved to have him by my side.

Then, a warm blanket is draped over me.

Not a blanket, a jacket.

I stare at Aiden's bare chest, lifting my brow in confusion. I peer up into his eyes, seeing the boiling rage in them.

I finger the cloth, knowing where it came from but not wanting to turn to look in Leo's direction. He probably isn't aware of how protective Aiden is, and the state Aiden is in right now isn't one to be fucked with.

He grips the jacket, ready to remove it, but stops himself. He wraps a warm hand around the back of my neck instead.

"I'm sorry I don't have anything to give you right now," He mumbles lowly.

It doesn't take long before we arrive at the condo.

Leo steps out onto the balcony to smoke. Aiden's face darkens at the sight of the small room, the one bed, the open bottle of wine and glasses beside it. The shattered bottle on the patio. His fist clenches as he gathers my things quickly.

"Let me help." My voice wavers as the adrenaline leaves my system. Fear and relief overwhelm my system. Now that I have him back, I feel safe again. Putting myself in danger was worth getting him back, but my mind is so done right now.

I watch Aiden in worry as he packs hastily, his chest rising and lowering harshly. My heart aches when he silently shrugs my hand off his shoulder.

Does he not see that he's hurt?
He needs to be looked at. I need him to be looked at.

"Do you still love me?" I wonder out loud.

He cups my face protectively. "Sweetheart, yes," He declares fiercely, pulling me into a tight embrace, inhaling my scent deeply. "More than anything. That's why I have to get you the fuck out of here. Now."

I shake my head. "But you're hurt. We need to go to a hospital."

Leo steps in then, nodding in agreement, though his gray eyes remain distant.

Aiden shakes his head, standing his ground. "You can patch me up. On the plane." He kisses my forehead gently before adjusting my dress as well as he can. "Go change." He orders in a soft voice.

I listen.

Honestly, I'm over this dress and gaudy jewelry.

Aiden smiles in approval when he sees me in his T-shirt and a pair of jeans. He grabs my bags, refusing to let me help, and we head to the discreet car outside. I climb in the back with Aiden while Leo takes the front. My body begins to shake as all the "what ifs" play out in my mind.

Sensing my terror, Aiden pulls me onto his lap, gently rubbing my arms.

I lay my head on his chest with a sigh, listening to the comforting beat of his heart. I inhale his familiar scent as he lights a cigarette, blowing the smoke out the open window. He no longer smells like mint, and the scent of iron is strong.

God, I can't imagine what he's been through.

"Emilia, baby, it's okay. I'm here now. You're safe." The rumble of his baritone calms me as he holds me tightly and securely.

I close my eyes, willing the tremors to stop.

I'm safe now.

For Aiden is here.

Aiden

I take my first breath once Emilia steps onto the plane, safe. I hiss from the stabbing discomfort of simply breathing. The torture my body endured is catching up to me. Haunting me.

I've barely been holding it together with the sole purpose of getting her out of Italy as soon as possible. She needs to be safe and protected, no matter the cost.

First things first, I need a fucking shower. I don't want her getting any more nasty shit on her and I'm not keeping my hands to myself tonight. I need her in my arms.

"Come," I beckon her to the back room.

She smiles and follows me closely.

I'm dying to see her naked.

I throw a smirk in Leo's direction just before I close the bedroom door and guide Emilia to the bathroom. Without taking my eyes off her, I turn the water on, running my hand under the stream to check the temperature. My breath hitches as she peels off her clothes. My eyes trace and linger on her curves as she stares at me with coy, innocent eyes.

I help her in, and we stand under the water in silence, letting the warmth cascade over our bodies. I sigh as the water carries away the blood and filth I've sat in for weeks.

I grip her chin, bringing her plump lips to mine. The feel of her soft lips sends shivers down my spine. I never imagined I'd be kissing my sweet Emilia again.

She grabs a washrag and begins lathering my body with soap. Her gentle, tentative touch almost brings me to tears after the past few weeks.

She's such an angel.

What did I ever do to deserve her?

The open cuts littering my body burn like a motherfucker as she cleans them. I hold back a hiss. She's being so fucking gentle I don't want her thinking she's hurting me. I don't want the gentle touches to stop.

"Your body… the bruises." Her broken whisper lingers in the air.

I cup her cheek as I gaze into her eyes.

Beautiful, broken, and mine.

"They will heal, baby. I will heal."

I don't know whose decision it was to allow her to come to Italy and face my demons, but there will be hell to pay when I find out. Leo probably had something to do with it.

"You're staring at me." She giggles, breaking me from my trance.

I kiss her lips before pulling back to study her face. "I missed you so much."

"I missed you too," She whispers and sniffles. Tears run down her cheeks and she swipes at them, but it's replaced by more water from the showerhead.

We fall into a fit of laughter at the insanity of things.

We're together once more.

She found her way to me.

She saved me.

I've never been this silent around her. But after the past few weeks, I just want to drink the sight of her in. I'd given up hope of ever seeing her since that night.

I bring my lips to her neck, nibbling and kissing, as I caress her soft body.

Fuck, she's perfect.

"I need to bandage your wounds." Emilia dabs my skin with a towel after we step out of the shower.

I smile at her concern. I don't think I've ever smiled this much in my fucking life. I lift her up and twirl her around. She giggles, but it's faint and distant. I know she's happy but she's reaching her limit.

I brush her hands aside and attack her hair with the brush, admiring the dark strands as I work out the tangles.

"I'm serious, Aiden. I need to bandage them," She tries to sound stern, much like a kitten sizing up a lion.

"Just give me a minute to enjoy you." I take the towel away, wanting to see her naked body again.

In a quick hungry movement, I press her up against the wall. With a groan, I capture her lips in a heated kiss, claiming her. I lift her legs and they automatically wrap around my waist. My bruised ribs cry out in agony, but I ignore them. I need her.

"Not now," Emilia pants, batting at me, trying to push me away.

"You deny me?" I growl down at her with a cocked brow.

She rolls her eyes and continues pushing at me.

I grab her ass in warning. "Where's this

attitude coming from?"

"You need to be bandaged." She insists, a tear rolling down her cheek. "I just need you to be okay," She whispers, her voice small and wavering.

It breaks me.

I cup her cheek, tilting her head to look into her eyes. "Emilia, listen to me." I use that calm, soothing voice she loves. "I am okay." I emphasize each word.

She shakes her head and sets her feet down to the ground. Turning, she rummages through the cabinets under the sink, sighing in relief when she finds the first aid kit.

I give in then.

This is what she needs to feel better.

And so it's what I'll give her.

I hoist myself up onto the counter as Emilia lays out the contents of the first aid kit. I watch as she carefully soaks a pad with alcohol and cleans my wounds once more. It's overkill, but whatever makes her feel better. I ignore the sting as I run my fingers through her damp hair.

She is so focused on the task at hand, it concerns me.

Once every cut is properly covered in a layer of antibiotic cream and thick gauze, she looks at her work in satisfaction.

"I would make a good nurse." Emilia claps her hands together with a slight smile.

I hop down, shaking my head as I pull her close. "You taking care of other people all day instead of me? No fucking way. Only me," I tease.

I love how her eyes light up. I know she loves how possessive I am.

She would make a wonderful nurse, but we both know where her real dream lies. I've missed her cooking so fucking much.

There's so many things I've missed.

But most importantly…

I lean down so that I'm on eye level with her. "So now can I fuck you?"

She smiles brightly and nods, pulling me close. She hoists herself up, wrapping her legs around me just as I push her up against the wall, feeling myself harden against her softness. I grunt in pain as the sudden movement jars my ribs.

Emilia is off me within seconds, her tone frantic as she flutters around me in worry. "Where does it hurt?"

"I'm fine," I lie through gritted teeth.

"Where?" She demands.

I shake my head, picking up a towel and running it through my hair. The simple action makes me hiss, my body feels constricted, broken. I usually lift her with ease, but when her legs wrapped around my waist my body felt like glass.

She pokes my chest and I stare down at her in confusion.

What is she doing?

Then she pokes my side where my injured ribs are and I flinch, doubling over from the pain.

"Ouch, what the fuck!" I snap.

Her voice cracks. "Are your ribs broken?"

I think this over. I could lie...

Will she let me fuck her with broken ribs? Probably not.

She shakes her head, deciding I've taken too long to reply. "They're broken, aren't they?" She places a gentle hand on my side. Her eyes trailing over my bruised body, discolored circles dot every inch.

"Yes," I admit.

"And you were thinking about lying to me to have sex?"

"Yes," I admit.

My reply elicits a chuckle from my girl.

What a beautiful sound.

"No sex until it heals," She chides.

I bark out a laugh. "I could just take it." I tease, enjoying the way she bites her lip. "You don't want me to fuck you, and yet you bite your lip."

She raises a brow before batting her lashes. "I never said I didn't want you to fuck me."

Where did this sassy girl come from?

I shoot her an amused smile.

She lets out a small laugh, but there isn't much humor behind it.

EMILIA

As much as I want to fuck her senseless, I see the hollowness in her eyes. Worry bubbles up inside me. Something is wrong.

After cleaning up and changing, we head out into the main area where Leo sits, sipping a glass of Brandy.

The relief I feel of being in the air and flying closer to home every second overwhelms me.

I grab myself a glass and down it, trying to ignore my discomfort at Emilia alone with another man for so long, before sipping on my second glass. I take a moment to celebrate the fact that I'm simply alive.

I narrow my eyes at Leo. I know it was an act earlier, but hearing him call my Emilia his wife makes me want to drive my fist through his smug face.

Fuck, the thought of her with another man is my worst nightmare.

Another fear is brought to reality when I search out Emilia, who is on the leather couch. My breath stutters at the sight of her pale face, her chest rising quickly as she brings her knees to her chest.

Suddenly, everything clicks into place.

I'm in front of her in two strides and go down on my knees.

Leo walks over, his eyes concerned. "What's wrong?"

Doesn't he know?

This is all his fucking fault.

"She's having a panic attack." I rub my hands up and down her back, but she isn't calming.

"Bu—"

I cut him off. "Shut the fuck up and get her some water."

I can't stand to be around this guy. He brings my girl into danger, and then wonders why she's having a panic attack?

Emilia's eyes are glossed over as she tries to breath.

"Shh, breath, baby. It's okay," I croon. "Everything is okay. I can't fucking believe you did this for me. How incredibly amazing and how unbelievably stupid of you." My breath hitches in my throat. *What if something happened to her?* "I love you so much, Emilia. Don't you dare fucking do anything like that on my behalf ever again. But you're truly amazing." I give her my best crooked grin, full dimples.

It takes her awhile, but she finally responds to my words as her breathing slows. She releases her knees as she takes in a few calming breaths.

Leo returns with a glass of water. "She's been fine this whole time." He remarks curiously.

EMILIA

I try to keep my voice calm. "Of course, she's been fine. Her only thought was to save me. Now that I'm back, her body finally has the time to process and adjust to what she went through."

He brings a hand to his chin with a hum. "She wanted to go so badly, I thought she could handle it."

The fucking audacity.

"She would do anything for me," I snap, looking him dead in the eyes, letting him know that I'm the end of the line for her. There is no one besides me for her. I've seen the way he watches her, as though he cares for her, as though he fucking knows her.

He places a hand on her shoulder, and my body tenses.

"I'm sorry, Em."

Em?

What?

"You call her Ms. Banks. Don't give my girl pet names." I spit, enraged that a guard would ever do that.

"I asked him too," Emilia's soft voice cuts in.

I wish I had the time to beat the shit out of this guy.

"I don't–" I cut myself off.

This isn't the time. Later sounds good.

Right now, she needs me.

Her voice is small and weak. "Aiden, I

don't know…I don't know what's wrong with me. It feels like I'm drowning. Help me." Her breathing picks up again.

Her words break my heart.

"I've got you, baby," I assure her, pulling her onto my lap as my hands caress her hair, shoulders, everywhere, to keep her calm.

Emilia

I focus on the swirls of ink on Aiden's arms, admiring the chaotic scenes on his skin as I try to calm my breathing. I relish in the feeling of his strong arms cradling me, filling me with a sense of security.

I trace my fingers over them. Aiden is a quiet man, but I've noticed the way his tattoos speak for him. I linger on the raven tattoo on his forearm and close my eyes, imagining the dark bird soaring in the sky. My eyes grow heavy as he plays with my hair, and I drift in and out of the men's hushed conversation.

"You can be mad at me, but don't be mad

at her. She would've gone without me," Leo murmurs.

Aiden tenses beneath me. "Please, for your own sake, do not tell me how I should feel towards her. She should have never been allowed to come here."

"With all due respect, she can make her own decisions."

Aiden chuckles lowly, his voice a whisper.

I stay silent, keeping my eyes shut, curious where the conversation will go.

"I don't know you. I don't want to fucking know you. But if there is one thing I will not tolerate, it's you thinking you have a say in what is mine." His arm tightens around me gently, but protectively. "This girl right here? Mine." He growls.

"Don't you think that's a little primitive?" Leo challenges casually.

"Fuck this new age bullshit. I support her, I care for her. So what if I own her heart and soul? She owns me, heart and fucking soul. That's how we work." He murmurs fiercely, his hand stroking my hair.

The exquisite feeling almost brings me to tears.

I can tell Aiden is struggling to hold himself back from hitting Leo as he speaks so freely about me. He's on edge, but as long as I'm on his lap, he won't move. I can imagine Leo pinching the bridge of his nose, and then Aiden doing the same. They're more alike than they think. If Leo wasn't being all weird and talking about me, I think they could be friends.

A long silence passes before Leo speaks up. "She's stronger than you think."

Aiden scoffs. "Of course she's strong. I know that better than anyone. But this is too much. Too fucking much. You don't understand her. She just had a panic attack because of *your* actions."

"Her actions saved your life." Leo's tone is cocky.

I frown slightly. *Why is he edging Aiden on?*

"You don't think I know that?" Aiden sighs.

"Exactly. She's a strong girl. Let her be strong."

Aiden throws his hands in the air. "That's not the fucking point! She doesn't *have* to be strong with me. It's my duty to protect her. She's free to do as she pleases with me. She doesn't have to be strong, because I'm strong for her."

"Lo–"

"I'm going to let you in on a secret about my girl." Aiden cuts him off, his tone laced with venom. "She won't admit it to you or anyone else, besides me, but she craves structure and order." His tone is the usual bitter melody he uses when talking business. "And I'm her structure and order."

Aiden continues before Leo can utter another word. "I'm done with this conversation. I just have one question for you."

I peek my eyes open to see Leo and Aiden in a staring match.

"Does anyone know that you brought her? I can't imagine Howard would allow this if he's alive."

"Howard is alive. Everyone is safe." Leo informs him.

Aiden relaxes slightly.

"We left on our own. No one knew."

"And why did you think that's okay?"

Leo scoots to the edge of his seat, clasping his hands in a challenging motion. "Because I can protect her."

"That's not your job."

"I'm sorry you feel that way, Sir, but that's exactly what my job is."

Aiden stands, holding me in his arms. "Thank you for keeping her safe, even though she should have never been here in the first place. It's no longer your job now that I'm home." He states. Carrying me to the bed.

With that said, I feel us moving before he lays me down in bed minutes later. I snuggle against his chest as he slides in beside me, relishing in his warmth. I fight against the sudden wave of exhaustion.

"Aiden," I whisper.

He raises his eyebrow as he peers down at me. "Sleep." He orders.

I can tell he's still on edge.

"I need to tell you something."

He tenses and I lift myself up on an elbow.

"I believed you were dead. I should've known better." I admit, ashamed.

He shrugs. "You were supposed to."

I shake my head. "I did, until I remembered my locket and came here," I pause. "…And then I found it in that dark room." I cringe remembering how sinister and lonely it felt. "I gave up. I thought you were really gone. I almost quit looking, but Leo…he made me continue."

He cocks a brow at me and kisses my forehead.

"I'm sorry I gave up on you," I whisper through my tears.

He chuckles, cupping my face with warm, inked hands. "Are you kidding me? You ran off to Italy after burying me. You found me, baby girl. Do you know how amazing that is? It was a stupid decision and I should spank your ass so raw you can't walk for a week, but I'm so happy." He pulls me close.

I give him a sleepy smile.

"I love you. You are mine," He murmurs

possessively.

Only then did I fall asleep in his arms.

I'm finally home.

I awake to warm hands languidly caressing my body.

"Couldn't sleep?" I peer up at Aiden with tired eyes.

He caresses my body with hungry eyes. The dim light casts a golden hue over his perfect frame. "Not with you right here looking absolutely perfect." He kisses and nibbles my neck.

I groan. "Aiden, we can't. Your ribs…"

He lets out a low laugh. "Just because I can't fuck you doesn't mean I can't do…" His hand grazes my inner thigh, "other things." He growls as his eyes devour me, hungrily. "I want you naked."

His emerald eyes watch my every move as I obey before sliding back on the bed.

"On your stomach," He instructs.

The sheets are smooth against my naked skin as I roll over. His stubble tickles me as he traces my curves with his lips, his hands gliding up my legs and over my ass. A pleasurable gasp escapes me when I feel his teeth gently sink into my cheek.

"You like that?" His voice is husky.

I raise my hips, silently asking for more.

A sharp smack greets my bottom instead.

"You didn't answer me," He growls, palming my ass.

I peer back, taking in Aiden's dark hair, a beautiful disaster. His throbbing length is heated against my bare leg.

"I'm going to ask again. Do you like what I do to you, Emilia?"

The way my name rolls off his tongue makes me squirm. Only Aiden can make a name sound sensual.

I don't answer.

I need to feel his hands on me, in any way, especially in that protective manner he does so well. Nothing excites me more than when he's this possessive of me.

I tilt my head innocently to the side while bringing my bottom lip between my teeth.

Aiden cocks a brow. "So, you want to play that game, huh?"

A smack rings throughout the room as heat flares across my other cheek. I moan his name as he slides a finger inside me.

"You won't win," He murmurs lowly as he fingers me. "Fuck, I missed this so much."

An arm goes under my stomach and I gasp as he flips me over onto my back.

"Aiden!" I exclaim in worry.

He goes straight for my neck, sucking

hard.

I know what he's doing.

"Be careful," I force out through ragged breaths. "Your ribs."

I throw my head back, moaning his name quietly.

His deep chuckle vibrates through me as he fists my hair. "You moan my name one more time and I won't hesitate to fuck you senseless right here right now. Broken ribs be damned."

I turn into putty under his very capable hands, squirming for more as he explores every inch of me.

"Stay still."

His full lips touch different parts of my body, gently biting and sucking. He pulls back to examine the marks he left on me, his eyes greedy and hungry. His fingers circle my nipples, pinching them sharply.

I fight back my moans as his hand trails down to circle my clit. The pleasure of his actions is so perfect, so exquisite I have to put a hand over my mouth.

A large hand traps my wrists, pinning them above my head, as his fingers continue working their magic on my most sensitive area.

"Don't cover your fucking mouth." His thumb flicks my clit just as he rams his finger in. "I don't care who hears."

His words bring me to the edge, and I

gladly fall off it, diving into euphoria from his warm touch.

I lay in bed, catching my breath, and push up onto my knees when Aiden stands next to the bed. He sinks his fingers through my hair and tugs as he guides his length into my mouth. I take in as much as I can, sucking and twirling my tongue around his length when I have a moment between him ramming it down my throat.

"That's right, baby. Fuck."

I peer up at him through batted lashes, enjoying the look of pleasure on his face. I suck harder, wanting him to finish down my throat but he pulls back instead. He grips his length, pumping it hard and fast. I watch greedily, moaning when he unloads himself on my face with a moan of my name.

"I'm going to go clean this up," I state as I feel his cum cool and drip down my cheek.

"I'd rather you didn't," He calls out teasingly.

"Why not?" I hop off the bed and grab a towel nearby to wipe him off.

He shrugs, his half smile melting me. "You could put on some clothes and go out there." He points to the cabin. "Let Leo see you with me all over you."

The humor is missing from his voice.

"Why would you want me to do that?" I ask, confused.

"So he can see my mark on you. Maybe then he'll stop fucking staring."

I laugh. "It's not like that, A."

He pushes up on his elbow, tilts his head.

Suddenly conscious about the nickname I gave him, I turn my face to the side to hide my red cheeks. "Sorry."

"No, I like it." He grins.

I gesture to the bathroom. "I'm going to wash this off."

He leans back, folding his arms behind his head, satisfied with himself. "Suit yourself. Your body is ravaged with my bite marks and hickeys anyways."

I flash him a sweet smile and wink. "I'm fine with that."

I grin when his face lights up.

I wash up before climbing under the covers and snuggling up against Aiden's chest, listening to the thumping of his heart as it lulls me to sleep.

This is probably the only time we'll be alone until we land and head back to the safe house.

I can't wait to see their reactions when they see him.

I jerk awake when Aiden begins thrashing against the sheets, still asleep.

Clicking on the bedside lamp, I watch as his face contorts, groaning and mumbling indiscernibly. Realizing his hands are searching the sheets, I slide closer. His hands clamp around my waist, pulling me closer.

"It's okay, Aiden," I soothe.

I'm not prepared when his eyes shoot open and he throws himself off the bed. I follow him closely, rubbing his shoulders while crooning gently to him to calm him. I can't imagine what he'd gone through in that awful cage. I hate seeing him like this.

He holds me tightly as he grows more aware of his surroundings and calms down. I pepper his face with kisses, whispering soothingly as he hugs me.

It doesn't take long before we doze off again, feeling more rested when we are awaken by the landing announcement.

I lean over and kiss Aiden's cheek as he rubs the sleep from his eyes.

"It's time to go home, babe."

Eleven

Aiden

Leo looks uncomfortable as we step into the cabin of the plane. I made sure Emilia wore my shirt just for good measure. I watch with amusement as his eyes trail to her neck where I left a mark, he turns away quickly pretending to be on his phone as we exit.

I know he heard her moans for me last night. Normally, I wouldn't want anyone to hear her sounds, but I had to let this guy know what's up. Emilia is a brilliant girl, but she lacks the ability to know when men are helplessly in love with her, myself included.

I understand his role in the actions that spared my life, but at the risk of her life? No. I just can't respect that decision. I can't respect any decision that interferes with my girls safety.

    I barely fucking slept last night. I don't want to burden her with my newfound nightmares, but nothing can break my spirit right now. I'm about to be reunited with Ash and Ricky and Howard, all with my girl by my side.

    Thinking about those four makes me realize what a lonely existence I lived before Em came into my life and filled it with more. Only ever caring about the next big investment or deal, never wondering about anyone besides myself. I'm successful because I was selfish, but she's showed me that I still have a beating heart.

    I wonder if they know I'm alive, I ask Emilia. She looks down, blushing. "Not yet, we didn't want to tell them such amazing news over the phone. Ash wouldn't believe me anyways." She giggles, trying to pick up her suitcase. I stop her and point to Leo. "Bags." I tell him, that's what he's here for anyways, right?

    The drive is long, but I don't mind as Emilia keeps her hand secured inside mine the entire time. I'm happy, but at the end of the day it's going to be a logistical nightmare for me if word of my 'death' has circulated.

    I'm hoping where Ricky took over that it's been quiet, with all the employees and financial advisors I have the business is capable of running efficiently on its own for a while, so there's hope that things will fall back into place even if I have to run everything through the safe house for a little while.

    These are the thoughts I consume myself with on

the drive from the airport, to try and calm my rushing heart at the simple fact that I'm alive. Business is easy to think about. Money, something I understand.

The normally timid girl sitting next to me, I don't understand at all. She risked her life coming to save me in Italy. Why? How am I so important to her that she would do something so brave?

Why does she adore me so much, when I'm such a fuckup?

My pride won't allow me to ask.

The driver pulls down the familiar long path leading to the cabin, I let out a sigh of relief. I've always loved this cabin. I bought it as a safe house just in case the need ever arose, but most of the time it's used for relaxing when I need to get away from it all. I don't know how I'm going to handle so many people being inside with me and Emilia, but I'm too elated to see everyone to think much on it.

I lift her from the SUV after we park, making sure Leo grabs her bags as we head for the front door. It's not quite dark yet but the sun is setting. The pink sky washes over the mountains and tall trees, it's so beautiful. A much better view than damp concrete walls and rusted chains. I rub my sore wrist, remembering how Emilia bandaged them on the plane.

I walk to the porch, standing off to the side as they enter.

Emilia

I step through the front door with shaky breaths, passing Aiden as he leans against the house, still in earshot. Leo comes in behind me, leaving the door open so he can hear us.

As Leo sets down my luggage, I survey the room. First, I look for Howard; but can't find him. I assumed he would be waiting at the door to yell at me.

After I call for them, Ashley appears with Ricky in tow. She wraps me in a tight hug. "I was so worried about you." She cries. I hug her fiercely, stepping back to look at both her and Ricky. Racking my brain, trying to decide how to tell them such unbelievable news.

"I'm so sorry I worried you guys." Guilt pangs in my voice, but they're about to be so happy.

Ashley rubs her hand on my shoulder, "You can't run away like that, I know times are hard, but we were worried." I give her a confused expression and silently thank Howard for lying to them for me.

With a weak smile, I sigh. "Where's Howard?" I ask, peeking my head around the room.

Ricky speaks first, his usually cool demeanor wavers. "He's... busy."

Okay, that was vague.

Time to tell them about Aiden. "I didn't run away Ash, I went to look for Aiden." I say this slowly.

Her face falls, "Em." A tear shoots down her

cheek. She wipes it away with her sleeve, more follow.

"No, no. Don't cry." I give her a warming smile.

I guide her to the couch with my hand, her eyes comb over me warily. "Em, I know it's hard. But we buried him sweetheart. I can't believe you didn't tell me you were going to look... I- wait we don't even know who took him, where did you even start?"

"Italy." I say, clamping my hands around hers. She tilts her head at me, "Italy." She repeats in a disbelieving tone.

Me and Aiden both decided this was the best course of action, to let it flow into her naturally versus just throwing him right in front of her. Even though she would be ecstatically happy, it could be traumatizing to see your 'dead' brother standing in front of you so abruptly.

Here we go. "You know that necklace he gave me?"

"The locket." She answers, her eyes slowly moving down to my neck.

"Is that a hickey!" Her eyes cut to Leo, shooting daggers. I smile at her quick thinking. Shaking my head, I brush my fingers against the locket. Lifting it to showcase the key slot, hoping that she's catching on.

I've never told anyone something like this before, I hope I'm doing an okay job. My best friend's well-being means so much to me. We've been each other's rocks throughout this nightmare. I smile brightly, from ear to ear as the two of them look in my direction, it's hard to contain my excitement.

"It was a tracker." I tell her. Instantly, she clamps her chest. Ricky opens his mouth to speak but stops himself.

"But Howard said the locket wasn't on his body..." She speaks slowly until reality hugs her in the face. "You found him?"

With a Cheshire grin, I give a bright nod. "Oh, we found him."

Carefully she leans forward, blonde hair blankets her tearful face. "Alive?" Her voice at a distant whisper, afraid to get her hopes up.

"Ash sweetheart, yes. Alive. Would you like to see him?"

She nods vigorously and with a triumphant smile I clap my hands and look back as Aiden rounds the threshold. Ashley falls to her knees at the sight of him.

Ashley

I can't... I can't believe it. I didn't realize I had fallen to my knees until Aiden got on the floor in front of me. Is it real? Is he real? I look over to Em, tears streaming down her cheeks. I touch the hardwoods, grazing my fingers over the rough grains, it's real. I can feel everything, I'm not dreaming, but how?

"We buried you." My voice cracks, an unfamiliar feeling of warmth shoots through me. He nods, his face trying to look upset on my behalf for what we've been through, but I can see he's having a hard time holding back his excitement.

I don't miss the bruises on his body, or the

bandages on his wrist.

I carefully throw my arms around him as he lifts me up to stand. I weep into his shoulder, then my hand wonders the air for Em. When she finds it, I pull her into us. Stepping back, I admire them both. My brother is alive, my best friend saved him. She's alive but how stupid, she really did go to Italy!

"Emilia Banks!" I try to be stern but my smile cracks through my façade, her honey eyes beam with life. "You must love him so much." I cry, so thankful to her for so many things throughout our friendship.

From breakups, to undecided majors, to great losses she's been my everything. Mine and Aiden's relationship has catapulted into something more, because of her.

"She's your angel." I tell him, Em blushes. Ever the girl who can't take a compliment, but that's what I love about her. Brilliant, beautiful and humble. Things have been rocky in our lives but never once did our bond even think of collapsing. She is my best friend, and now my brother's protector as much as he is hers.

I look to Aiden, the sight of him taking my breath away. My body shakes as he holds my shoulders, I notice Ricky standing behind me with his hands behind my waist.

Ricky and Aiden exchange a hug, words were said but I couldn't catch them in the frenzy of our reunion.

"Who took you?" Ricky ask, his voice shaken.

Aiden shrugs, unable to answer. The severity of his wounds makes me shiver. *What happened to him?*

But nothing, absolutely nothing compares to the overwhelming joy I feel to have them both home and safe. I am on the verge of breaking down from everything going on, but I am too elated to feel anything but joy.

I pull Aiden to the side and study his face, so many things I wanted to say to him, but it was too late. It's not anymore. "You know in that video." He nods solemnly, clearly guilt ridden.

"I'm sorry Ash, I just..."

"No, don't explain or apologize. I get it, you wanted all of us protected. But what you said, about how you haven't always been there for me…"

He takes in a sharp intake of breath, uncomfortable with such a heartfelt conversation... I don't care. "Listen, I know you didn't have it easy growing up after your mom passed. I know how shitty dad was, I'm sorry I never visited."

"I never wanted you under the same roof as him." He states, his tone cold.

"I know it was hard for you to visit me and see the interaction with my mom and me. I know you've spent your life building an empire for yourself, but this has to be it, Aiden. Whatever you have to do to get out of this, you have to find a way. Nothing like this can ever happen again, I can't believe I'm even able to say this to you." I've rehearsed that in my head so many times, in the hopes that he could hear me in heaven or the insane notion that one day he would walk through the door just like this, I guess it wasn't so insane of a thought after all.

He smiles, slightly rolling his eyes. Surprisingly, I

feel his arms wrap around me. "Thank you, Ash. Thank you for understanding."

I keep my arms carefully wrapped around him and my eyes flutter over to my smiling best friend as she watches us, gently bouncing on the balls of her feet from excitement.

Then the guilt takes over.

I hope she can forgive me for what I did.

Emilia

"You what!" For the first time in my life, I'm screaming at my best friend. *What was she thinking?*

She looks me over with a weak smile, "We had no idea where you were, what choice did I have?"

"Absolutely any other choice besides this one." My eyes roll, giving a full view of the lonely cabin bedroom that I've been staying in.

"When is she coming?" I huff, crossing my arms.

Ashley looks around, trying to determine the best way to tell me. "She'll be here within the hour."

Aiden peeps in, I'm sure he heard our shouting. Hell, the whole state probably did. I look to him in desperation. "My mom will be here in an hour." I pout, fear coursing through me.

"Oh." Is all he says, then he tries to slip out of the room.

"Oh?" I shout, and when he cuts his eyes to me, I

relax. Why does his dominance help me to relax? Maybe it was like what he was saying on the plane. I crave structure and order; he is that structure and order. But none of that matters right now.

A wave of nausea runs through me, "Aiden." My throat instantly dries. "Will she be safe coming here?" I throw my hands up in frustration, realizing I don't even know where we are. I've been so caught up in unspeakable grief that I never paid attention to anything. We left so late that night going to Italy, the road signs were just unfamiliar street names.

His velvety voice flows through my ears. "Yes babe. She'll be safe, Howard is on his way to get her." Oh, how I missed the way his words can calm me in an instant. So that's where Howard was.

Wait. "How did you know where he was?"

"Ricky." He replies.

I look between them. "Anything else I should know?" I start to collect myself as they shake their heads.

Taking in a calming breath, the scent of cedar fills my nostrils. "So, where are we?"

Aiden pinches the bridge of his nose, "The safe house is located in Oregon still, it's an hour from Corvallis."

I take a relieving breath, knowing she's safe. "She's going to kill me."

"You're going to have to lie sweetheart." He tells me, his gaze travels around the room.

"I suck at lying!"

They both look between each other and

simultaneously say, "We know."

Aiden picks up a piece of my clothing, examining it. "Emilia, tell me why your things are in this room?"

"I've been staying in here."

His fingers slip through his tousled hair, "You we're meant to stay in the master bedroom, it's better."

I throw my hands up. "None of this matters! I wanted to stay in this one. The most important issue is that I'm going to be a dead woman come sixty minutes."

Aiden gives a smirk; I know he thinks I'm being dramatic, but he doesn't get it. "It's not going to be a big deal. Ash, what did you tell her?"

She looks around the room, attempting to avoid the question. "I... Well."

"Spit it out." He sneers, his tone dark. I know I'm upset with her but too much has happened for any of us to be hostile towards each other.

"Okay, let's take a breather." I sit next to Ashley on the bed, Aiden leans against the wall. "I'm sorry for freaking. I just don't want her to hate Aiden if she thinks I just ran away. She's probably worried sick and on top of it all, I don't want her in danger.

"I understand completely, you don't have to explain to me, I was just so worried. I figured you went home, so I called her. She got a little panicked thinking something happened to you."

I nod, "Where does she think Aiden was?"

"Well after she calmed down, she asked. I didn't know what to say, I told her you guys left together even though…"

Aiden nods his head, thinking. "Okay, that's good."

I run my hand through my hair, reminding myself of Aiden. "I know I'm eighteen, I'm an adult but that's not why I'm freaking out. It's just… me and mom are all we have for family, after we lost dad, she held onto me so tightly it was suffocating." I sigh, remembering the enormous impact the loss of my father had on us. "I understand now why she did it, but she worked so hard going to therapy and going through the proper steps of grieving that I don't want her worrying about me." I look to Aiden, "And she really likes you, I don't want her opinion on you to change."

"It can be salvaged." He assures me, pulling my hands from where I've buried my face in them.

"How?"

He shrugs, so calm. "We can say it was a misunderstanding." He looks over to Ash. "Anything you can think of?"

Ashley thinks for a moment, then a light clicks on in her head. "Well, you got that scholarship!" She squeals, then instantly clamps her hands over her mouth.

"Scholarship?" Aiden cocks his brow at me.

To be honest, I haven't had time to think about that. "I got a full ride to Portland State."

He pulls me from the bed and wraps me in his arms, I push back when he winces from the pain. "That's wonderful babe!"

I shake my head, "Not really."

"Why not?"

"I'm not going." I say in a small voice.

He looks down at me, narrowing his eyes. "The fuck you aren't."

Ashley shifts uncomfortably on the mattress.

I try to reason with him. "Look, we don't know who took you. We have no clue what the future holds. We can't just return to our normal lives. I can't."

"I can't!" He exclaims. "You can." He gestures between the two of us, "They don't know you, either of you."

A bitter laugh escapes my lips. "So what, you'll just live here while we move back?"

"No, just.... None of that is important right now. I'm so proud of you and this will work to your advantage."

"How?" I ask.

"Okay, so she thought you two were at a summer retreat for a month, right?"

I nod.

"Okay, it's been a few weeks so we will just tell her that once I found out about your scholarship, we decided to have a celebratory vacation. No harm in that, right?"

"Right." I say, slightly de-thawing.

Then I frown, "That still doesn't help the phone call Ash made, what will we say about that?" A groan escapes me, "Plus, the grounds here are littered with bodyguards."

He thinks for a moment. "Okay, let me worry about all of that. For now, we celebrate my return." He gives a cocky grin.

    After a few glasses of wine to calm my nerves, the familiar sound of rubber on pavement drowns my ears. A car door slams, then another one. The tapping of my mom's heels against the stone entryway makes my heart almost burst out of my chest.

Thirteen

I discreetly slide the glass of wine away when Mom steps through the front doors, her eyes frantically looking around. She locks her gaze on mine, and a sigh of relief escapes her lips.

Something soft and warm wraps around my neck, and I look down to see a scarf. I lift a brow at Aiden in confusion.

Hickeys, He mouths.

Got it.

She rushes to me, looking between Ashley and I. "What's going on?" Her voice is shaky.

I resist the urge to throw my arms around Howard's neck when he steps through the door. He does look a little angry.

Aiden is beside me, holding something in his hands.

"Hey Mom!" I pull her into a hug, feeling her melt against me in relief.

I keep quiet, remembering Aiden's words and letting him take the lead on this.

Her eyes search my face before turning to Ashley. "What is going on?"

Aiden smiles down at her. "Hello, Ms. Banks."

She gives him a confused look.

"Are you okay?" He frowns.

She throws her purse on the bar top and straightens. "Well…I received a phone call saying that my daughter has been missing for three days. No one bothered to call me before that, and now, she's here." She shoots us a skeptical look. "I'm happy that she's safe…but someone needs to start talking."

I give Ashley an innocent look and shrug.

"I'm sorry Ashley said that." Aiden shoots her an angry look before turning to my mom. "Emilia got some good news, so we're throwing her a party. Ashley was in charge of getting you here for the surprise."

Oh, he's good.

She rolls her eyes and turns to Ash. "Of all the things you could have said, why would you make me believe my daughter is missing?" She huffs, dumbfounded.

Ashley gives her a weak smile. "Sorry."

Mom shakes her head. "Wine." She gently demands, a smile tilting on her face.

We came back at such a perfect time. We would have been absolutely screwed if we stayed in Italy for another night. Mafia be damned. My mother would have personally killed me.

I introduce her to everyone and after getting a few more hugs, she settles down. Thank God.

Sitting on the barstool with her legs crossed, she peers around the cabin while sipping her glass of wine. "This is beautiful. Where did you find it and why aren't you girls at the retreat?"

"It's Aiden's." I beam proudly.

Her eyes widen slightly before she collects herself.

I know what that means. *Did you spend the past few weeks here instead of the retreat I paid for you to go to?*

"We left the retreat a few days ago to celebrate!"

"So, what's this good news?"

Aiden hands me a piece of paper. It's a printout of my scholarship letter.

With a smile, I hand it to mom.

She sets down her wine glass and grabs her readers from her purse. As she skims over the document, tears form in her eyes.

"Oh, honey!" She exclaims, not looking

up from the paper. "This is incredible!" She wraps me in a tight hug. "You can finally follow your dreams."

I can feel the relief and happiness in her words as she holds me tightly.

She pulls away and playfully slaps Ashley's arm. "I forgive you, but my God, you need to work on your lying skills. You almost gave me a heart attack! Poor Howard here saw me cry within the first two minutes we met." She flashes him a smile.

It's odd that she knows Howard now, but at least she thinks he's simply Aiden's driver and not the head of his security.

The visit flies by in a flash, and at around ten, she asks me to go somewhere private with her. I guide her to the balcony, wishing it wasn't dark so she could see the view. She would love it.

"First thing I wanted to talk to you about, Emilia." She gives me a stern look. Shit. "I know you're an adult. I get it, your friends are here, you're celebrating…" She sets her glass and purse down on the small patio table. She opens her mouth to speak but closes it.

The silence stretches out and I see a blush form on her cheeks despite the sparse lighting.

"Are you two being careful?

I throw my head back, mortified. "Mom."

She cuts her eyes to me.

"Of course, we are." We always are.

"Good." She nods, letting that conversation end. Thankfully.

I look around the cabin, changing the subject. "There's plenty of guest rooms for you to stay in. Howard can bring you back tomorrow."

She frowns. "Oh, honey, I wish I could stay, but I can't. I've got to return home. Tomorrow is the grand opening of our new wing."

"A new wing? At the shop?"

She bounces on her heels. "Yes! I've been waiting to tell you in person. The shops been doing so well since Aiden's investment that I decided to buy the lot next door. We're adding an interactive butterfly exhibit. You know how much I love them, and with the warm climate of the greenhouse, we will be able to have more tropical flowers. I'm so excited!"

I love watching how animated she gets when talking about her shop. I'm just so happy for her and for a moment, my life is normal.

"It's late though." I reason, not wanting her to go just yet. So many things have happened that she doesn't know about.

"Hardly. I'll be home a little after eleven if we leave soon. Howard…" She pauses. "He's a nice man."

My eyes widen. I haven't seen *that* look before.

"Oh! Before I forget." She pulls an

envelope and a small box from her bag and places the contents in my hands. "This came for you at the house. The return sender is Scott Investment Corporation, so I assumed it was for you. I know we do business together, but those letters are normally sent to the shop. I was tempted to open it when Ashley told me she couldn't find you, just to see what it was." She laughs.

I'm glad she's blissfully unaware of how much danger I've been in lately.

"The box is for your birthday." She smiles. "From me." She looks down. "And your father."

I set the envelope down on the patio table and grab the box. I open it slowly, tilting it in the direction of the porch light to get a better view. I catch a golden shimmer, igniting tears in my eyes.

It's a bracelet. A couple of charms line the golden threads.

"Your father bought this for you when you were a little girl." Her smile falls as she wipes tears from her eyes. "I was supposed to give it to you on your eighteenth birthday, but I didn't have the strength. It's the last gift you'll ever receive from him and it broke my heart."

I twirl the bracelet in my hand as I fight back tears. "It's beautiful. Tell me about the charms."

"This one," She gestures to a tiny rose gold whisk, "It was my choice. I added it recently." She lets out a small laugh. "And now, look at you. You made it, baby. You get to follow your dreams."

"I love it." I whisper, my lips quivering.

"And this one…" She pauses, pointing to the diamond encrusted yellow rose. "Is of course your father's choice."

"It's beautiful." I throw my arms around her in a tight hug before pulling back to let her fasten the bracelet on my wrist.

I admire how it looks sitting against my skin, near my ring.

As we head back inside, she chuckles while stumbling. I think she had a little too much wine.

After she hugs me no less than three times, Aiden places his arm through hers and guides her to the car, with Howard close behind.

I return to the porch alone with a glass of wine. Anxious to see what the Manilla folder holds. I move the prongs and pull out a sheet of paper.

Ms. Banks.

Aiden's handwriting.

What is this? My eyes narrow to adjust to the dim lighting.

'If you've received this letter, I'm no longer

here. I wanted to give Emilia fair time to tell you what happened, so this will come to you later. I didn't want her to be financially troubled and so I made it so that she will never have to worry about money again.

Enclosed is a check for you, so that you don't have to worry about money again either. Please don't try and return it. My assistant will send it back each time. I'm sorry to have to leave her alone. Please watch over her as you always have.

Thank you for raising such an amazing woman.
Aiden Scott
Scott Investment Corporation

I slip my hand inside the envelope and pull out the check.

"The letter was fine, but don't look at the check."

I turn to see Aiden leaning against the balcony door with a smirk on his face.

"I was wondering when your mom was going to tell you about that. I assumed it was unopened, or she would have fucking flipped when she got it."

"How long have you been there?" Tears fill my tired eyes.

He shrugs, holding out his hand.

I shake my head. "Not only were you going to take care of me, but my mom too?"

For weeks, my days have been filled with nothing but anguish. Now, ever since he returned to me, I've felt nothing but happiness.

"Of course. She made you."

His simple yet powerful words bring tears to my eyes. I look down, shaking my head. That's when I see the numbers on the check.

Two million dollars.

"Aiden!"

He throws his head back with a laugh. "I just told you not to look at it."

"She would have never accepted it."

He nods. "I know. That's why I had it set up where if it didn't get deposited or she sent it back, another would be delivered until she did."

"Why did you send it to the house?"

"I didn't want to risk someone at her workplace opening it."

My mouth forms an 'O' before I set everything down and make my way to him. I go on my tippy-toes and cup his face. "You don't realize how amazing you are." I declare.

"Amazing?" He scoffs, stepping away from me. "Emilia, I can't even fathom why you're still with me."

His words take me aback.

"Do you not want me to be?"

His smirk reveals deep dimples. "You're so smart, but sometimes you can be so oblivious. Yes, I want you. I want you every second of every fucking day, Emilia Banks. That's the only thing I do know." He paces the porch, running his hands though his tousled hair. "What I can't figure out is why you stay."

He's normally so confident. What happened to make him this way?

Stopping such a large man takes a bit of effort as I reach up to peel his hands from his face. "Don't you get it by now, A?"

He looks at me, his expression grim.

I soften my voice. "You're it for me. You're made for me. It's that simple."

He gives a small laugh, no trace of humor in it. "It's not that simple, Emilia." His voice grows stern. "I almost got you killed. I put you in danger."

I shake my head. "No. You made some bad business decisions, before you met me, before you got close with Ash again. You didn't know your life would involve all of this." I gesture towards the living room where everyone is. "You didn't know you would have us. And now you do."

He pulls me into a hug, breathing me in.
"That's what I'm scared of. I have everything to lose now."

Fourteen

Laying on my side, I take in Aiden's sleepy features. His rough edges that are usually softened in his sleep now look haunted.

I've tried everything to fall asleep, but between my mom's impromptu visit and Aiden's confession of his worries, my brain has trouble winding down. I'm fully aware of how dangerous our lives are right now, but he doesn't need to worry about me going anywhere.

Careful not to wake him, I slip out of the bed and tip-toe downstairs for a glass of hot chocolate. I rummage through the pantry, looking for anything sweet, and pull out a bag of chocolate chips with triumph.

EMILIA

I stroll through the quiet cabin, trying to quell my restless mind as I sip on the creamy treat.

Spying Leo on the porch, I step out. "Can't sleep?"

He shakes his head, a small smile playing on his lips. "I'm on watch duty."

"Isn't this a safe house? Is that normal?"

He shrugs, lighting up a cigarette.

I inhale at the rich aroma.

"I like to keep on my toes, just in case." He winks, blowing the smoke away from me.

Remembering the taste from Italy, I grow curious. "Can I have one?"

With a smile, he pulls one out and places it between my lips. The lighter flicks on and he brings the flame to the end of my cigarette.

An unnatural gust of wind tickles my face and the flame disappears.

I turn slightly, spotting the cause.

Dressed in a pair of sweatpants that sit so perfectly low I can see the well-defined V below his tattooed stomach, Aiden stands with his eyes narrowed. I snap out of my daze when his finger brushes against my lips as he takes the cigarette away and places it in his mouth before lighting it. He scowls at Leo as he takes his first drag.

"She doesn't smoke." Aiden spits.

I catch Leo's amusement as he nods.

Aiden doesn't miss it either. "Let me

make one thing clear." He takes a menacing step forward, crossing his inked arms over his broad chest. "You're not going to corrupt her."

A carefree smile forms on his lips. "She asked for one the night we stayed in the hotel together. I didn't tell her no."

I blink.

Seriously, Leo?

Aiden's narrowed eyes cut to me.

I smile innocently, trying to salvage the situation. "It reminded me of you. I missed you."

Aiden places a hand on the back of my neck, grazing my exposed shoulder with his fingertips and sending a chill through my body. "But I'm home now, beautiful."

I smile at that.

"And it's a disgusting habit. I don't want you picking it up."

I nod. He's right, but I was curious.

After a moment of silence, Aiden rudely waves Leo off and I shoot him an apologetic look as he steps inside the cabin. Aiden leads me to the far side of the patio by my hand, his jade eyes searching behind me to make sure Leo is really gone. Carefully, he lifts me onto the ledge of the porch rail.

"Careful. Don't hurt your wrist," I remind him, trusting that he won't let me fall.

He holds up his arm, the white bandages still intact, before wrapping it around my waist.

The guard rail is high, putting me at eye level with him. The shirt I'm wearing rides up as he steps between my legs.

"Did he ever touch you?" He growls, his hand firmly on my thigh.

I swallow nervously.

"I don't mean the shit that happened at the mansion. What had to be done is what had to be fucking done, I guess."

I think for a moment. "Not in the way you're thinking."

"Tell me, Emilia." His tone is deadly. "And don't lie to me."

I bite my lip, trying to hold back a smile at his possessiveness. I missed him so much. It fades as my stomach grows sick as I think of how I'm going to explain this.

"Well, the first night we stayed together in that condo…"

"Separate rooms, right? Because from what I recall, I saw only one bed. Was there another room attached that I didn't see?"

I pause, distracted by the sharp edges of his jaw and his defined cheeks as he takes one last drag of his cigarette.

I bite my lips, nervous. "No. They only had one bedroom available."

"Bullshit," He spits.

"I'm not lying." I frown.

"No, but he is. I'm sure some other place

had two beds. I assume he made the reservations?"

Aiden throws his head back with a bark of laughter when I nod.

"He slept on the couch?"

Guilt drowns me, unsure how to explain how innocent that night was. I shake my head tentatively.

"The floor?" His tone grows darker, if that's possible.

I place my hands on his warm chest, trying to cool his anger. "Let me explain before you flip out."

"Fucking. Answer. Me."

I take a deep breath and let it slip.

"We slept in the same bed."

Aiden chuckles lowly. The same maniacal sound I've grown accustomed to when anyone tries to mess with me.

"Please." I plead, wrapping my hand around his arm, his muscles tensing with his growing rage.

His smile widens, dimples in full view. With a nod, he gestures for me to continue. I can tell he's close to breaking, thinking of a million ways to kill Leo.

I tell him about our failed reconnaissance mission, and how I believed he was gone for good. That my life was over.

"I needed the comfort, Aiden. You have no idea how dark my thoughts were as I looked out over the balcony." My eyes water. "I was drunk. It seemed easier to just…jump." I admit, my voice low and ashamed.

He hugs me tightly, kissing my neck. "I'm sorry, baby. I'm so fucking sorry."

"We just slept on the bed. That's it. Nothing happened."

"Okay." His voice is surprisingly calm.

I blink, gazing into his eyes. "Okay?" *Well, that was easy.* "Thank you for understanding." I sigh in relief.

He laughs. "Don't get me wrong. I understand why you did it, I trust *you*. But I'm still going to kill him."

"Aiden, I fucking buried you."

He cuts me a warning look at my harsh tone before bowing his head at my words.

"Then you were alive again. Do you know the joy that went through me? Then you were gone again. Leo was there for me. Do you have any idea what my mind was like? I don't know what you went through, but I wouldn't judge you for needing a moment of peace."

He shakes his head, opening his mouth to speak.

I cut him off. "Leo knew. I think that's why he took the bottle away and handed me the cigarette. A reminder of you was what I needed. He was going to sleep on the couch. I told him no. I was…afraid of what I might do. I laid on his chest, and we fell asleep. That's it."

His jaw twitches. "So, he didn't…touch you?" His shoulders relax slightly.

I smile. "Of course not. No one ever will." My smile fades and a memory flashes in my mind. "He did help me shower though."

"He fucking what?" Aiden snaps.

"Clothed!" I exclaim. "After I found your empty cell, I shut down. I was covered in muck and blood, and…I'm sorry. Don't blame him. He was just trying to protect me."

His hand circles my throat possessively. "You haven't seen fucking protective, Emilia Banks."

I bite my lip, reveling in the heady feel of his strong hands on me.

"Fuck this." With a growl, his lips crash down onto mine, devouring me.

"What are you doing?" I moan, feeling him harden against me, yet concerned about his broken ribs.

"Claiming you." With one hand, he hastily pulls down his pants. "I'm not waiting any longer to fuck you. To bury myself so deep inside of you, there will never be room left for anyone to try and take you away from me."

"No one ever will," I assure him breathily.

He has nothing to worry about. I'm his, heart and soul.

"I need to mold myself into you. Stretch your perfect cunt with my throbbing fucking cock to prove just how fucking taken you are."

I feel my blood heat as I grow wet at his words. I've missed this.

His warm hand slides up my thighs, pulling my panties aside. His fingers graze my slit, sending shivers through me. I gasp as he nudges himself against me and pushes in impatiently.

"Already so fucking wet," Aiden moans. "So fucking ready for me."

I moan his name as he thrust harder, eliciting a territorial growl from him. "Take me," I beg.

His rough calloused hands caress my body as he slides into me fully. It isn't methodical or sweet. He's rough and uncalculated, something that never fails to turn me on. It's always passionate, but this is so much more than what I've ever experienced.

I know he'll stop if I make the slightest inclination that I'm in pain. He's so big that it's a struggle to fit all of him inside, but the fullness is so blissfully perfect I couldn't bear if he stopped.

"This is where I'm supposed to be," I announce, my voice is different, smoother…rougher.

"What do you mean?" He moans, his

movements grow desperate.

"You." I rake my nails across his back. "Inside of me."

"Fuck, Emilia."

"I'm meant to be right here, Aiden. My body is yours…I am yours." I reassure his jealous mind as he pounds into me, desperate grunts escaping his full lips.

"As I am yours." His voice breaks.

I gaze up into his eyes; they're glazed over. I blink in surprise when a tear rolls down my cheek.

"I missed you." I moan, digging my nails into his back.

He grunts, pounding harder into me. My moans echo through the quiet night as he doesn't cover my mouth like he normally does. I bring a hand up to muffle myself, but he peels it away, placing it on his back.

With every hard thrust, his arm tightens around me, keeping me safe. It's a feeling of freedom being suspended so high in the air. Putting all of my trust in Aiden to keep me safe while sending me into euphoria. His hands are everywhere and nowhere all at once, it's as if we're floating on air. I'm utterly transfixed, we are tangled, one.

"I love you." We mutter at the same time while gazing into each other's tear-filled eyes.

Aiden

Leo may think he can have Emilia, but that will never happen.

She's mine.

I don't care how it sounds, but her body, and her everything belongs to me. I own her, as she owns me.

With every thrust, I relish that fact.

Her trust for me is unrelenting. She is sitting on a thin porch railing, being nailed to it by me. My arm holds her in place while my cock holds her up. What more could I ask for in a woman?

She gives me her complete and total fucking devotion.

I'm not mad at her for what happened. She was desperate. She buried me. Then, she had such a pure hope that I was alive, only to find that locket necklace with me nowhere in sight. It had to be fucking devastating.

I hate the things she's been through, because of me. But I'm home now, and I will protect her with my dying breath.

"You feel so good wrapped around my fucking cock," I murmur against her neck. Needing Leo to know who she belongs to, I mark her. Her neck, her chest. Everywhere my mouth lands, I mark. My fucking territory.

After, I make sure to fix her clothes as we head back upstairs. I'm going to have a little talk with Leo once she falls asleep.

I gaze down at Emilia, gently caressing her body as she dozes off. "Can I at least cut off his hands?" I smile as I think about it.

"No."

"I can't kill him or cut off his hands…" I shrug as she swats my arm sleepily. "I'll fire him." I come to a compromise.

She pushes herself up and grabs my hand. "I know you don't like him, but he saved your life. You don't have to worry about me and him. I think he was just being sweet because I was so distraught. He doesn't like me that way."

I raise my brow in disbelief.

"It was completely innocent. I swear it wasn't anything like that," She promises.

Of course, I believe her, my sweet naïve girl.

It wasn't like that for her, but for him? No, no, no. He will understand what happens when someone tries to take advantage of my sweet Emilia.

Yes, he helped return me to her, but I simply can't forgive the danger you were in. I can't get the image of your dark, soft hair laying against his chest by the ocean in Italy out of my head. That should have been me, not him.

I kiss her forehead as she falls asleep in my arms.

Then, I slip out to find Leo.

Emilia

My eyes flutter. "I'm so tired, Aiden." I yawn, wrapping my hands around his neck, I don't know why he's woken me up. A heavy scent of bourbon lingers around him as we lay tangled in the bed sheets.

"Shh, babe. Just a little while longer." He holds a finger up. Then a clock chimes; showcasing its midnight. He flips himself over, sitting in between my legs.

"Happy Birthday, Beautiful." He smiles, pulling me in for a kiss.

I look at him, completely stunned. "How did you

know?" I ask, twirling the promise ring that we haven't yet talked about around my finger. I want to ask him so bad about it, but he was going to give it to me the night he was taken... is it a promise ring? Or just a gift?

"I know everything about you." His lips trail my neckline. "What you like." He places a hand on my throat, "What you dislike." His husky voice toying with me, "What you need from me." His warm hand cups me, his touch awakening my body.

Walking downstairs the next morning takes a moment, last night was perfect but having sex multiple times in one night has me walking on wobbly legs.

Taking a seat at the barstool I look over at Ashley as she attempts to make something at the stove. Her hair in a bun atop of her head, with pajamas adorning her tall frame. I would offer to help, but I legitimately can't walk straight.

I look around for anyone else, only spotting a few quiet guards dotted at the entrance to the cabin. I don't have to look for long as Aiden walks in.

From the looks of him I can tell why I woke up to an empty bed this morning. He's been busy working out, only wearing gray track pants. His hair lays messy on his head and his entire body is glistening.

I bite my lip as I watch him looking at me, the way his emerald eyes seem to always drink me in sends chills down my spine. Rubbing his hands together, he walks up to me, placing a warm hand on my thigh.

Leaning down he whispers into my ear, "How you feeling today, angel?"

I wasn't sure if I should tell him what happened last night after we went upstairs. Shortly after he fell asleep in my arms, which isn't the usual. Normally it's reversed, me on his chest and his arms wrapped tightly around my waist.

He had a terrible nightmare, all he kept repeating was "No, No, NO." I want to get him to talk to someone about what he went through, but he refuses to disclose even the smallest bit of information with me about his time in the torture chamber in Italy.

He's staring at me waiting for an answer, I didn't realize I zoned out. I nod, "I'm good." I smile, taking a deep breath. He's so close, his scent is intoxicating, and he's been working out. How does he do it? Always so... perfect.

He moves a hand from behind his back, showcasing a solitary yellow rose. He's good, so good. The way my heart melts in that moment takes my breath away, pure adoration is the only way I can explain my feelings for him.

"Em, can you help me?" Ashley's desperate voice breaks me from my longing thoughts. She's facing away from us, busy at the countertop.

"Go help her." I plead with him in a whisper, he cocks his brow at me.

"I don't know how to cook." He whispers back, but it's awkward because he doesn't understand why we're whispering in the first place.

I look down to my legs and after my eyes return to him, I see realization dawn on his face. He leans in, kissing my cheek and whispers, "I fucked you too hard last night."

A huff sounds from somewhere behind us, "Okay, is someone going to help me cook?" Now she's turned in our direction. Looking irritated.

Aiden waves her off, "Yeah. Yeah."

"You're going to help?" She's holding a spatula in her hand, flicking it towards a grinning Aiden. Shrugging she says, "Okay, chop the fruit."

I enjoy watching the two of them together, wondering when the last time was that they did something like this together.

Lost in thought I barely notice when a plate is placed in front of me, I look down. A big floppy pancake with two chocolate chip eyes and a banana smile stares into my soul.

Oh no.

She was making my birthday breakfast. Why did I think this was a one-time thing last year and not the start of a tradition?

Aiden squeezes in next to me at the bar top, holding his own plate of pancakes, sans smiley. "Why this?" He gestures to my plate, mimicking the fruit smile.

Ash raises a brow at him. "It's her birthday pancakes, don't judge." She smiles at me. "Happy Birthday by the way!"

"Thank you, Ash."

Aiden tilts his head at me, grinning. "Smiley face

pancakes?"

"Absolutely!" I say, smiling. Inside, I'm dying.

Ashley turns to the stove, continuing her assault on the poor pancakes. I don't know why I didn't notice what she was doing before. Aiden takes a bite, I watch as he chews slowly, his nose turning up slightly. Then he begins to head towards the trash can. I lean into him, whispering. "Don't you dare spit it out."

"Going to grab Ricky!" Ash squeals, dancing out of the kitchen.

When she leaves Aiden looks at his pancakes, his brows creasing. "What in the fuck?" he says to the plate, I hold back laughter.

"I don't have the heart to tell her they're awful." I scan the room to triple check that we're alone. "I was a little homesick on my birthday last year and Ashley asked what I normally did. I told her my mom made pancakes..." I trail off, gesturing to the mound of whatever is on my plate.

"You should tell her, these should be fucking illegal." He jokes. I swat him on the arm. "Fine. I'll tell her. You shouldn't have to endure this on your birthday."

I narrow my eyes. "You tell her, I won't talk to you for a week."

Laughing, he slides his pancake into the trash. "Baby, in what world would you not talk to me for a week?" Immediate silence grows between us. My thoughts rewinding to the weeks I spent thinking he was dead. His thoughts, unreachable.

Distant laughs drown out our silence. Aiden

brings my hand to his lips, taking his time to kiss each knuckle before everyone crowds the kitchen.

Ashley hands Ricky a plate, he gives her a fake smile. He must know. It's not for lack of trying, I've showed her before how to bake and cook but she gets so damn excited about these pancakes... who am I to hurt her feelings?

A frown forms on my face as Leo makes his way into the kitchen, with a fresh black eye taking up residency on his face. I turn my attention to Aiden, who is now eating an apple. "What?"

I look around, "Living room?" I gesture, he nods.

It's not very private anywhere in this cabin. It's designed beautifully and there's plenty of space, but everything is so open. Looking at Aiden pointedly I try and keep my voice down. "I told you not to hurt him."

Tattooed arms cross his chest. "No, you said don't kill him. Does he look dead? I hardly hurt him, serves him right."

"He saved your life, Aiden."

He scoffs, "I punched him for touching you. For his involvement in my rescue, I drank a bottle of bourbon with him." His eyes narrow. "You saved my life, not him."

Rolling my eyes, "I think you hate him because you're so similar."

he scoffs, "Don't fucking compare me to him."

"No, no. I just-"

Aiden cuts me off, slashing his hand in the air. "I hate him because he thinks we're going after the same girl. *If* he understands now, things will be okay."

"Em!" We head back into the kitchen when Ash yells my name. I lock eyes with Leo for a brief moment and give him an apologetic smile. But besides the black eye and bruised jaw he seems totally fine, smiling away.

Ash leans against the counter, eating a bowl of cereal. "So, you're not eating the pancakes?" Aiden asks, his tone light.

Here we go, "No, I hate pancakes. They're Em's fave though." She smiles at me, returning her attention to the Frosted Flakes. Aiden gives me a 'that explains it' look.

"So… I have an idea of what to do for your birthday!"

Aiden and Leo both stand a little taller, looking at her. "And what's that?" Aiden asks, his tone weary.

"A bonfire!" She squeals, scooting closer to Ricky. I can tell she's excited for something besides sitting in this cabin.

Aiden looks at me, his face twisted. "If you want to go out, I could arrange something." He's trying to make me feel better about being stuck inside the cabin but it's only temporary, right?

I shake my head, "A bonfire here with all of you sounds perfect."

"Babe, you don't have to cook on your birthday." Aiden peeks over my shoulder, looking at the stove.

He laughs. "Spaghetti?" I swat his arm for making

such a cruel joke.

"I'm never making fucking spaghetti again, it's bad luck." I state, remembering the last time I did, the men came and took him from me.

His eyes go wide. "Since when do you say fuck?"

"I don't know." I'm honestly not sure why I said it.

Aiden laughs, his fingertips trailing my shoulder. "The cussing." His tone is accusatory. "It's that boy isn't it?"

Now it's my turn for an eyeroll. "He's like a couple years younger than you." I point out, picking the spoon up to taste the garlic butter sauce.

Leaning down, he plants a gentle kiss on my neck. "He hasn't corrupted my girl, right?" His tone is light, but his emerald eyes study me.

"Of course not." Why is he looking at me with such concern over a curse word? Does he think Leo has some sort of influence over me?

Smiling, he pulls me in. "You know I could have arranged something, a nice dinner so you didn't have to do all this."

I raise my brow, "You said we can't leave."

"We're in the middle of nowhere. With just me and you, with enough security it would be safe."

"I'm assuming since you didn't protest the bonfire then we're definitely safe?"

He nods, "We're sitting on a hundred acres. This land is completely guarded."

I ponder that while glazing the salmon. Everyone

shuffles in the dining room. Ashley helps me set the table and we all dig in.

When dinner is done, I go to clean the dishes, but Aiden isn't having it. He sends me off to get ready with Ash as they take care of it. I imagine what he looks like washing dishes, the soap suds on his hands. His muscles constricting as he reaches up to put a plate away.

"Which one?" Ashley's voice breaks my longing thoughts. She's holding up two very short dresses.

"Ash it's a bonfire, not a club." I giggle.

She rolls her eyes, "You're nineteen, Em. It's your birthday! If we have to celebrate it here, I'm getting dressed up and so are you! We've been cooped up for too long!" She dramatically sweeps the clothing in front of her, I point to the blue one.

"And for you?" She says, rummaging through her things, "This."

She tosses over a white summer dress, "I was going to wear a sweater and shorts." I tell her, but as I look to what she handed me I smile at how cute it is. Nothing daring or too much, it's just right for me, a little short but she's tall so that comes with the territory.

After running a hot wand through my brown hair, I slip on the short white dress. I sweep the smallest bit of make-up over my face, knowing Aiden prefers me without it. Honestly, I don't care for it much either.

We make our grand entrance downstairs. The boys wait for us at the bottom as if we're going to prom. Aiden is looking perfect as usual in his casual attire. Black jeans with a black T shirt, I bite my lip at the sight of him.

EMILIA

Aiden's mouth slightly opens as he takes in my outfit. As I step on the last staircase, he extends his hand to help me down while simultaneously tugging my dress down. "It's too fucking short." He states, grabbing his chin in thought. "But it's your birthday and you look..." He grabs my ass, leaning in to whisper in my ear. "absolutely fuckable."

"This way." He smiles, placing a hand on the small of my back. I'm guided to a dark room but by the small flickers of light I already know what's in front of me. A birthday cake. The room breaks out in song and normally this would embarrass me, but I feel so much love and happiness that I have to smile.

In the dark room, barely illuminated by candlelight, Aiden's hands clamp on my waist. He leans down into my ear and whispers in a husky voice, "I can't wait to have you wrapped around my cock later." He nibbles my earlobe and then he continues to sing the song in my ear. His voice is rough, rugged, full of want.

"Make a wish!" Ashley sings, I was so flustered by Aiden's words I didn't realize the song was completed. I snicker when I look back at him, thankful the darkness hides my blush.

Leaning down I make my wish, the warmth from the candles disappears and Ricky flips the light switch.

"Bonfire time!" Ashley squeals in delight, grabbing Ricky's arm and heading towards the back door.

I walk quickly to keep up with Aiden's long strides, my hand in his. We make our way through the woods, the light from the fire dances from a distance.

Aiden sighs at the sight of Leo walking with the other guards but I'm proud of him for not firing him.

Sixteen

Aiden's hand wraps firmly around mine as we walk into a clearing in the forest. The large bonfire centered in the middle cast a golden light around the circular meadow we're in.

Lush grass sits beneath my feet as I walk around admiring the area. I was expecting a normal bonfire, maybe some marshmallows to roast. I should have known with Aiden, nothing is a small thing.

I look to his dimpled smile, admiring all he's done for me. "Happy Birthday." He tells me, guiding us to a beautiful wooden bench that sits on the edge of the large fire.

I was expecting for the wood to be rough, but it's smooth and glossy as I run my palms across it. "Where did you get these?" They remind me of the wood on the cabin, I note a few blankets laying across them.

"I made them this morning after I knew you

wanted a bonfire." He shrugs, "I know it's not much and you would probably prefer something more fun-"

I cut him off with a kiss, in awe of his raw talent. "I didn't know you could make stuff like that!" He rubs my shoulders as I look around. Multiple tables line the outer area of the meadow with different types of food. A hot chocolate station is set up, a smores station, various other drinks and food line more tables

My favorite part is a banner with 'Happy 19th Birthday, Emilia.' written on it. I have to hold back tears from how thoughtful all of this was, my damp eyes trail to a small table that's playing music. Next to the speaker is Ashley's laptop, showcasing pictures of all of us on a slideshow.

"That was my idea!" She squeals, cracking open a beer and sitting on Ricky's lap.

"Thank you. So much. You guys didn't have to do this for me."

"Aiden did everything else." She tells me, with a cocky smirk. "You've turned him soft."

"I'll show you soft." He warns, lightheartedly.

Ricky looks between both of them, shaking his head. "I'm not picking sides." He says, smirking at Ash and tickling her when she rolls her eyes at him.

"This is so perfect, Aiden." I can't believe he would do all of this for me.

"You're perfect." He tells me, his posture relaxed. It's nice seeing him in this state, just calm.

An unfamiliar man steps in front of me, placing a warm mug of hot chocolate in my hands. "Kahlua?" He asks, showcasing a bottle of liquor. I look over to Aiden unsure of who this man is, how did he bring people here? Is it safe? Aiden slings his arm around me with a smile.

"Emilia, this is Dylan." We exchange hellos, Aiden continues. "He's been my chef for years, catering parties and events but there are few things better than his cocktails." I nod to Dylan with a bright grin, ready to celebrate and forget everything.

I slide into Aiden's lap and sip my alcoholic hot chocolate. "It's so good!" I tell him, you can barely taste the alcohol and I can tell the hot chocolate was homemade.

"Only the best for you." He replies, grazing his long fingers down my shoulders. I smile, watching my friends as they relax, this isn't something we've been able to do... ever. Even Leo is joining in on the fun. Howard is on his phone, grinning. Ashley and Ricky are making out.

Tilting my head to the side, I find Aiden already watching me.

The drinks keep coming, I switched it up a bit and now I'm drinking chocolate martinis instead. The music flows freely through the speakers and I feel a small hand wrap around my wrist. I look up from Aiden's longing gaze to find a tipsy Ashley holding my arm. "Let's dance!" she squeals.

Aiden's hand wraps around my waist, stopping me. "Aiden! Let her up, it's her birthday."

His eyes dart to where Leo sits, he's talking to Howard. They're both drinking beers and laughing. Aiden nods, and hesitantly releases me into the clutches of his sister.

We dance the night away, drinking our martinis and dancing around the fire. My eyes glide to Aiden's every so often and even though Ricky has been in deep conversation with him, his eyes never leave me.

I find myself dancing a little sexier than I normally would. The alcohol has made me loosen up, unwind. He beckons me, I walk over and sit on his lap. "That's enough." He tells me, with a grin on his face.

"You're no fun." Ashley chimes in, her speech slurred. She falls into a fit of giggles when Ricky tosses her over his shoulder, carrying her back to their wooden bench.

I nuzzle into Aiden's chest. Then a song comes on that makes Ashley get hyper again. "Leeeet's dance!" She slurs, leaning against Ricky. He laughs, pulling her close. "You need to relax babe, you've had too much to drink."

The melody is upbeat, and I dance to the music on Aiden's lap, singing the lyrics past the fire to Ashley who does the same on the other side.

We do this for a while, chatting, singing, just being young and free for once. Eventually, Ricky and Ash disappear into the woods laughing as they trip over twigs. I continue to dance to the intoxicating music.

Aiden leans forward, bringing his lips near my ear. "If you keep bouncing on my lap like that, I'm going to have to slip your panties aside and fill you." He tells me, I laugh at him.

Leaning close to his ear I reply, "Aiden, you

almost didn't let me wear this dress. I highly doubt you would risk someone else seeing you do something to me." I'm a little tipsy, not drunk at all but I have a bit more confidence right now.

"Don't act like I won't take you right here." He kisses my bare shoulder, my body twitches as he whispers in my ear. "It would be so easy to just..." He pulls a warm blanket over us, reaching his hand between my legs.

I feel him pressing against me, rock hard. "I could just grab you here." He removes his hand from between my legs and grabs my waist, slowly he picks me up once and lowers me back down. "I could wrap you around my cock and bounce you myself."

"Stop." I say, with no conviction. We have to get out of here. I look around at the drunken scene in front of us. Ashley and Ricky long gone into the woods, Howard asleep in his chair, a few guards dot the property and Leo. When my eyes meet his Aiden wraps his hand around my throat gently, claiming me. Leo looks away quickly.

"Oh my God, I think Leo saw that." I tell him with a whisper.

Aiden shrugs, "I know."

"Stop being so mean to him." I'm trying to be serious, but my voice is sultry.

"Don't tell me when I can and can't touch you on his behalf. I can fuck you whenever I want, you know that right?" He's right about that. Whenever he wants and I will gladly accept.

Aiden looks around once and then focuses his

attention on me, "I want to show you something."

Helping me up, he places one hand on the small of my back and guides me through the meadow and into the forest. A flashlight in his other hand lights our way. "Where are we going?"

"Patience, birthday girl."

Moments later I hear water gently lapping from a distance. Walking through a wooded archway, I gasp when a lake comes into view. It's midnight black outside but the moon is full and cast a glow on the deep waters. It's breathtaking.

"I love this." I tell him.

"This is more private, yeah?" Does he come here a lot?

I can't help myself, my insecurities getting the better of me. "Do you take a lot of girls here?"

"I've never had a girl at my safe house, much less this many people. It's driving me fucking insane not having you alone."

I smirk. "Why didn't we have the bonfire here?"

He gives me a pointed look, the kind of look that says I should already know the answer. "I didn't want anyone to see you naked."

Without a moment's notice he releases me and walks towards the water. "Get in." He grins, ripping his clothes off. His sun kissed skin glistens against the silver glow of the moon.

I shake my head, a little afraid of what may be lurking in the dark waters. He claps his hands once and then rubs them together. "Either you can take that fucking dress off, or I will rip it off of your body. Your choice." He threatens me with a devilish smile.

I pinch the soft fabric in between my fingers, slowly pulling it up as Aiden watches me with a cocky smirk.

Water gently laps against my shoulders as Aiden holds my waist, pulling my nude body flush against his. I hold the black ink on his arms as the lake showers our bodies.

The gentle current surrounds us, cascading over us. Aiden's naturally warm body mixes with the cool water, creating the perfect temperature.

"I love you, you know that right?" There's so much power behind his words.

"I love you more."

He runs a wet hand through his dry hair, gently messing it up. "Not possible." His movements are slow, normally he's fast to attach himself to me like a viper but now with his length hardening against me and his eyes dark he just looks... hungry.

The only sounds around are lapping water, rustling trees, and the chirps of animals who are still awake at this hour. Until Aiden grabs my hips and slowly lowers me onto him, I gasp from pleasure.

"I told you I would bounce you on my dick." He breathes, in a velvet tone. I put my head in the crook of his neck, breathing him in while his strong arms dip me up and down.

He gives me my birthday present, in the form of

him, underneath the bright moon.

"Quit trying to find the ground."

"I wanted to stand, I." I look around, taking in a deep breath. "I need to talk to you." I tell him, with a nervous smile.

Cocking his brow in inquiry he holds me tighter. "Whatever you have to tell me, I can hold you during."

Okay, here goes. "So... the ring."

He nods his head, looking out towards the water for a moment. "The ring." He breathes, longing in his voice. "I've noticed you wearing it." He looks back at me and smiles, "I also notice you haven't taken your locket off either."

I stifle a laugh, "It's how I found you. I know it has a tracker now, but I don't care."

He waves his hand above the water, "Disabled. Too risky in the safe house. That's why I had IT guys come in and check everyone's phones, it's also why Ashley can't snapchat." He laughs, "She won't shut up about it."

I playfully swat his arm. "Please, I want to know what you were going to say before you got kidnapped." I hate saying those words, I can tell Aiden doesn't like it either because even though we're surrounded by darkness his sharp edges become more defined. His emerald eyes turning deep jade.

"I wasn't fucking kidnapped."

Taken a back, I slightly gasp. "What do you

mean?"

He rolls his eyes. "Not like that Emilia, I'm just..." He bites his lip, trying to find the words. "Let's get out." He suggests.

I rummage around in the dark searching for my clothes. "Dang it!" I yell at the sight of my soaked dress. When I took it off, I placed it way too close to the shoreline, it's absolutely drenched.

Aiden slips his pants on, opting to go shirtless. Happy Birthday to me. "You have a clean dress on that branch." He points behind me and I laugh at his joke.

"Seriously Aiden, this thing is soaked. I don't know how I'm going to go back."

He walks past me in long strides, I follow his movement and see that in fact there is a dry dress sitting on a branch. He places it in my hands and kisses my cheek. "I brought it here earlier, I knew your birthday adventure would end here." He winks. "I also knew you might get a little dirty." He helps to slip it on over my body, the cool cotton feels soft against my damp skin.

Hand in hand, we find a weathered tree laying near the water. I take a seat and fold my hands in my lap neatly.

I take in his serious expression, just moments ago he was laughing and cracking jokes, but we need to talk about this. "I say I wasn't kidnapped because I went with them willingly. I couldn't risk them finding you, searching for you." His entire body shakes, "They put..." He looks down, shaking his head. He's deciding if he wants to talk about this. I've spoken with Ricky and Howard; he hasn't talked to either of them. I know it's haunting him in his dreams. His thrashing and jumbled words worry me in the middle of the night.

"What I fucking hate the most is that we don't know who it is." He changes the subject; I'm not going to push him. If I know anything about growing up with a father who was a cop it's that people will talk when they're ready and pushing him wouldn't help a thing.

"Yeah, I mean what are we supposed to do?" I say nervously, "Like, do we stay here forever?"

"Let's not talk about that on your birthday. And to circle back around to the kidnapping thing." He gestures with quote signs. "I'm a grown ass man... I can't be kidnapped there has to be a better word for it." He's playing around again, thank God.

"Mannapping." I mumble, he chuckles. Actually chuckles, it's so unusual to hear such a sound coming from him. I look into his eyes, admiring the twinkle behind them as he takes my hand in his and brings it near his mouth. He kisses every finger, landing on where I placed his promise ring.

"This was supposed to go differently." He tells me, his eyes full of love.

"How so?"

A shrug, "I know I'm not the most romantic person, Emilia. Truthfully I've never wanted to be anything for anyone before you." A dimpled smile appears, "That night." He shifts around, it almost looks like he's about to bend down on one knee. This is a promise ring, right? My heart is beating erratically and slowly at the same time.

Is he going to propose? I place my hand over my mouth, a small gasp escaping my lips.

"I'm not proposing to you, Em."

My eyes begin to water; I can't help it. It's not that I'm upset that he's not, it's too early for a proposal; but I got caught up in the moment and now I'm embarrassed.

"No, no baby, I worded that weird. I just saw that look on your face, I didn't want you to be disappointed."

A laugh escapes my lips, "You could never disappoint me." I tell him.

"I always disappoint you." He scoffs, then shakes his head. "Forget that." He twirls the ring around my finger. "I bought this ring to symbolize my loyalty to you. Nothing in this world matters to me besides you and your happiness Emilia, I mean that in every sense of the word. You have changed my life; you have no fucking idea how much. I promise you I will always do what's best for you." His jaw twitches, what does that mean?

"You're not..." How do I say this without sounding absolutely desperate? Screw it. "You can't leave me, Aiden. Even if it's best for me."

A smirk adorns his face, "Yeah, I know. I couldn't if I wanted too." He lets out a small laugh, "Do you like the ring?"

"I love it."

He extends his hand, helping me up. "Let's go back to the cabin. I want to cuddle the fuck out of you."

Seventeen

I lie next to Aiden in bed after an uneventful but relaxing two days of recovery from the birthday bonfire.

The master bedroom is gorgeous, much like the entire cabin. But this room has Aiden's touch. I'm not sure how he pulled off an industrial modern look with the rich woods of the cabin, but he did. A California King fitted with black silk sheets sits flush against the wall, while black and white artwork hangs around the room.

With my head pillowed on his chest, I trace his defined V with my eyes. The large windows that adorn the walls and the plush interior makes the cabin feel like home.

Aiden has been recovering his business, getting everything handed back to him. Fortunately, no one knew of his 'death', so things were up and running per usual. I can tell he's enjoying these relaxing days with me, but I can't help but wonder if the city is where he wants to be.

How can life go back to the way it was when we're being chased by faceless ghost?

I circle the ink on Aiden's chest to distract myself from my nightmarish thoughts, landing on a favorite of mine. A bird sitting on a branch with its baby, similar to the dark raven on his arm, but it seems happier.

Aiden flinches lightly and I pull my wandering hand back. I look into his wide eyes. After a deep breath, he moves my hand back to it and I continue to trace the outline.

A long silence passes before he speaks.

"It's for my mom," He admits in a quiet tone.

I figured as much but I never pushed, wanting him to tell me when the time was right. "It's my favorite."

"It was my first tattoo. She'd always sing to me, so I got a songbird." He shrugs, pulling me flush against him.

"It's beautiful, Aiden."

My hand aimlessly caresses his body, passing over the untold stories on his skin.

"I want one." I declare, peering up into his emerald eyes.

He raises a brow. "A bird?"

A laugh escapes my lips. "No, a tattoo."

"Fuck no."

I blink in surprise and push myself off him. I gesture to his body. "You're covered in them."

"It's different." His fingers trail my blank canvassed skin. "You don't need to cover up your body."

I tilt my head. "Is that what you're doing?"

"In a way, yes."

I cross my legs, wanting to learn anything he's willing to tell me. "Tell me about them."

He points to his tattoos, smiling at some while frowning at others.

"This one, I got with Ricky." He grins. "It was a dare, and it's fucking stupid, but it's one of my favorites."

My eyes follow the trajectory of his finger and a giggle slips free when I look closely. Twisted vines creep up his rib cage in a haunting manner. Near the bottom, hidden beneath the tangled vines, sits a little smiley face.

"Don't laugh," He warns playfully.

"How have I never noticed that?"

"The artist hid it well, but I'll never cover it."

The vines hold my attention. It reminds me of my mom and her love for flowers, but it's dark and twisted.

"Why the thorns? Why not add roses?"

"You see the size of the smiley, maybe a nickel would cover it? The tattoo's too happy for my liking, that's why he chose it." He looks away in thought. "I wouldn't remove it. Ricky is my most trusted friend and," He shrugs, "I wanted something closer to my actual personality than that."

"You think your personality is dark and twisted?"

He remains silent.

"Do you want more?"

He nods. "Yeah, when I drew the design for the vines..." He visibly draws back when the words slip from his lips, as though he'd let his darkest secret slip.

I beam, leaning forward slightly. "Drew?"

He thinks hard, rubbing a long hand over his face. "I draw sometimes," He admits hesitantly.

I move closer, admiring the work. "It's so intricate."

"It's the tattoo artist. They're really good and…"

I flash him a bright and hopeful smile, not liking that he's doubting himself. "Can I see the drawing of the new tattoo you want?"

"Maybe some other time," He clips.

I bite my lip, unsure if I should push. "Won't I see it on you all the time after you get it tattooed on?"

He rolls his eye dramatically. "I've never shown it to anyone. I don't know why I even blurted it out like that."

Scooting closer, I cup his cheek. "Because you trust me. Let me in, baby." My voice cracks. *Let me in so I can face your nightmares with you*, is what I want to say.

He chews on his lower lip before finally saying, "It's under the bed. My side."

I pull the leather-bound binder in triumph, slowly and carefully flipping through the pages, admiring his work.

Impatient, Aiden pulls it out of my hand and bypasses half of the sketches. I hold myself back from pestering him when I catch a glimpse of a portrait of me. Maybe later. He's made so much progress tonight. If only I could get him to talk to me about Italy.

"Here." He hands the book back to me.

I smile at the solitary yellow rose, a few water droplets on the delicate petals. The detail is stunning. My mouth hangs open at this secret I never knew.

"It's beautiful." *And it's for me.* I fight back my tears.

"I wanted to get it here." He points to the

top of his dark tangled web of rose stems. "I drew this sketch for you, so you'd have an exact replica to hang up or whatever."

"That's the most beautiful thing I've ever heard." I beam up at Aiden, grinning when I see his cheeks heat a little.

"It's one of my favorite things to give you. Seeing the way your face lights up with a single rose…" He smiles, a genuine, full dimpled smile. "I love that smile."

He captures my chin, pulling me towards him as he leans in for a slow, gentle kiss. He pulls back, growing serious. "And out of respect for your father. I hope that's okay."

I throw my arms around his neck, careful not to crumple the paper. "Of course it's okay! It's perfect!" I pull back, hesitant. "But if you break up with me—"

A deep laugh cuts me off. His eyes soften as he drinks me in. "Emilia, all of the times you bring this up, it's always *if* I left you. I don't know what world you're living in but…" He smiles, "In reality, the one who should be leaving is you. I carry to much danger and destruction around with me."

I'll help you carry it, Aiden, I whisper in my heart.

"And if you did leave me, I wouldn't allow it," Aiden declares fiercely. "There is nowhere else for you, besides with me. End of fucking story."

I grin, loving when he goes all caveman on me.

A thoughtful smile appears on his face. "I'm sorry if that sounds mental, but I just can't bear to be apart from you, Em."

Breaking the tension, I climb onto his lap and pepper him with kisses.

"Okay, let's go!" I exclaim after pulling back to catch my breath.

He chuckles. "It's midnight, Emilia."

"So?"

"We need guards."

"Get Leo." I roll my eyes.

He growls.

"Howard?"

He considers it before shaking his head.

"Let's sneak out." He's caving, I need to work fast. "I'm sick of hiding out. It's midnight and we're in the middle of nowhere. Let's just…go."

He hums. "I could fly my artist out here. There's also a local artist who I've used a few times. I'm sure he'd be willing to do a house call."

I sit straighter, shaking my head. "No one knows where we are. We've been stuck in this cabin for weeks. I've heard your security detail talking. I know we're safe here."

We've been surrounded by people every day. I want it to be just us.

He throws his head back, giving in.

"Fine."

I shimmy into a pair of jeans and throw a T-shirt on, grabbing Aiden's hoodie for good measure. Fall is my favorite time of year.

"Let's go from our deck," Aiden suggests.

I nod.

We descend the back staircase leading to the side of the cabin. A guard is at the front stoop. It's definitely not Howard since this man has a head full of black hair.

"What do we do?" I whisper, holding back a laugh when Aiden smiles mischievously. "What?"

We slip into the garage, and I admire the newer luxury cars, classic cars. I look to the side to see Aiden beside a shiny black motorcycle, a wide grin on his face.

"Nope."

He slides a helmet over my head. "You know I'll never let you get hurt. Besides, the cars are too loud. We have to take this or walk."

My eyes pan back to the intimidating looking bike. I've never been on one before, and the way the slick black metal twists around the frame terrifies me for some reason.

Screw it.

"Let's do it."

Opening a small metal door flushed

against the wall, Aiden grabs the two leather jackets inside and zips me up in one. He laughs when he sees it swallowing me.

I tip toe beside him as he straddles the bike, inching it down the driveway with his feet. It's so quiet I'm worried my giggles will get us caught as Aiden makes silly faces at me under the dim moonlight. Before I know it, he's gesturing for me to hop on.

"How?" I tilt my head, wondering where to place my feet.

He smiles, dimples prominent even in the dark. "Come here." He twists, picking me up and placing me behind him. "Just hold on to my waist. If I lean to the side, just go with me."

I wrap my hands tightly around his waist.

He laughs. "There's no need for the death grip."

When I don't ease up, he laughs once more. The bike lightly purrs to life as he starts it up. Thankfully, he guides us slowly, drifting down the curvy roads with ease.

He places a reassuring hand on my leg. "Feel better?" He asks, his head tilted to the side. Although the scenery zips by and the wind glides over our helmets, I can hear him through the Bluetooth in my helmet.

Lifting my visor, I let the cool wind tickle my face. It's calming and the way the trees fly past us is freeing. With anyone else I would be terrified. But with Aiden, I know I'm safe.

Pressing against his back, I yell over the wind, "Faster!" My voice happy and my mind free.

He revs the throttle and we accelerate. I lay my head against his back, watching the scenery fly by. It's beautiful, and probably gorgeous in the daytime.

A town comes into view, small but bustling. People turn in our direction as we pull up. My eyes pan around the area, taking note of the tattoo shop in the corner of the small strip. Aiden helps me off, staying alert as the drunk men finish smoking and head inside.

"Everything is okay," I reassure him, watching his eyes soften as I place my helmet on the handlebars.

We walk into the tattoo shop hand in hand.

The first and only time I was ever in one was when my mom got an in-memory tattoo for my dad. Now, I'll be getting one too. It's even more special because Aiden designed it.

Black leather chairs dot the shop with various booths set up. A woman is working hard on a man's back, not noticing us walk in. A man steps out from the back, his eyes light up when he sees Aiden.

"Mr. Scott! To what do I owe the pleasure?" He seems so chipper to be working so late, but I'm guessing this is his normal schedule. A mustache twirls into a spiral above his lip, making him look fancy.

"Hey Bo, swinging in to get some new ink." Aiden shakes his hand.

Bo looks over at me, his smile brightening. "I've never seen you with a lady before."

I giggle as he bends down and kisses my extended hand enthusiastically. Surprisingly, Aiden, who is usually extremely protective, is smiling from ear to ear.

"So what can I do for ya?"

Aiden hands him the paper.

"Full color?" Bo examines the drawing.

"Yes. It will be my only color tattoo." He winks at me.

My heart seizes beating. Not only is he getting something for me, it will be his only vivid tattoo. I refrain from melting in front of the two men.

Bo whistles, throwing his head back. "It must be an important tattoo."

Aiden gazes tenderly at me. "Yes, it is."

Bo turns to me as I bounce on my heels nervously. "Anything for you, young lady?"

Aiden shakes his head.

"I want to get it too," I blurt out.

"She's joking. Just me," Aiden insists.

I place my hand on his shoulder. "Aiden,

it's okay."

Bo laughs, walking away to let us have a moment while he lays out his items.

"I don't want you to ruin your perfect skin," He whispers.

"I thought we were coming here for me to get one too!" I argue, annoyed.

He shakes his head.

"In the past month, I've almost died twice. You died like eight times." I have to laugh at the irony. "And now we're in our own version of witness protection. I'm getting the freaking tattoo."

Aiden chuckles, giving in.

Bo walks back over, placing black gloves around his hand. "I see from your expression that you got your way?"

"I always do." I wink, eliciting an annoyed groan from Aiden.

"Who first?" Bo gestures towards his booth.

"Me." Aiden deposits himself on the black leather chair.

"May I ask the story behind this? For your first color tattoo, it has to be important."

"I'll let her explain." He nods to me.

I try to keep my composure. "My father, who passed, used to buy yellow roses for my mom every week. He would always take one from the bouquet and give it to me." I smile at Aiden.

"Now he brings me a solitary yellow rose."

Bo smiles proudly. "I'm sorry to hear about the passing of your father. I'm honored to do this for you both."

I watch in awe as Bo traces the outline of the rose, turning the black twisted vines into something more. The solitary yellow rose sits at the end of a stem, bursting to life with the vibrant color.

"It's beautiful," I whisper, tears in my eyes.

Aiden stands, checking himself out in the mirror. That image is doing something to me.

Bo changes out his gloves and preps the new equipment while Aiden helps me onto the leather chair.

He leans down, whispering in my ear. "I'm allowing this so I will choose it's placement, understand?"

I nod, unable to think with his body so close to mine. I didn't really know where I wanted it anyways.

Bo comes over, grabbing the same piece of paper and looking it over again, "Where would you like it?" He asks me, looking over my blank canvas skin.

Aiden speaks up, "Her ribs, same placement as mine." I look over at him and smile, it will look perfect there.

"Ready?" Bo ask as I turn on my side

towards him. I nervously bite my lip.

"First tattoo." He nods, noting my nerves, "That's why Mr. Scott was worried. Don't be scared, it won't hurt..." He assures me, his voice calm and his hands steady as he begins to clean the area. "too bad."

Tears stream down my cheeks as I gaze at my reflection. The rose is just as perfectly detailed on my skin as it is in Aiden's drawing. The sight of it takes my breath and my words away.

"It's perfect," I gasp.

I can't help but feel sad as Bo covers mine and Aiden's tattoo with gauze. I can't wait for the bandage to come off so I can admire it some more. I love how feminine it looks on my ribs yet so masculine on Aiden. It didn't hurt as bad as I thought, but I did shed a few tears from the constant prick of needles. Aiden didn't even flinch, of course.

Cool air sweeps across my face as we head outside.

"Thank you."

"I know I said I didn't want you getting a tattoo, but it looks so sexy against your skin. I can't wait to see it when it heals." He pushes me up against the brick wall and kisses my cheek. "I'm so fucking happy I have you alone tonight." His hands come to rest on my waist as I rest against him.

Our sweet moment is interrupted when three drunk men step out of the bar, hooting and hollering at the sight of us.

"Give us a show!"

Aiden steps in front of me protectively, on high alert.

To my horror, the men walk towards us, beer bottles in hand. They're belligerent and whistling at me.

"Get in the—" Aiden cuts himself off, realizing there is no car. Only a bike.

"You don't want to do this," He warns, taking a menacing step forward when one man asks if I'm for hire.

They laugh.

I bite my lip in worry. He is outnumbered. If I can get past him and run back to the shop, I could get Bo.

"What's the problem man? Don't want to share your whore?"

Aiden chuckles darkly. "Close your eyes, Emilia."

I don't have time to obey as Aiden's fist connects with the man's face the next second, knocking him out cold.

"Anyone else?" Aiden gestures to the men with a 'come at me' motion.

I gasp when one of the men slams his glass beer bottle against the brick wall, creating a weapon, before lunging.

Aiden seems unfazed as he efficiently disarms the man, tossing the bottle onto the sidewalk. He turns around to make sure I'm okay at the absolute worst time.

"Watch out!" I scream as the third man hits him over the head with a beer mug.

I wait for Aiden to pass out, budge, or flinch…but he doesn't. It seems to hype him up as he turns and lunges for the man. They collide with the pavement, thankfully free of glass shards, and he wraps his hands firmly around the man's throat.

I tug at him, trying to pull him away as more bar-goers step outside to watch the action. The commotion is becoming too much, and Aiden's bloodthirst is palpable.

I lean down, whispering over the cheers as the man gasps for air, "You're drawing attention to us." My voice is shaky, I'm terrified of anything happening to him.

That seems to knock him from his trance.

Aiden stands, dusting off his jeans before grabbing my hand, leaving the unconscious man on the ground. Within seconds, he slips our helmets on and helps me onto the bike. Once we are safely away from the commotion, he stops on the side of a dark and empty street.

I swing off, my hands shaking from the adrenaline.

He pulls off his helmet and looks me over. "You okay?"

I nod. My eyes widen as they adjust to the dim light from the headlights and full moon. "Oh shit!" My fingers trail to the stream of blood coming from Aiden's head. "You're bleeding."

He twists, opening a compartment in the bike, and hands me a small first aid kit. With the help of the moonlight, I clean and bandage his wound, sighing in relief when it stops bleeding.

He takes my hands in his, kissing it softly. "I'm sorry."

I laugh, stepping closer to him as he straddles the bike. "No, they totally deserved it. I was just scared for you." I hum in thought. "Well, maybe they didn't deserve to die. But you just wouldn't stop."

He grips my chin. "Sweetheart, I've told you a million times, there is absolutely nothing I won't do to protect you."

I smile, though my eyes narrow in warning. "You have to be careful, Aiden. Nothing can happen to you." I bite my lip as I think on the past few weeks. "Again."

"Baby, it was just three drunk men. I wasn't even going to fight them until they disrespected you." He looks down at his busted knuckles. "I'm sorry you had to see that."

I shake my head, tilting his head up. "I thought it was kind of…hot, the way you always stand up for me."

His eyes narrow as he steps off the bike, placing his helmet on the handlebars. He towers over me as his hands languidly explore my body.

"Is that what you like Emilia?" His voice is husky. "You like when I protect you?" He looks around the dark surroundings. "Let's get you home so I can fuck you."

I nod, biting my lip in anticipation.

Aiden grips the throttle tightly the entire way home. His muscles are constricted, I can tell he's still on an adrenaline high from the fight.

The trees pass in a blur and it isn't long before we pull into the long drive.

He stops the bike midway before demanding, "Off."

His helmet is already on the ground when he flips the kickstand down and swings off the bike. He reaches for me with hasty hands.

I squeal as he lifts me.

"Shh, we're not far enough into the woods," He orders, clamping a hand over my mouth.

His lips press against mine while his tongue dances with mine as he stalks through the dense forest. He sets me down in a small clearing, laying his leather jacket against the lush grass. The stars twinkle above, and the full moon illuminates our surroundings.

He moves the hair from my face, his bruised knuckles gently grazing my skin, "I want to taste you," He whispers, his minty breath warming my neck as he peppers me with kisses to calm our nerves from the fight.

His long fingers travel to the top of my jeans, unbuttoning them as we make our way to the ground in a rush. He yanks them off and discards them to the side before sliding his hands up my shirt to cup my breast.

"You have no idea all the dirty things I think of doing to your body every day."

"Like what?" I murmur, my breathing quickening

He buries his face in my neck. "You don't want to know."

My panties are ripped off a few moments later, and his finger slides inside of me, eliciting a whimper.

"More," I demand.

He raises his brow at my boldness. "More what?" His voice is sly, deep, frantic.

"I…" It's so difficult to speak when his finger is circling my opening while his tongue twirls around my nipple. "I want you inside of me."

Without a word, he pulls away.

I'm thankful as I can't take much more of his teasing.

"I'll be inside of you soon, sweetheart." His eyes burn with hunger. "But first I want you to cum all over my tongue."

He pries my thighs apart, greedily devouring every inch of me. "I love it when you're exposed for me. Only for me." He licks his full lips as his head lowers.

The scratch of his scruff between my thighs is heavenly as his tongue glides across my inner thigh. His tattooed hands are fueled by adrenaline, his tongue by pure want. He grips my thighs firmly, holding them wide apart as I squirm and tremble beneath him.

I know he enjoys pinning me down, I love it too.

I run my fingers through his hair, bucking my hips as pleasure overwhelms my body. His name escapes my lips, eliciting a wild groan from him, which turns me on even more.

He pulls back, the cool air sending a wave of shock to my core.

"Why did you stop," I moan in despair, my head falling back.

A smirk takes over his face. "When I'm down there, I can't see what I'm doing to you." He bites his lip. "I love watching what I do to you Emilia."

He returns to his position between my thighs, but this time, he doesn't bury his face between them. Instead, his deep green eyes peek up as he rolls his tongue around my clit.

I throw my head back with a squeal.

"Look at me."

I struggle to keep my dazed eyes trained on him as he makes me come undone. His grip grows tighter, his tongue moving faster as my body begins to shake. Our eyes never leave each other. The moment is so intimate, so beautiful that he's on top of me in seconds when I collapse onto the ground.

He slides up, kissing every inch of me as he goes. My lips, my neck, my breasts. With a deep groan, he stands.

"Where are we going?" I pant, still recovering from the intense orgasm.

He lifts me silently, carrying me back towards the bike where he sets me down so that my back faces him. His warm hand clamps around my neck, gently yet possessively, sending shivers down my spine.

"I need you to bend over the bike." He demands.

I eye it worriedly.

What if it falls over while I lean against it?

"Kickstand is down," He murmurs, reading my mind. "Now bend for me."

I obey, bending over the bike as Aiden's hand rests on my right shoulder. His hot, throbbing length presses against me before sliding inside of me. He grips my hip, drawing me into him with every thrust. The pleasure is overwhelming, and my knees begin to shake.

A moan escapes my lips, echoing through the air.

"Aiden," I gasp, "I don't know if I can stand."

He laughs, deep and maniacal.

The pleasure in his eyes pushes me over the edge when I peer back at him. My knees go weak, and that's when I learn his real physical strength. With one hand clamped on my shoulder, he pounds into me, while lifting me slightly off the ground with his other hand around my stomach.

My hands stay on the bike while he fucks me like a ragdoll. I look at my clenched fist laying on the leather seat, I realize I'm not even holding it anymore. His hands clamp down on various parts of my body. It's fueled by anger and I love it.

His deep voice cuts through the silence, pure pleasure mixed with a possessive growl. "You enjoy being fucked like this?"

I try to speak, but the uncontrolled way he's pounding into me makes it impossible. Unable to communicate, I nod vigorously through my moans.

A rush of cold hits me when he pulls

back. A deep grunt escapes his lips as he unloads against my back. I melt when he grabs a small towel from the bike and cleans me off. He leaves me to recover and quickly grabs our clothes before we return to the cabin.

I'm surprised when he drives up to the garage and parks. "Why did we come back in so loud?" I climb off, hanging up my helmet

Shrugging, he kisses my lips. "Sweetheart, I own this cabin and pay the salary of every man here. I'm free to leave as I please."

I swat his arm playfully, a smile on my face. "So why did we sneak out?"

"I thought it was cute, you wanting to be spontaneous. I didn't want to tell you no." He smirks.

I roll my eyes. I should have known better.

"I had already texted the guard at the door that we would be leaving."

"What if they get mad?"

"Who?" He laughs, guiding us towards the front door. "Fucking Leo? I respect my security." His jaw clenches. "Except Leo of course, but that's beside the point. But I also pay them to do as I say. No one will be mad at me. If they are, they're dismissed."

I know he said it doesn't matter that we were out, but he only told that one guard.

"Be quiet," I whisper, glaring when he

quietly laughs. I don't want to worry anyone. It's so quiet that I fear the lock clicking will wake everyone up.

We step through the threshold and Aiden raises his arms up with a cocky smirk.

"See, no one's–"

A lamp flicks on, illuminating a corner of the living room.

Howard sits in a leather chair with a newspaper, a disappointed look on his face. He looks like the quintessential angry parent.

I frown. *How in the heck was he reading it in the dark?*

"Emilia Banks," Howard chides seriously.

Aiden laughs.

"Where were you? It's the middle of the night!"

Howard glares me down, not once looking in Aiden's direction.

"Get on him!" I huff, pointing a finger at Aiden while trying to hold back my laughter at how angry he is.

Howard smiles. "He's a grown man."

I scoff. "I'm grown!"

Yet the way I yelled that sounded anything but adult-like.

"That's not the point. You're a young lady. I would have had a search party if I didn't already check the garage and notice Mr. Scott's bike was missing."

I try to speak but he doesn't let me.

"It's not safe," Howard states, but there's no conviction behind it. He knows Aiden would never directly put me in harm.

"I had Aiden," I reassure him.

"I know, Ms. Emilia." Howard pinches the bridge of his nose.

Leo casually walks into the room, his hair disheveled. "What's going on?"

I watch as Aiden's amused expression turns to one of hate.

"They decided to go out to God knows where without informing anyone."

I can sense Aiden's irritation.

"I informed the guard. This isn't an issue."

"You should've taken a guard with you," Leo directs his words at me sleepily.

I gently wrap my fingers around Aiden's clenched fist, calming him slightly.

"I am her guard," He smiles down at me. "We're going to bed. End of discussion."

Howard brings me in for an unexpected but welcomed hug, which I return.

"I'm sorry Ms. Emilia, I was just worried." He squeezes tight, the pricking pain of the fresh tattoo makes me squeal. He looks at me with worry and I lift my shirt to showcase the white gauze. "What's this?" Howard frowns in concern. "You're hurt?"

EMILIA

Leo walks over in a few quick strides.

Aiden throws his hands up.

"A tattoo," I state quietly.

They look at me in astonishment.

"What is it?" Leo asks.

Aiden steps in, wrapping his hand around mine. "She'll show everyone tomorrow."

"Your mother will be upset you didn't tell her," Howard mumbles under his breath.

I tilt my head and step forward. "And how would you know that?"

Aiden tries to pull me away again, but I hold my ground.

"I may be keeping in touch with her. I hope that's okay?"

I ponder this for a moment, letting the information settle in my mind. "Like talking talking or like talking?"

"I'm an older gentleman. I don't understand what that means."

Aiden chimes in then. "He's got a crush on your mom."

"You knew?" I gasp.

"He told me earlier. I was going to mention it, but he was planning on talking to you tomorrow. I respect his wishes. She has no idea he's into her."

I blink. I'm totally fine with it. Howard's been a father to all of us. A father who is a trained killer and security guard, but a good man. I can't deny that Mom did look at him in a certain way when she was here.

The tension is palpable as they wait for my response.

"Howard, we'll talk more later. But if you like her, tell her. She's been alone for a long time and you're a good man. Take her out."

His smile at my words lights up the dim room.

I look down at my feet. "But you need to wait until all this blows over. Don't put her in the danger we're in, and don't let her know about any of this."

I almost clamp my hand over my mouth when Aiden's expression falls. What I said really hurt him.

"Of course, Ms. Emilia."

"Emilia." I correct, biting my lip.

He nods before he and Leo leave the room.

"Bed?" I suggest.

Aiden shakes his head "Go ahead. I'm going to grab something to eat first."

I know he's lying and he's going to pick apart what I said, blaming himself for everything bad that's come my way recently.

"Bed," I insist.

Rolling his eyes, he listens.

I climb in the bed once we've changed and washed up, patting the sheets. I eye his tan skin and bandage as he pulls off his shirt. I can't wait to admire the rose again.

"I didn't mean that about you." I lay my head on his chest, careful to not touch his new ink.

"It's true though. What you wish for your mother is something I can't give you. Your safety." He scoffs. "Such a simple thing any man should be able to offer his other half and I can't fucking give you that."

I roll my eyes. "We're not doing this tonight, Aiden. I love you. You do everything in your power to make my life amazing. I know we're in a rough spot right now, but this isn't your fault. None of it is."

"Everything is my fault, Emilia."

I kiss him softly. "Being in this safe house is just a precaution. You said it yourself, you don't know who took you but I'm free to go. I'm safe, and I'm not going anywhere without you." I gaze into his eyes. "Wherever we end up, we're going together."

Eighteen

I hurry down the steps to grab a glass of water, afraid of Aiden having another nightmare.

"What's wrong?" I set the glass down and rush to Ashley, who just walked in, looking upset.

She runs a hand through her golden hair. "Everything." Her voice is distant.

I hop onto the counter, giving her my full attention. "Spill."

She sighs, studying the kitchen. "It's just that being stuck in this cabin... I mean we just moved to another city, and now we're in the middle of nowhere. We should be applying for fall semester at a new school." She takes a deep breath.

I nod in understanding, biting my lip. "I understand. Aiden's working on getting us out of here. It just needs to be safe."

"I get that. But like, can't we do something for fun?"

An idea pops in my head, but I shrug it off.

Ashley perks up. "I saw the gears turning, Em. Spill."

"Aiden will kill me." She smiles wider. "Ricky will kill you."

She shakes her head and clasps her hands together, pleading, "Get me out of this house."

"Well, the night of the bonfire, Aiden took me to a lake."

"A lake?"

I smile, remembering the sweet memory. "Yeah, he wanted to surprise me. It's really pretty!"

"Okay, eww. Don't want to know anymore. But a lake! Is it far?"

"Nope! Just a few minutes' walk."

Her smile brightens the room. "Let's get our swimsuits!"

"I don't know, Ash," I say hesitantly, deep in thought.

What harm could it do? We're in a safe house surrounded by a hundred acres of woods.

Ashley pouts, her frown deepening with

every long second.

"Fine," I cave, keeping my voice hushed as we giggle.

"We need swimsuits," Ash whispers.

We peek up the stairs, where our men are sleeping.

"On second thought." She guides us back to the kitchen. "We'll just swim in our undies!"

I nod. "Can't risk waking up the lion."

Her hand grips a bottle of tequila.

I shake my head in disgust.

"Oh, come on!" She pleads.

"It's not the alcohol that's the problem. It's the choice." I set the tequila down, and grab a bottle of whiskey instead.

I fight back a yawn, thinking about staying inside and getting some sleep, but caffeine should be enough. "Grab a few cans of Coke," I instruct Ashley.

She gives me a mischievous grin, and soon we are sneaking through the bottom floor. Rounding a corner, I spot a guard asleep by the front door. We may not need swimsuits, but we definitely can't walk in the woods barefooted.

My heart races when he stirs in the chair, our silent laughter is not helping the situation despite the need to be quiet. I grab our shoes quickly, peeking at the guard. We're in the clear; he's passed out cold. He's the only one down here, as there isn't a need for 24/7 guards at a safe house anyways.

We step out the back door and into freedom.

Trotting quietly through the backyard, I take in the emptiness around us.

"It feels so weird to be alone."

Ashley nods, humming as she skips along. Our laughter echos through the quiet woods with the moonlight as our guide, scrambling not to trip on sticks.

"Seriously, we're constantly being watched by the most serious men I've ever met."

She turns to me. "Em, I know I haven't said this before, and I know your life has been turned upside down…"

"So has yours," I remind her.

"Yes, but he's family. I want to thank you for sticking by his side through everything. I couldn't have asked for a better best friend or a better partner for my brother."

Such sweet words make me smile.

She cracks open the bottle and we take turns taking a swig as we walk. The warm liquid burns my throat. I pop open a can of coke to wash it down, grateful for the hit of caffeine. It's around three in the morning and the day's events are catching up to me, but Ashley needs me and that is so much more important than sleep.

It doesn't take long for us to reach the clearing near the lake.

"We're here!" I exclaim, taking another swig from the bottle.

Ashley rips off her pajamas and runs straight for the water. "The last one in is a rotten egg!" She squeals.

"Not fair!" I shout, tearing off Aiden's shirt and tossing it aside, as I hightail after her. I splash her. "You cheated!"

"Get in!" She yells.

I shake my head, thinking of my tattoo.

"Wait!" She slurs, stepping towards me. Her finger grazes the gauze. "When did you get this?"

"Earlier tonight," I admit, guilty for leaving when she has cabin fever.

"What is it? Can I see?" She smiles, allowing me to momentarily forget about my guilt.

"I'll show you tomorrow when Aiden cleans it!" I smile. "It's a yellow rose."

Her lip pokes out.

"Don't cry," I warn, knowing that in my tipsy state, I'll cry too.

"Aiden took you to get it?"

I nod. "We got matching ones."

"Like the same tattoo? Isn't that bad luck? Like it's adorable and all, but are you guys doomed now?"

I laugh. "That's if you get someone's name apparently." I giggle. "I won't be doing that." I wade in carefully, stopping when the water hits my hip.

Our laughter booms and echoes off the pines. The shimmer of the moon is enough for us to see.

Ashley floats on her back with a sigh, her hair drifting against the calm current. "This is exactly what I needed!"

I hand her the bottle of alcohol still in my hand and we drink more than we should. "Now this. This is what I needed."

Ashley raises her brow. "I thought you didn't like to drink."

"Things change." I shrug. "And I don't really. But on special occasions, it can be fun."

We laze around in the water, catching up on things we've been too busy to talk about.

"How are you and Ricky?"

She looks up to the sky, obviously reeling about how happy she is. "He's incredible! He doesn't talk much but I think he's just generally shy around people, but he opens up to me."

I nod in understanding. Aiden hates the world, minus me. "Maybe when everything calms down, we can go on a double date?" I suggest.

She nods fervently.

With half the bottle gone and our chest aching from laughing, we step out of the lake. The crisp autumn air sweeps across our wet bodies. We lunge for our clothes, shivering at the cold. I scan the dark ground for Aiden's shirt as Ashley dresses.

"What color is it?" Ashley joins in the search, stumbling over her own drunken feet.

"Black." I sigh, knowing it's a pointless endeavor, but honestly too drunk to care at the moment. "Screw it!" I giggle, stumbling towards her with wobbly legs.

Leaning against each other for support, we head home, attempting to keep our giggles quiet as we get closer to the cabin. On our last turn, an opening in the trees reveals the silhouette of a large man.

My eyes widen, looking over at Ashley who notices the man as well. We're soaked, and I'm in my underwear and bra. We have no phones or anything to fight back with.

We're completely defenseless.

The tall silhouette stalks towards us as we stagger back, drunk and uncoordinated.

I decide screaming is my best option. I part my lips, inhaling the crisp air readying myself to let out the most blood-curdling scream I can manage, as the leaves crunch beneath the man's feet signaling just how close he is.

To my absolute happiness, Aiden's familiar deep voice rings out in the darkness. He sounds absolutely pissed, but at least we're safe.

"You don't leave this cabin without

permission, Em!" Aiden chides.

I'm kind of drunk, and I kind of want to kiss him right now.

His eyes widen at the sight of me. "Where the fuck are your clothes?"

It is probably the wrong thing to do, but Ashley and I burst out into giggles.

He continues his lecture. "Not only did you put yourself in danger, but Ash as well." He sighs, taking in the way I sway back and forth. "And you're drunk. Just fucking wonderful."

Ash raises her hand, her words slurring, "Chill, Aiden, it was my idea."

He directs his attention to her. "You didn't know where the lake was." She falls quiet. "You, inside. I'll let Ricky deal with you." He states, waving her off.

Ashley shoots me a small smile and a wink as she leaves.

I look back up to Aiden, gulping when I see his emerald eyes burning into me. "You fucking know better."

I roll my eyes, mustering up my courage. "We were going crazy in this house."

With a swift movement, he backs me up. My back presses against a tree, though his large hand protects my bare skin from the scratchy bark.

"You're making me crazy, Emilia." His eyes trail over my body.

"It's not that big a deal. We were safe."

He looks intimidating but I've never felt threatened by him, he's soft for me. "You aren't allowed out of my sight."

I roll my eyes.

He presses against me, his knee pushing my legs open as he settles between them. He eyes my bra and underwear.

A sly grin spreads across his face. "You roll your eyes at me one more time, and I will bend you over my knee."

I lean in and whisper, "Maybe I want you to."

His eyes darken as I pull back, my words exciting him. He gently wraps a hand around my throat, my favorite thing.

"You want me to punish you." His voice is half sexual and half angry.

At the sound of leaves crunching, Aiden turns to shield me.

"What's going on here?" Leo asks.

Aiden relaxes before ripping off his shirt and tugging it over my half-naked self. "Nothing that concerns you. Leave."

I peek my head around to say hi.

Leo speaks first. "Em?"

Aiden growls in warning.

Leo smiles, looking pointedly at me. "I mean, Ms Emilia, are you okay?"

I'm glad Aiden is facing me, so he misses

Leo's accusing face.

Aiden whips around, his vicious gaze trained on Leo. "Don't ever fucking ask if she's okay around me." He cups my cheek gently, flashing that dimpled half-smile I love.

"I'm just worried you're scaring her." Damnit, Leo. "Look at her chest, she's breathing erratically."

Aiden throws his head back in a fit of laughter. "She's not scared. She's turned on. Something you wouldn't understand about her and never will. Now, make your exit."

Damn it, Aiden.

"You act as though she's your property," Leo remarks.

Aiden squares his shoulders, looking him dead in the eyes. "That's because she is."

"That's so fucked!"

They step closer to each other, with Aiden closing the last gap with one menacing step.

"You're just upset because I'm the only man who knows how it feels to be inside of her," He spits. "So stop fucking trying. I see you, Leo. I've been you. I know your games. Stop waiting, she'll never come to you."

Have they forgotten I'm here?

Leo scoffs before they turn their attention to me.

Aiden's words send anger through my whiskey-filled veins.

Throwing my hands up, my eyes narrow at Aiden. "I'm fucking done!"

Aiden gently grabs my arm as I turn to stomp away, hesitant because he knows he upset me, but his anger is palpable.

"Don't you dare walk away from me."

"This is me." I step out from his hold, hissing. "Walking away."

Leo chuckles.

Aiden's glare is venomous. "Emilia Banks."

"Aiden Scott," I challenge.

Turning on my heels, I step a few feet away.

I wave at them. "Once you two sort out your issues, I'll return."

Crossing my arms, I stomp away. I turn to look at the men who are still glaring each other down. "Leo, look, I know you don't get it. But Aiden's never scared me, ever. He is fiercely protective, and I love that."

Aiden lets out a triumphant laugh, his cocky grin melting me even though I'm pissed.

"And you." I point a finger at Aiden, who crosses his tattooed arms, a warning for me to smart off. "You've got to chill out. We went drinking in the woods and swimming. The mafia isn't in the fucking woods."

Aiden shakes his head.

"What about the property comment?"

Leo shakes his head in disbelief.

I look to Aiden, his eyes full of remorse.

I give a small wave.

"Goodnight gentlemen."

I sit on the porch, sipping wine straight from the bottle.

It's been thirty minutes since I left the guys alone. I don't think I've ever been this drunk. All I wanted was one fun night, but the tension between Aiden and Leo is becoming too much.

"Need something stronger?"

I turn to see Leo, clutching a decanter filled with dark liquor.

"Why not." I giggle at his question, grabbing the glass he's holding out.

He sits beside me. "I'm sorry about earlier. I know I pushed it. I'll try and respect your boundaries." His tone is clipped.

"Why do you not like him?" My words slur with how trashed I am.

He shrugs, a smile creeping up his face. "We're just too different."

His words make me laugh. They're more alike than they think.

"How so?"

Raising a brow, he grins cockily. "Sure you want me to answer that?"

I nod.

"And you won't get mad?"

"I pinky promise."

He takes a swig from the bottle. "I, for one, would never call you my property." He scoffs.

I grab the bottle from him and take a swig, having finished the small glass he poured for me.

"I just don't want you to think no one would love you, but him."

My mind is too hazy to comprehend his words.

He takes my silence as the end of the conversation. "Look, I'm not going to say anything else. It's your business. I just want to know if you're happy?" His warm hand grazes my leg.

A hiccup escapes my drunken lips.

Nineteen

Aiden

I lay in bed, mulling over what happened. I feel fucking awful for upsetting her earlier. I only partially meant what I said. Still, I shouldn't have said it, but Leo gets under my fucking skin.

Unable to take it any longer, I finally decide it's time to find Emilia. She never came to bed last night. I was surprised I fell asleep without her there. but by the clock readout saying It's four in the morning, I must have slept pretty damn well.

Where the fuck is she?

I stumble down the stairs in the dark, the boards creaking under my feet. The quietness makes me a little nervous.

As I near the kitchen, I hear the most perfect sound, her laughter. Following the happy sounds of my beautiful girl, I step out onto the porch, prepared to make a long speech about how sorry I am.

The crisp moonlight cast a bright glow across the wood flooring, illuminating my worst fucking nightmare.

Leo is standing in front of Emilia, her bare legs wrapped around him as she sits on the railing. The same position I had her in our first night back from Italy. My eyes widen at the sight of him thrusting into her.

Inside of her.

It isn't her laughter I'm hearing.

It's her fucking moans.

"What the fuck!" My broken voice echoes through the dense forest.

I clamp a hand on Leo's shoulders, pulling him away. To my horror, he doesn't budge and simply keeps thrusting into her.

He turns back, a smirk playing on his face.

Emilia looks over his shoulder, looking directly at me with glazed eyes as he fills her. Her mouth opens and she moans his name.

"I'm sorry, Aiden. You just can't protect me like Leo can."

Her hideous words cut into me like a hot knife. My feet won't move as I watch the horrific fucking scene unfold in front of me.

She smiles at Leo in adoration. "He's a better man than you," She moans, burying her face into his chest.

I fall to my knees, distraught.

Leo continues ramming into my girl as he turns to me. "Fuck, she feels so good."

I roll into a ball, covering my ears as I hide my face between my knees to block their voices out.

Someone fucking make it stop.

I shoot up from the bed with a gasp, covered in hot sweat. I reach out for her, but she's already leaning over me, shaking me awake.

A sliver of moonlight showcases her face.

Thank God she's here.

I lay back down, my body still shaking as she tries to soothe me.

Every night, since I've gotten back from Italy, this has been my routine. Nightmare after fucking nightmare. Always in a different location, but always the same dream. The thought sickens me.

I know I shouldn't be obsessed with being the only man to ever touch her, but it makes me happy knowing that. And fuck, I know she would never do that to me. But it feels so real when it's happening.

She wonders why I fucking hate Leo.

This is the reason.

But it's just a nightmare. It isn't real, yet it's driving me mad.

I want to tell her. My biggest insecurity is her leaving me for another man and it's reflecting in my dreams. Not that I would ever fucking allow that to happen.

But the truth is, Leo kept her safe in Italy. It's the only reason I keep him around. But the opposite side of that is that I couldn't keep her safe. Yes, I locked her away before they took me away, but I put her in that situation.

How much longer until she realizes what a fuck up I am and leaves?

I've seen the way he looks at her. I know how he feels. But is it my own fears I'm seeing or the truth?

Reality and my dreams mix, creating a haunting routine for me.

I train my eyes on hers. She's waiting for me to reply but I need a moment. A moment to look into the eyes of my entire heart to calm myself, before I rip Leo to shreds over a fucking dream.

Emilia

I calm slightly when his eyes shoot open. It feels like years before his lips part.

"You're here." His tone is so defeated, it breaks my heart.

"Of course I am. Where else would I be?"

He shakes his head, refusing to answer me. He rubs the sleep from his eyes. "When did you come up here?"

"Not long after you. I'm sorry about our fight."

Sleep has sobered me up a little. I went to bed the second Leo touched my leg last night, to sleep with Aiden in our bed. I don't remember the exact words spoken during my drunken state, but I hope I remained respectful towards mine and Aiden's relationship.

Aiden insists that Leo likes me. I just didn't see it until last night.

I'm planning on talking to him, to let him know nothing will ever happen. But is it my fault? Am I giving off those kinds of vibes?

This conversation doesn't need to happen now, especially with Aiden so upset. It's extremely late and I'm a little tipsy. These nightmares are constant, multiple times every night. I can't imagine what happened but it's clearly haunting him.

"Aiden, I've tried to be patient. We need to talk about Italy. What happened?" My question throws him off.

"Italy?" He pulls me closer.

Why won't he open up to me?

"Your nightmares. I know it's from the torture you went through in Italy." I frown. "You don't have to hide from me, A."

He gives a slow nod. "Yeah…Italy." His jaw twitches. "Can I just hold you?"

I melt into his embrace.

"I'm so sorry about earlier. I didn't mean anything I said." His breath is warm on my neck.

"Don't apologize. It was dumb. I'm sorry too, though."

Silence takes over the room.

"Still, I should never have said something like that about you out of spite to anyone…especially him." He holds me fiercely, my back to his warm chest.

Tears stream down my face when I feel his body shaking. My heart breaks at the sound of him crying.

No, not crying.

Sobbing.

Aiden

It's been a few days since my chat with Emilia that night. I've spent the better half of those days organizing my business so we can somehow get back to reality. If it were just me and her, it wouldn't be an issue. But it's not.

I finally have her alone.

Emilia's been busy all-day, cooking for twenty people in the house. Guards, us, new security. The cabin is fucking packed. She even made a sweet little cup of coffee for Leo.

I'm spiraling.

I need to keep calm.

How can I explain I don't like her serving him without sounding like a fucking moron?

I want to do anything but sleep.

The nightmares are becoming too real, keeping me high strung. I'm starting to mix reality with my dreams. I know she wouldn't. But it's him I don't trust. At the same time, he did keep Em safe in Italy so I can't ignore that.

I watch as she gets ready for bed. I admire her tattoo; it looks insanely good against her tan skin. I have no idea why I argued with her about getting one.

"Come here," I beckon with open arms, wanting to feel her.

She slides in, fitting to me like a glove. Her brown eyes peek up at me through batted lashes. I need to talk to her about everything, not directly as I don't want her to see anymore faults in me, but I need to be assured.

"Why are you with me?"

Her eyes widen and she sits up. "Why are you asking this?"

Shrugging, I pull her down against me. "I need to know what qualities you see in me."

"There's so many, A." She trails a finger across my chest. "How safe I feel with you."

That's a lie.

I play with her hair as she lays on my chest, her words haunting me. The cool feeling of her locket necklace laying against my skin makes me smile momentarily. She never takes it off.

"You don't have to lie to me." I can't blame her.

She props herself up on my chest, facing me. "What did I lie about?"

I laugh at her attempt at trying to be sweet. "About you feeling safe with me," I get out through gritted teeth. I fucking hate admitting that.

She gives me a curious look. "Aiden, never in my life have I felt safer than when I'm with you."

"None of the shit would have happened if you never met me."

She rolls her eyes. "I wouldn't even know who I was if I never met you."

"Still, there's no way you feel safe around me. Everything you've been through is a direct implication of my bad choices. I would die before ever letting anything happen to you but–"

She cuts me off by cupping my face in between her small hands. "Aiden Scott, I'm not lying to you. There is nowhere in this world I'd feel safer than with you by my side. Remember, every time I was in danger, it was when I wasn't with you. You weren't there when the Matterazo brothers took us. And the other time when those men…" She takes a deep breath. "When they took you, you sacrificed yourself for my well-being. You put me in that room and locked me inside to keep me safe." She kisses my cheek. "There is no one in this world who'd protect me as fiercely as you do."

I hate to fucking ask this. I hate being insecure and unsure but she makes me vulnerable.

"What about–" I quiet my voice, even though it's late. "Do you feel safe around Leo?"

She lays on her back, mulling over my question. "Kind of."

I lay on my side, watching her expressions.

"But not like when I'm with you. More of he's my bodyguard and he'll protect me as well as he can."

I smile. "Is that the truth? I won't be mad."

"Yeah. I'm not going to lie and say he isn't capable of protecting me, because he is. But not to the depths you're willing to go. For him, I'm a job. To you, I'm your lifeline."

I smile at her words. "So naïve my sweet girl." I twirl her hair, telling her the truth she doesn't want to hear, "You're more than a job to him."

She shrugs. "He'll learn."

I hold her tight.

He better fucking learn quick. I plan on firing him when the new security team gets here. The main tangible reason being my nightmares. *How fucking crazy is that?* Plus, he has an innate ability to overstep his minuscule place in Emilia's life.

I will my anger to subside. "I don't know what I did to deserve you. I put you through so much, Emilia. How much longer until you leave for someone less complicated?"

She laughs, doubling over.

I cock my brow. "What's funny?"

Laying her head back down, she runs her finger over my tattoos, circling our yellow rose. "What's funny is you thinking I would ever leave, A. You're it for me."

"You promise?"

Fuck, I sound like a bitch.

"With everything in me." Her eyes flutter

close.

I feel like I'm losing control for the first time in my life. My entire empire is centered around my control of power.

Growing up, I had nothing. My father made sure we did without. It isn't Mom's fault for loving him. Apparently, he was a nicer person before the alcohol took over. But I've only ever known him as a monster.

I have no communication with him. He kicked me out once I turned sixteen. I wanted to go live with Ashley and her mom, but I didn't want to be a burden. So, I got a job as an intern at an investment company and lived with Ricky and his family. If it wasn't for them, I don't know where I would be. That's why I'm happy he's with Ashley, he's a good man.

I saved my money throughout my internship and put myself through a semester of college, hoping to get all A's. I had a perfect GPA throughout high school, and between that and my work in college, I earned a full ride to Stanford. All my accomplishments, and it's never enough for me. I must be more; I always have to be more. Better, richer, more successful, with each passing year.

That's why I'm so obsessed with wanting Emilia to have the world. She deserves everything. I hate that she feels guilty when I buy her things. I never want her to do without. It makes me physically ill thinking of her not having whatever she needs, yet she wants so little for herself, always caring about others and putting herself second.

For years, I've struggled with why Mom would always run back to my father. I think I understand more now, with the overwhelming love I feel for Emilia. You can't help who you fall in love with.

I'm just lucky the one who has my heart would never break it.

Mom's death was caused by my father's actions. She died in a crash while driving in a storm after a fight with him. Her only fault was loving the wrong man.

I've worked to be a different man than my father was, but is the cycle continuing? Is everything I've put Emilia through something my father would do? Is my selfishness of having her contributing to her downfall?

I have a plan to get her life back on track, more stable.

I swear if one person argues with me, I will flip my shit. Emilia won't be able to stop me, which is why I'm waiting until she falls asleep before going to talk to the guys.

Emilia

Hearing a commotion downstairs, I dress and creep down quietly to see what's happening. I peek into the living room and see Ricky, Howard, and Aiden in a heated discussion. Leo sits on a barstool nearby, watching on silently.

Aiden's voice is the first thing I hear audibly,

"I don't think anyone in this house has a say in what I can and can't do." Aiden runs a hand through his hair. "Except for Emilia."

I smile.

"Aiden." Ricky sighs. "I'm not trying to

tell you what to do. I just don't know if it's safe to do so."

Howard shakes his head. "I have to agree with Mr. Scott. Sorry, Ricky, but as head of his security, I have to say it will come with its risk, but she will be safe."

The men grow silent when they notice me walking towards them.

"What's going on?" I tilt my head in curiosity.

"Nothing." Aiden clips.

I wonder if he has a plan for me that doesn't include him.

Like that would ever happen. I wouldn't allow it.

I head to the kitchen to make some coffee. After that, I'll figure out what's going on. I pour five cups.

Aiden appears beside me, looking on edge. "What are you doing?"

What is going on?

"Making coffee."

He runs a hand down his face. "Go back to sleep, babe."

"No." I need to know what's happening. I place a cup in his hands, which he quickly sets down, before giving out the rest of the cups.

This seems to irritate Aiden further.

Discreetly, he leans down to whisper into my ear, "Grab your shoes." His voice is uncontrolled.

I look at him questioningly. His wild eyes and the slight shake of his head stop me from arguing. I head to the foyer to slip on a pair of toms.

Putting his boots on, Aiden grabs a set of keys just as Leo steps off the barstool and throws on his jacket.

"You're not coming," Aiden states in an amused tone as he holds onto my arm.

Howard smirks.

Leo shakes his head. "She needs a guard if you're taking her out."

Aiden stiffens, cutting his eyes to Leo and he straightens to his full height. "I'm her fucking guard," He spits. "Get in the damn car, Emilia."

I obey, putting their hushed discussion to the back of my mind. Right now, the important thing is figuring out what's causing Aiden's stress.

The sun is cresting the mountains when I step outside with Aiden following close behind me.

Slamming the front door shut as though to end his discussion with Leo, he opens the passenger door for me. I slide into the familiar leather seat of his classic Challenger, the first car we ever rode in together. So much has happened since then it's hard to even believe.

I'm knocked from my longing memories as the door slams shut. Keeping his eyes trained on the driveway with narrowed vision, Aiden starts the car and the engine revs to life.

We sit for a moment, his back leaned against the black leather, his tattooed arm dangled over the black wheel. He's so lost in thought I need to bring him back here with me. I buckle in and hear him let out a low laugh.

"Middle." He orders, pointing to the seat next to him.

I happily slide over.

His stance is still rigid, but he leans over to strap me in. It's almost as if he's admiring the restraints he's placed on me.

No other words are spoken as we peel out of the driveway.

I look out the open window, breathing in the fall scents and the cool crisp air flowing through the car. I can only imagine the vibrant colors of the trees lining the drive.

I admire Aiden's control over the vehicle, the way he navigates us through the twisty mountain roads. Every so often, as he switches gears between my legs, his thumb brushes against the inner part of my thigh, eliciting a fire against my skin.

I'm not scared of the speed, I know he would never put me in danger but I'm curious. My eyes widen.

One hundred and five.

I can't deny how incredibly sexy he looks

with his tattooed wrist between my legs as his hands work the shifter.

Miles pass behind us before he finally speaks. "I'm so fucking sick of being in that cabin. Everyone thinks they have a say over you, my business, everything." He runs a hand through his tousled hair. "I can't fucking do it."

I look at his hands again, one on the wheel and one on the shifter. The dark road ahead illuminated by only dim streetlights and yet he handles every sharp curve with precision.

He calms the farther he drives.

Everything is clearer now.

He's navigating these roads with precision and control. That's what he needs, order.

Maybe I'm wrong, maybe it's his nightmares. I know he was tortured. I see the scars he doesn't want to talk about every time he takes off his shirt. No one knows what happened. He won't talk about it, and I don't want to push him.

I may not be able to give him what he needs to fix everything, but I can give him the one thing he's craving right now.

I run my hand slowly up his leg. "Is this what you need?"

"I just…I need fucking control."

His hand on my thigh causes a warm sensation to spread through my body. I place my hand on top of his, sliding it further up.

"Control me," I plead, knowing this is what he needs.

Aiden

My foot slams on the break, causing us to come to a skidding stop on the dark empty road. In a quick movement, I have her pants off and drag her on my lap.

She squeals with delight as my hands squeeze firmly around her waist. "Is this what you need?" Her breathing heavy.

Fuck. Yes, it is.

Running my hands through her soft hair, I breathe in her scent.

I hate not being able to take her anytime I want. I fucking hate being locked away in a cabin with everyone else. If it were just me and her, we could do whatever we wanted, but everyone is always there. Too many guards, too much of Leo trying to tangle himself in our lives.

I can no longer ignore the idiotic problem that has been bothering me. "Why do you pour his coffee for him?"

She staggers back, her back hitting the steering wheel with a soft thud. "I...I don't kn...." She stops herself.

I grip her chin. "Why?"

Biting her lip, she shrugs. "I just do."

"Not anymore, okay?"

"Okay." She looks up at me, through thick lashes.

The way she looks, with her lips pouted makes me want to do very…very dirty things to her mouth.

She moans as I slip my hand into her panties.

"Is that what's wrong with you?"

I'm about to pleasure her and yet she selflessly wants to make sure I'm okay.

"Emilia, there are so many fucking things wrong with me. The biggest issue right now is your lips are moving but my cock isn't filling them." I calm down slightly. She does that to me. I know she loves it when I talk to her this way.

Nothing in my life has been consistent lately, but when I tell her to do something, she always listens. She is my constant in life. The way she smiles before lowering her body in the middle seat is the most stable thing in my life. Her undoing my pants brings back the power and control I've lost since the fucking mafia tried to destroy my life. It may be fucked up, but her utter devotion and submission is nothing short of absolute perfection.

She smiles, bringing her full lips down to my hard cock, bobbing her head up and down in a smooth rhythmic motion.

Thank God I bought a cabin in the middle of nowhere, but I still need to get us off the road. I compose myself as I pull off to the side. My plan changes as the car begins to move and she continues to suck me. She tries to lift up, but I gently push her head down. I keep driving, relishing the feeling of her warm mouth.

I tug on her hair. Faster. Faster. Faster. The precision of my movements behind the wheel, my hand holding her head on my cock, moving my hands only to switch gears. Nothing else around us.

Control.

This is what I need.

I pull over, shutting the car off in a haste before lifting her perfect body onto my lap. The moonlight shimmers against her skin in a delicious way. I rip her thin panties off with a territorial grunt. A pleasurable moan escapes her freshly fucked mouth as I lower her onto my throbbing cock, filling her.

I admire her velvet lips, still plump from sucking me off, as they part to moan my name. She's unbelievably tight, wet and ready for my cock.

She looks at me with those eyes, eyes that tell me how much she wants me. "Choke me," She begs.

I wrap my hand around her throat and squeeze gently. My tongue caresses her bottom lip down to her neck as I kiss her, while simultaneously bouncing her on my cock. Jealous of my shirt hiding her perfect tits from me, I rip it off before gripping her waist as she holds onto the headrest.

Our movements are feral, filled with lust and love, as we collide. Our bodies tangled as skin on skin delivers us pure bliss. She reaches for my hand and places it back on her throat, bouncing her small body herself.

Fuck.

"Say my fucking name," I demand, gripping her breast in one hand and her neck in the other.

"Aiden," She moans.

"Come," I demand, loving how she submits to me, how her body obeys me.

She slows, her forehead touching mine as she cries out in blissful pleasure, coming undone on my cock.

I push her hair out of her face. "Suck me off until I'm done with you."

She pulls her bottom lip between her teeth as she slides off me. I clean myself off with the ripped T-shirt just before her lips slide around me.

"I taught you fucking well," I praise, gripping her hair to make her movements slightly faster. "Fuck," I moan, teetering on the edge as she brings herself farther down. The sound of her gagging turns me on more as she takes all of me in.

"Fuck, Emilia. That's…" I can barely speak, the pleasure overwhelming. "That's right, baby. Open your throat for me."

With one final thrust, I unload down her throat while she swallows me.

"You ripped off all my clothes!" Emilia laughs.

I kiss her forehead. "I like you naked."

Rolling her eyes, she grabs a black shirt from the backseat and pulls it on. "At least you didn't rip my jeans."

She slides into the middle seat and leans against my shoulder. The night is quiet. I know she wants to know what I was talking about in the living room.

"Aiden." She meets my gaze. "I need to know what's been going on with you."

Good, I dodged that bullet. She's more worried about me. Of course, she is.

I tell her about my dad, my mom, my fears. I lay all of my insecurities at her feet, with no fear that she will step on them.

She kisses me. "So…do you want to tell me what's been happening in your nightmares?"

"I don't…" I hesitate, not wanting her to think I'm insane. Her reassuring tone helps.

"I know it's hard, babe. But you have to talk about what happened in Italy at some point.

Your nightmares are too much."

"My nightmares." A gentle humorless laugh escapes my lips. "They're not about Italy, Em."

"Please, talk to me, Aiden," She begs, trailing her gentle fingers across my hand.

I take a deep breath. "They're about Leo."

Her brow raises. "Leo?"

I look out of the dark window for a short moment before she turns my face back to meet her eyes. "Ever since I saw you with him in that fucked up basement, they've haunted me."

She leans in. "Why?"

"I locked you away to be safe. Not to find me."

"But if I–"

I cut her off. "I know, then I wouldn't be here now. It's not that I'm not thankful. I'm simply explaining the events that led to this."

She nods in understanding.

"I kept you safe. Then Howard hired Leo, since extra security was part of the procedure for you and Ash if something happened to me. But the thought of you two alone in a room…" I clench my fist. "And the way he's just always fucking there." I laugh darkly. "But he hasn't made a move on you. He's your guard. His one job in life is to worry about your safety. I'm the one who's being jealous and rendering him incapable of doing his job."

She nods. "So, what's happening in the dreams?"

"Yeah," I pull her close. "I keep having dreams of you choosing him–"

Emilia cuts me off with a kiss. "That will never happen, but continue."

"In my nightmares, you…" I look out the dark window. "and him…"

Emilia

Never mind, I don't want him to continue. "Aiden, if I had any idea you were being tormented like this…" I take a breath. "Babe, just fire him."

He raises his brow. "Over a dream?"

I nod. Who cares? There are plenty of other people we could hire. "Yes. Why didn't you talk to me about this?"

Aiden shrugs. "It's just a dream. I didn't want to sound dramatic."

"Never, I would never think you were dramatic." I grip his hand. "So, fire him. Know that it's not real and I would never betray you," I assure him, enunciating my words. "For the benefit of your mental health and our relationship, just fire him."

His head leans back against the headrest I

was gripping in pleasure moments ago. "I don't want to look weak."

"Weak?" I scoff. "You will never be weak in my eyes. If it makes you feel better, he put his hand on my leg when I was drunk the other night."

"He what?" He tenses. "Why didn't you tell me?"

"I thought your nightmares were because of Italy. I didn't want to hurt you when it didn't matter, and I was honestly too drunk to remember our conversation before he placed his hand on my leg," I ramble. Maybe I shouldn't have said anything, but if it happened to him, I would want to know.

"Okay." He twirls my hair through his long fingers. "I'll fire him in the morning. It's late we should get back."

His knuckles turn white as he grips the steering wheel once I've settled back in my seat.

"You okay?"

Silence.

"I'm trying to imagine why you didn't tell me he touched you." His tone is clipped.

I sigh. "It wasn't inappropriate."

He scoffs. "Don't fucking stick up for him."

"I'm not. I just…he's a friend. I know you think he has feelings for me, but he doesn't. I thought so too, but I always put my hand on

Ashley all the time when comforting her," I assure.

He doesn't respond, instead he steps down on the accelerator as we fly down the driveway. It isn't long before we pull to a stop in front of the house.

He kisses my forehead before hastily exiting the car, death raging in his emerald eyes. He moves with absolute purpose as he stalks up the stairs while I stumble behind him.

"Where the fuck is Leo?"

Aiden

"Come into my office," I call out to Leo, bypassing hostility and keeping my tone neutral.

It's silly for me to get so worked up over an employee. I fire him, and it's done. This will be nothing more than a simple career change for him. Hell, I'll recommend him to some of my friends.

I step into my office and close the door behind Leo, leaving Howard to keep Emilia entertained in the living room. I take a seat on my faded leather chair and place my elbows on the cherry wood.

I eye him as he remains quiet, sizing him up.

Yes, he gets in our business and yes, he

oversteps but I'm a levelheaded man... sometimes. I can't help the slight respect I have for him when he brought Emilia to Italy, kept her safe, and saved me.

He should have never brought her, but without him, she would be lost, and I would be dead. It's a lose-lose battle here. Most importantly, I have respect for Howard and he's who hired him.

Leaning back, I run a hand over my tired face. "Leo, listen–"

He cuts me off, shaking his head. "Mr. Scott, I know you're about to fire me. I know you can't stand me."

I nod in agreement.

"But you just can't."

Why is he so desperate to stay? What are his intentions?

"And why can't I?" I ask in a bored tone.

He looks around, sucking in a deep breath as his grey eyes level with mine. "I take my job seriously. I'm sorry if that comes off as overbearing to Emilia's and your relationship."

I hold back a scoff. "Overbearing?" I laugh. "You, Leo, are downright intrusive, meddling, and frankly obsessed with her safety." I lean forward, shooting daggers at him. "Why?"

Maybe I've been looking at this in the wrong light?

He flicks a wrist in the air casually. "As I

said, I take my job seriously."

"Yes, your job is to protect her. But I'm your boss. You realize that, don't you? You don't have to protect her from me."

He opens his mouth to speak before stopping himself. "Yes." He lowers his head. "I'm sorry, and I promise not to overstep again."

I shake my head. "That won't be a problem at all. You're fired from Scott Investment Corporation. Effective immediately."

His face falls, hurt by my words.

I wonder if there's more that meets the eye than what he's letting on.

"Tell me, Leo." I smile. "Are you in love with my Emilia?"

Twenty-One

Emilia

The golden morning light filters in through the floor-to-ceiling windows as Aiden lays beside me in a peaceful slumber. I get up quietly as not to disturb him. His emotions were so full last night; rage, lust, love.

So many things came to an end last night. Leo will be leaving today. Even though Aiden has nothing to worry about, it's for the best. We have too much going on for him to be worried about other things.

I don't know what happened last night as Howard had made sure I went to bed. Aiden stumbled in an hour later, collapsing into bed as he pulled me in tight. His only words were 'he's fired and leaving tomorrow', before he was out cold, snoring.

Wrapping myself in a thick robe, I head downstairs, passing Leo's empty room on the way. I wonder if he already left.

"Hey, Em." Ashley's sleepy voice greets as I enter the kitchen, a sleepy smile adorning her face.

"Want to do something today?" I need to get out of here, even if only for a little while.

The danger of the Mafia. Leo. Aiden's nightmares. So many negatives surrounding me, yet so many positives. It's hard to wrap my head around. I prefer this beautiful retreat for what it is, a vacation home. Somewhere to destress, not hide away.

Ashley tilts her head.

"What?" I place a hand on my hip.

"Oh…nothing. Ask my brother when he wakes up. Love you." She waves before sleepily trudging up the stairs.

I can't tell if she sounds mischievous or sad.

"Emilia." Howard greets with a warm smile, pulling a muffin from the bowl as I take my first sip of warm coffee.

"Is Leo gone?" I blurt.

Howard's face falls slightly. "Yes, but it's for the best. Those two young men just can't get along. Power struggle, you know?"

I nod fiercely. *I know so well.* "What are we doing today?" I casually change the topic, hoping he'll reveal something.

He smiles, zipping his lips in a dramatic fashion.

Heavy footsteps sound to my right and I turn.

"Quit trying to ruin your surprise." Aiden smiles sleepily, planting kisses on my jawline as he steals my coffee.

"Surprise?" I look between the men.

Aiden nods, pulling me towards the back door.

The crisp fall air wakes me further as we step outside. I snuggle against Aiden's warm bare chest. He never gets cold, he's like his own personal heater.

He pulls me back to examine me. "I wanted to see if you wanted to go on a date with me tonight?"

He sounds sweet, being so formal. I can't help the wide grin taking over my face, "Of course! Where to?"

"A little restaurant in downtown. An Italian place. It's really good." He looks hopeful.

My face falls slightly, feeling bad for Ashley. She needs to get out too.

Aiden kisses my forehead. "It's a double date."

My smile brightens. "What do I wear? Is it fancy?"

I start piecing together an outfit for an upscale restaurant.

He shakes his head. "I've hand-chosen your entire outfit, it's upstairs. If you don't like it, you can wear sweatpants for all I care. You look beautiful in anything. I just wanted you and Ash to have a fun night, away from all the bullshit."

"Is it safe though?"

Lifting my chin up with his fingers, "Em, please do not question my ability to keep you safe." His voice stern, yet soft. "I know things have been fucked but I promise you you're safe."

"I'm worried about everyone's safety, not my own. We still don't know who took you."

He looks out at the foggy mountainside. "We're starting to get an idea, but that's for another discussion."

"We can discuss it now."

He shakes his head. "Please, baby. Just one night. I need one night of normalcy for all of us. I have important things to discuss with all of you tonight. Just trust me…okay?"

I don't think I've ever been this excited for a date. Ashley and I have been getting ready all day. You would think we were going on a month-long vacation.

"Which color?" Ashley holds out a vibrant palette.

Horrible at picking shades, I point to a few pretty ones.

She laughs, shaking her head. "You're lucky you're naturally pretty or you'd look like a clown."

I quirk a brow, pointing to her perfect features. "Okay, miss America," I toss a pillow at her before we fall into a fit of giggles.

"Which dress?" Ashley holds out two floor-length gowns. She grows nervous as I take my time to think. We both already know she'll look stunning in the deep blue dress.

I hum. "I don't know, Ash, I don't like either of them." I joke, leaning back against the throw pillows as I fake a yawn.

"Ugh! I know your sense of style isn't as bad as your make up choices." She teases back, tossing the black dress on the floor before holding the sapphire blue one against herself in front of the mirror. "I know you like this one better. Your eyes tell all." She winks.

A soft knock sounds at the door just as Ashley is about to start applying her make up.

"Come in!"

Aiden walks in with Ricky in tow.

Ricky whistles, lifting her face for a kiss. "Wow, you look fucking gorgeous, babe."

She giggles. "I'm wearing sweats and have

absolutely no makeup on."

He shakes his head. "I stick to what I said. Absolutely gorgeous."

"You need glasses," She jokes before returning to her meticulous routine. I can tell how happy she is with Ricky from the smirk she can't seem to shake.

Aiden walks over to me, bending to whisper in my ear, "You're the prettiest."

I shake my head.

"I heard that!" Ashley yells, "But I agree."

"Did you like the dress I picked for you?"

I grin, having seen it earlier. It's perfect, a little loud in color but it matches my tan skin. It fits as though it was made for me.

"I love it!"

"Hear that? She loves it," Aiden boasts.

Ricky rolls his eyes.

I give him a questioning look.

"Ricky and Ash said you'd hate it. They thought you would prefer black."

"Why?"

"Because you're shy, and red is a not so shy color," Ashley chimes in. "I know you're going to look stunning in it, but I thought you'd hate it." She shrugs, chucking a pillow at Aiden when he laughs.

"I still know her better than you," She crows, sticking her tongue out.

"No fucking way." Aiden swoops in to

steal a kiss.

I laugh at their sibling rivalry over me.

"We're leaving in an hour, girls."

"Sounds good."

I don't know why I'm so nervous about tonight. Aiden gives me butterflies every time he walks in the room. I hope tonight goes perfectly.

I admire my reflection. I never would have imagined myself in such a stunning deep red dress, but it's my new favorite. I'm amazed by how well he knows me to pick out something I never would have got for myself but when it's on…it's perfect.

Coupled with heels, jewelry, a handbag and Ashley's beauty skills, tonight is going to be amazing.

A knock sounds on the door as I'm slipping on my heels. I smooth out my dress and turn, excited for Aiden or Ashley to see me. My jaw drops as Leo saunters into the room.

"I thought you left?"

"I…I had to come back to say goodbye." He takes a few steps towards me. "It didn't feel right to leave without saying anything."

I smile awkwardly. "Does Aiden know you're here?"

He rolls his eyes. "Come on, Em, I'm not a threat. You know I'm not. He just gets nervous about me." He eyes me. "You look beautiful by the way."

I look to the side, unsure of what to say.

It takes him a moment to speak again. "I needed to tell you something."

I cock my head to the side in question.

"I wanted to tell you to be careful." His voice is low and cautious.

"Careful?"

He pinches the bridge of his nose. "Going into the city tonight."

"How did you know about that?" I ask, confused.

"Aiden's been planning it for a while."

I give him an odd look.

"I was your guard, Em. I know these things because it was my job. Please don't let him brainwash you into thinking I'm the bad guy here."

"Are you insinuating that he's the bad guy?"

Silence spills through the room, implying that is indeed it. Wanting this conversation to end as quickly as possible, I give him a pointed stare. "It's a date. We're not going into an underground fighting ring."

He rolls his eyes, stepping closer. "I'm not worried about the date."

I gesture for him to elaborate.

"It's Aiden. Doesn't he seem a little…"

He rubs his chin in thought. "Controlling?"

I scoff. "You know nothing of our relationship."

"I'm worried you don't see anything besides him." He sounds desperate.

I laugh. "Why would I? He's everything to me."

"That's the fucking problem. Why don't you be with someone who doesn't bring you danger? All I want is your safety, Em." His tone is desperate, but his words infuriate me.

"Why are you acting like this?" I'm completely taken aback.

"I couldn't say these things before, but since he fired me…" He closes the gap between us, his gray eyes filled with purpose. "I can say whatever I want. You deserve a better life, a calmer life."

"I have a perfect life!" I announce, my cheeks reddening in anger.

He scoffs. "Perfect?" He gestures around the room, his accented voice raising in volume. "Emilia, you're in a fucking safe house. None of this is good for you. Go home. Go home to your mom and your normal life. No man is worth this."

I look down at my feet.

This is pointless, he'll never understand.

He exhales deeply, pinching the bridge of his nose. "You're impossible."

I stagger back as he stalks towards me, coming a little too close for comfort. His tall frame towers over me as he leans down. A blanket of overwhelming confusion washes over me as his unfamiliar lips crash against mine.

My mind blanks out.

The kiss last for mere seconds, before my mind kick starts once more. My hands push against his chest and Leo stops immediately, stepping away. He shoots me a look of sorrow.

I gasp as I see Aiden in the doorway behind him, looking heart-wrenchingly broken and enraged.

Twenty-Two

Leo continues, "There's more to this world out there. Find a boring guy who keeps you safe," Leo begs, his voice filled with pure panic. He's completely oblivious to the angry man behind him. Perhaps he knows and doesn't care.

A streak of black rushes in front of me and Leo's body is slammed against the cedar walls a second later. Aiden's large hands pin him by his shoulders as he stares him down. His sculpted back is to me, but I can see his shoulders rising and falling rapidly.

Leo scoffs, trying to remove himself from his grip and completely ignoring Aiden's snarls.

"See what I'm saying? He was fucking listening in on us!" Leo shouts at me.

Aiden slams him harder into the wall.

"Emilia, Go!" Aiden demands.

Is he mad at me?

I stay. "Aiden." My voice is small, scared.

I hope he knows I didn't want that. He can't think I've betrayed him.

He turns his head towards me, his face contorting with rage.

"I didn't—"

"No." He cuts me off with a wave of his hand.

My heart is about to beat out of my chest. *Does he hate me now?*

"Baby, I know you didn't. It was all fucking him." He cocks his head towards Leo, who rolls his eyes in return. "Now go!" He turns his full attention back to Leo.

I don't want him to get hurt. Not like Leo could do much to him, but still...he is a trained killer.

Aiden's tone is venomous. "To respond to your stupid fucking remark about me listening in, I walked to *our* bedroom, heard what you said to *my* girl, and waited. I wanted to let her handle this. But since you decided to kiss her, I stepped in."

Aiden looks back at me, sighing when he sees me still standing there, awkwardly twiddling my thumbs. A smile takes over his face as he takes in my appearance. "You look stunning in red baby girl."

I melt, almost forgetting the situation we're in.

"You've got to be kidding me!" Leo grunts.

Aiden laughs. "You know the funniest part about this is when I asked you if you loved my girl…"

When did he ask that? What's going on?

"You told me you did. You didn't lie. I thought about killing you then. Maybe I should have."

"Em." Leo begs for me, ignoring Aiden.

"No!" Aiden snarls. "Don't you dare speak to her."

Aiden looks at me, mouthing the words 'close your eyes'.

I obey, hearing a loud thud moments later. I squint my eyes, afraid to see what happened, only letting out a relaxed breath once I've fully taken in the scene.

Aiden stands over Leo's fallen body that is slumped against the wall.

I squeal, worried. "Is he dead?"

I'm not a monster. I don't care that Aiden hit him, he fully deserved it. I just don't want anyone dead. Period.

Aiden steps over his body, dusting off his

perfectly tailored black suit. He offers me a hand before guiding us to the car, his voice devoid of amusement. "He's just taking a nap."

The crisp fall air makes me shiver; my adrenaline going a mile a minute. I slide into the sleek leather seats of Aiden's Mercedes, waiting quietly as Howard and Aiden speak in hushed tones.

Aiden climbs in quietly and we speed off.

I lean over, unbuckling my seat belt.

"Put it back on." He clips before softening his tone. "Please."

I obey. "Are you okay?" I ask in a small voice.

"Are you serious, Emilia? Are *you* okay?"

Okay, so he doesn't hate me. "But your dreams…"

He shakes his head. "Fuck my dreams. My girl just got kissed without her permission. I'm fine, I promise. But seeing that made me mad *for* you, not at you, sweetheart."

He takes my hand, kissing the back. "You really do look absolutely perfect tonight."

I blush at his words.

I sit up straighter, suddenly realizing we're heading to the city without the other half of our double date. "Where are Ash and Ricky?"

"They drove separately. I wanted you all to myself tonight…but I needed Ashley there too. They left about twenty minutes ago."

EMILIA

I hum, wondering what he wants to tell us.

We arrive at the restaurant half an hour later and Aiden escorts me past the tall cherry wood doors and the gorgeously decorated main eating area. A smiling hostess dressed in a sleek black dress guides us to a door in the back, handing me a glass of red wine, before gesturing for us to go on up.

I can practically feel Aiden's eyes burning into my ass as I walk in front of him. It makes me feel good and I crave for his touch.

We step out onto a beautiful rooftop veranda where a lone table sits. Hundreds of candles dimly light up the area with their warm golden glow. Red roses mixed with yellow bloom even on a crisp fall night. It's cozy and intimate.

It makes me think of Mom, suddenly missing her so much.

Warmth engulfs me as we step closer to the table. I notice the tall heaters dotting the area, and Ricky and Ashley lost in each other.

The guys really went all out on this one.

Ricky notices Aiden's hand when we sit down. "Why are your knuckles bruised?"

Unsure of how to explain things, I jump right in. "Leo kissed me."

Ashley spits out her drink. "When?"

"He arrived back at the cabin to tell Emilia goodbye, right after you guys left," Aiden cuts in.

"Ugh! We always miss the good shit!" Ashley complains before looking at me intently. "You okay?" Her smile sympathetic.

"Totally fine."

And I mean it. I wiped my mouth about two hundred times already.

"He dead?" Ricky takes a sip of his whiskey, bringing my attention back to the conversation.

"Nah." Aiden smiles. "But he'll be gone when we get back, and we won't see him again. Let's enjoy the night. No more talk of that fucking idiot."

Courses and courses of food arrive. Seafood, soups, salads, steaks, along with some of the most delicious desserts I've ever tasted.

I hum happily as I taste everything.

Hands down the best restaurant I've ever been to.

"Now for what we brought you here for." Aiden announces, swallowing the last of his Bourbon.

Ashley and I are practically on the edge of our seats in anticipation.

"We are leaving the safe house."

Ashley squeals. "When?"

"How?" I gasp, stunned. "I love the idea,

but we still don't know who took you. Is it safe?"

Aiden and Ricky look at each other.

"I had a body-double placed at my apartment," Aiden states. "He goes to my office too. No one has tried anything. I kept him heavily guarded, but there have been times he stood by a window for a little longer than I normally would have and went out without a guard, and he's fine."

I still don't understand. "How good can this double be? Wouldn't someone looking for you figure out that it isn't you?"

"Show her." Ricky gestures to Aiden's phone.

Aiden reveals a photo of the double who looks exactly like him.

"Holy shit."

Ashley peers over, scoffing, "What the fuck? He could steal your life!"

Aiden laughs, sliding his phone in his pocket. "I've been using him for years. He's even done stand-ins on business meetings for me. Really good guy." He smiles. "Handsome as fuck too."

Aiden's emerald eyes slide over to mine. "We can go back to the city…or we can get a house in the suburbs, close to your mom's."

"You call that a house?" Ricky laughs, tossing back the last of his whiskey. "That thing is a fucking mansion."

So, they've been planning this for a while.
My heart feels full.

Aiden rolls his eyes, turning his attention to me. "As long as you're there, I don't care where the fuck we go. Your schooling will work in either place." He looks at me through thick lashes, "So what is it, Emilia? *Mansion* or back to the city?"

"Which will it be?" Aiden waits for my answer as we sit on a plush rug in front of the roaring fireplace.

As much as I love the city, settling down with Aiden in a home sounds incredible. I know we're young, but it's not like we haven't been living together since I first met him, and I'll be closer to Mom.

"A house." I grin.

Aiden smirks, tangling his hand with mine. I watch as the flames dance in his eyes, mesmerized by the striking emerald and dancing red under his thick lashes.

"I'm really glad you said that." He slips a velvet box into my hands.

I open it slowly, confusion washing over me. My fingers trail over the intricate black key that sits snug inside a silk bed. Its ornate detail belongs to that of a treasure chest. I hold it closer to the flickering light, admiring the vines weaving around it.

"I don't know what it's for."

He places a warm hand on my cheek with a smile. "It's the key to your new home."

My eyes well with tears as I lean in to kiss him. "What if I said the city?"

He laughs, placing the key back in its box. "Then I would have made a really bad investment buying that man—" He coughs. "I mean house."

I eye him through narrowed eyes. "You were going to say mansion. Was Ricky right?"

A cocky grin forms on his sculptured face. "It may be a little bigger than your normal house, but we can grow into it."

My heart aches in a good way. He wants a future with me, though we've never spoken about it before.

I work through the knot in my throat. "You mean…with kids?"

"With everything. The white fence, the wedding." He pulls me into his lap. "And a million kids."

My tears flow freely at his confession, having never felt so much joy springing through me.

"Don't cry." He wipes my tears away.

"I'm just so happy."

"Me too, baby."

Practically bouncing out of my dress, I chirp, "When do we leave?"

He halts my movements, his firm hands on my hips making me melt. "We leave the day after tomorrow."

I cheer. "I can't wait to see it. Can we go tomorrow instead?"

He shakes his head with an indulgent smile.

It dawns on me what day tomorrow is. Thanksgiving. I'm cooking everyone a huge dinner, and…

"Oh no! I need to call Mom." My voice is panicked.

Aiden looks around the room, whistling nonchalantly.

"What?" I peer at him curiously.

"You won't have to call her. She's already coming. I was going to call her, but Howard made the specific request to do so himself."

"Why is he so precious?" I sigh in relief. I wonder how Howard will act around her. This will be interesting.

"Why are you so precious is the real question."

Our conversation comes to a halt as he plants gentle kisses along my jawline and neck.

"I'm so happy you said yes."

His hands caress the soft material of my dress. He slips one thin strap down before grazing my bare shoulder. My body tingles at his touch, chills running down my spine. I rub my palm against him, feeling him harden under my hand.

"Fuck, Emilia."

The way he says my name does something to me. I always hated my full name until him. He trails the letters out, always putting emphasis on the last letters. It rolls off his tongue perfectly…just like my moans are rolling onto his tongue right now.

He lifts us up momentarily to take his pants off as I forcefully get his suit jacket off. It takes seconds to unbutton his black dress shirt.

"Get this dress off of me," I beg, needing him inside me.

"Suck me," He demands, gripping his length.

"Dress," I counter, about to break from the tension I feel.

He shakes his head. "I want it on you. You look so fucking elegant." His words are calm, but his chest is rising heavily.

I twirl my tongue across his length and listen to his breathing patterns change. He hikes my dress up, revealing my bare bottom. I specifically didn't wear any panties tonight so we could have fun after dinner. He pushes me further down onto him while slapping my bottom, eliciting a moan from me.

"That's for being too sexy for your own good." His words are playful, but I know he truly thinks I'm the hottest thing ever.

I wish I saw myself that way, and tonight…I want to.

Dripping from his touch, I straddle him.

"What do you want me to do to you?"

"Destroy me," I whisper, my confidence building.

"Gladly," He growls.

My back hits the plush rug and he hovers over me. My dress is pushed up far enough for him to enter, but he teases me instead. Nudging himself against my center yet hovering there, driving me insane.

"You have too much control," I moan, unable to wait much longer.

He shoves himself in with one hard thrust. "You think I have real control when it comes to you. When it comes to you and your perfect fucking body?"

I moan his name.

"Do you know how many times in a day I've wanted to bend you over a nearby table and fuck you senseless?" His fingers stroke my clit, the feather-like touches making my body shake. "It's unhealthy how much I've imagined my cock filling you." He groans.

I come undone at his calculated movements as he hits a spot deep inside of me, causing my eyes to roll back. He watches with wild eyes as I scream his name. I don't have time to recover from my intense orgasm as he pounds relentlessly into me like a ragdoll.

I'm completely lost in the moment.

"Where do you want it?" He moans.

"What?" I moan, unable to think properly. Everything feels so good.

"My cum." He speeds up.

"Your choice."

He pulls out, pumping his cock. I watch in amazement as his eyes roll from pleasure, his mouth slightly agape as he finishes all over my brand-new dress before we collapse in a heap of heavy breathing and lust.

"You ruined my dress."

He admires his work. "I like seeing you ruined by me." He shrugs. "In case you forgot I own you."

He grips my dress and rips it from my body. I gasp at the sheer power of this man, turning me on.

He positions himself in front of me, kneeling on the rug.

"I own your body, and I can do what I please with it." He smiles, bringing his head in between my legs.

"I don't think I can handle anymore." I bite my lip.

We both know I crave every inch of him.

His laugh is deep, and dark, sending delicious chills up my spine. "I tell you when you've had enough of me, understand?" His hands hold my legs firmly apart as his head moves down and his tongue devours me with expert precision.

"Aiden," I moan, throwing my head back as my hands run through his hair.

"Look at me while you cum all over my tongue." He demands before bringing himself back down to twirl around my center more.

I obey, watching the light dance over his dark hair. He grips my legs tighter as my body shakes from the pleasure, pushing them apart so he can lick every inch of me as I moan his name.

His head rests on my leg as he looks up at me while I catch my breath. My hazy eyes look around the cedar room, taking in the rich features and breathing in the woodsy aroma. "I'll miss the cabin, the lake, and all the fun we had here."

Aiden leans forward and kisses my forehead. "We still own it, babe. We can come back whenever you want."

Twenty-Three

Aiden hovers beside me. "You know, a caterer would have made this easier for you." He tells me, wrapping me in his arms after I close the oven door.

"There is no way I would let your chefs be away from their families today. We're perfectly capable of cooking." I smile, gesturing to Ashley. "See! I even have Ash on chopping duty."

She giggles, showcasing her very large knife. Aiden laughs, "Yes, and when she cuts her finger off, I'm not driving her to the hospital."

I wipe my hands against my apron as Mom rushes in through the front doors, her eyes search the open floor as she darts in my direction. I turn to Aiden with a smile,

"It's tradition, you'll find my family is very fond of those." I assure him that I'm okay and this is what normal people do on thanksgiving. I wonder what he usually does.

Mom slips into my arms, hugging me fiercely. "Honey!" she squeals, bouncing by Howard's side. He insisted on picking her up of course. In her hands, she holds two bouquets. One, which I know is for me. A blooming bouquet of yellow roses draped with greenery. The second, a vibrant set of tulips. Howard.

She hands the roses to me, I bring the fresh-picked blooms to my nose, inhaling their sweet and dewy scent.

As she rushes into Aiden's arms for a hug, I smile. She knows just how much I love him, from our talks on the phone. The calls were sporadic when we first arrived at the cabin, but things have calmed down immensely.

The news of the body double has helped to quell my nerves.

Howard and Aiden walk away, giving us a moment. I grab two vases and arrange our bouquets accordingly.

Mom walks to Ash, a little more pep in her step. "Ashley, how are you? How's your mom?"

"Good and good." She smiles, carefully chopping carrots. "You?"

"Wonderful.' She replies, full Cheshire grin.

My eyes glide over the flowers, thankful that Howard got her some. The yellow roses remind me of something. "Oh! Look!" I tell her, taking off my apron and placing it on the counter.

I slowly begin to lift my shirt up and she swats my hand, her eyes panning around the kitchen. "Emilia Acholeis Banks!" She scolds, making me and Ashley both laugh.

"It's okay. I just want to show you something." I smile, lifting my shirt to showcase the vibrant ink.

She places her hands over her mouth at the sight of the small yellow rose on my side. She trails her fingertips over the ink. "It's gorgeous, Emilia."

"I knew you would love it!"

She nods, "The artist did a wonderful job with the drawing, just wow."

"He really did," I say, wishing I could tell her it was Aiden. For some reason, that's a secret for him, and it's not my place to say.

Ashley pipes in, "Aiden got the same one." Shit.

Mom places her hands on her hips, mulling it over. "He did." She repeats to herself, looking out the large glass windows onto the patio where Aiden, Ricky, and Howard stand. Huddled around a tall heater and smoking with drinks in their hands.

Aiden looks different today, more casual but still edgy. His hair is a tousled mess, but it's perfect. He opted for a navy sweater, which I love. He said it matched my cream dress, and he was right. I've never seen him in anything but suits or black T-shirts. I prefer him shirtless, of course.

My mom coughs, breaking me from longing further. "Yes." I say quietly, unsure how she will respond to matching tattoos.

A smile creeps up her face, "Well as long as you didn't get each other's names I don't care."

A laugh escapes my throat, "I would never!"

"Ouch! Fuck!" Ashley yelps, and somehow Ricky is already rushing through the kitchen to her side.

He looks panicked as he grabs a small clean towel from the drawer, "Are you okay?"

"Mhmm." She whimpers, always trying to be the tough one. Aiden walks in trailing behind Howard.

He takes one look at Ash, "How deep is it?"

She sighs, taking pressure off the wound to show him. A little blood comes out, but nothing major. Ricky instantly begins cleaning it. "I'm sorry!" She tells me, as they walk towards the bathroom.

"I should have known better than to give you a sharp object!" I yell back as they disappear down the hall. I hear her laugh, and I know she's okay.

Aiden walks over, throwing away any food that may have blood on it. "What are you doing?" I ask him, watching him roll his sleeves up and dip his hands under the running stream of water.

"Cleaning up to take over Ashley's job." He smiles, "She's out of commission now and I'm starving." he draws the last word out, and then winks at me.

Mom steals my apron, throwing it over her burgundy dress. "What do I need to do?"

I smile, watching her in the kitchen with me. This is something we've always loved to do together. "Help me with the Turkey?"

We sang, danced, chopped, cooked and caught up

while cooking Thanksgiving dinner.

Ashley even came back and helped pipe icing on the cupcakes since that didn't require any sharp utensils. I swear that girl can do everything, except cook. I love her for it though.

The long wooden table is decorated with a ridiculous amount of food, eight places have been set. Me, Aiden, Howard, Mom, Ash, and Ricky all crowd around and take our seats. It takes some persuading to get his 'guards' who my mom thinks are his friends to sit and eat, but they do happily.

We cut back on security for tonight, men still line the property but it's Thanksgiving and we need normalcy. Besides, Aiden's body double is still unharmed. We may never know who took him, or why. Personally, I hope we never come to find out.

"A toast!" Ash's voice draws me from my thoughts. "To health and family. And this delicious looking food." Glasses clink, and we dig in. Enjoying the delicious food and relaxed conversation.

Everyone is almost too full to move. Mom is at her usual, running full speed. "So, are we putting a tree up here?" She asks, her eyes panning around the massive dining room.

I warned him about the usual tree decorating immediately after Thanksgiving dinner. It's not that I hate it, I absolutely adore it and Christmas is my favorite time of year. It's just that... we won't be in the cabin but for one more night.

I relax when Aiden speaks up. "Actually, if I could have a moment with you." He sets his napkin down on the table, "Maybe on the balcony?" He suggests. I stand to join, but he stops me.

Mom nods with an eager smile. Howard takes her attention momentarily; she giggles as he whispers something to her. Seeing her so carefree, it's amazing.

Leaning over, Aiden whispers in my ear. "I need to speak with her, give us ten minutes."

He escorts Mom outside and I fidget in my seat until I can't take it anymore, I need to do something. Howard coughs, "Emilia, set your plate back down." His voice is soft, playful. "You cooked; we will clean."

Ashley looks at me, nodding her head to the stairs. "Hey, Em. Can you help me change my band-aid?"

Ricky looks at her with a cocked brow, "Babe, it was barely a papercut. You don't need to change it."

She rolls her eyes, standing up and gesturing for me to follow. "What are we doing?" We creep up the stairs towards mine and Aiden's bedroom.

"We're going to eavesdrop; don't you want to know what they're talking about?"

I ponder this for only a moment, "duh." I respond, I mean I know he's going to tell her about the house but I'm curious about her reaction. Trying to keep quiet, we slowly open the back door and crawl on our hands and knees onto the small balcony, which sits directly above the first-floor patio.

"I'm not going too. You're a grown man, and

successful. I know you've got your head on the right track but I'm also not an idiot."

Aiden gives an appreciative nod; I can see them through the slits in the rail. They're both huddled by the heater and in deep conversation. My mom continues, "My husband was a detective, he dealt with bad men all the time." *What are they talking about?*

"Ms. Banks-"

She cuts him off with a gentle smile. "Aiden, I know you're not a bad man. I know you love my daughter. But I also know that last time I was here, there were men everywhere. Men who acted as if they were your friends but they seemed more like bodyguards to me."

She takes a sip of her wine, gauging his reaction. I know that inquisitive look of hers. Reminding me of being in high school, about to get one on Pamela's famous interrogations.

But unlike me, who would break at the slightest guilt from lying to my mother, Aiden keeps a straight face and a casual demeanor. "I'm a man in a position of power, Ms. Banks. It was a decision I made to keep Emilia safe, as a precaution of course."

She nods, "So you're not in any trouble?"

"No, ma'am." He doesn't hesitate, I almost believe him myself.

"Okay well, thank you for telling me the truth."

Aiden smiles prematurely, thinking he's won the battle.

"However," Mom glares at him, setting down her

glass of wine and standing firm in front of him. "Emilia doesn't have her father here on earth to say the things that need to be said to her first love,"

"If you hurt her, or ever put her in danger I will hunt you down to the ends of the earth." She tries to be serious, but her facade is crumbling.

"Go, Mama!" Ashley mouths. I playfully swat her arm; thankful they didn't hear. But I agree, and what she said was sweet. I don't give her enough credit for how amazingly intelligent she is.

She was married to a cop for decades; she knows more than I think she does.

"Now, what is it you wanted to talk to me about?" she asks, back to her usual happy attitude. Howard walks outside, bringing her a fresh glass of wine. When he goes to leave, she tugs on his suit jacket. Bringing him closer to her, she snuggles against him which gets a collective 'aww' from me and Ashley.

"Actually, I was going to ask your blessing-" She cuts him off with the palm of her hand. My stomach drops, as well as Ashley's.

"For marriage?" She chokes.

A small smirk creeps up his face, "No. Your blessing of me and Emilia buying a home together." He frowns slightly, "But just so you're aware. My intention is to marry your daughter in the future. That conversation will happen later, of course. But I hope your reaction won't be quite so... that." He jokes, slightly. I can tell this makes him nervous. My heart spins with joy hearing him talk about me becoming his wife.

She hugs him, "No, no dear. You just caught me off guard. I see the way you two are. I know that you're both headed in that direction and I personally think moving into a home together is a great idea before marriage. It will give you a good test to see if you're ready for that kind of commitment." She looks off into the night air. "I never want to hold her back from love. Life is too short, just please tell me you'll be moving close? Don't take my baby girl far from me."

Aiden visibly relaxes. "Never. We found a place about thirty minutes from you."

"Anywhere I'm familiar with?"

"It's off of Wellington Crescent." He tells her.

She lets out a low whistle. I'm unfamiliar with that area but apparently, she's not. "When will you be going to look at it?"

Howard laughs slightly, making my mom look between the men.

"What?"

Aiden clasps his hands together, "I may have already bought it, we leave tomorrow." His words are rushed. Boy, is he nervous or what?

She shakes her head, with a smile. "And what if I would have said no?"

"Then you would be the first and only person on the planet to ever witness me beg." He replies.

She gives him an appreciative nod, placing her arm on his shoulder. "I'm happy for you two."

Howard walks inside with a giggling Pamela interlaced in his arm and Aiden takes a moment to smoke. I watch with intensity as his eyes trail across the dark yard, wondering what he's thinking of.

After looking around the empty porch, Aiden grabs his phone, dialing a number and placing the device to his ear. "Hello." His voice is cheeky.

"We should go inside." I whisper to Ashley; I don't want to listen in on his personal calls. Besides, I'm sure it's nothing but business.

She shakes her head, still holding a grin. "I want to hear." She whispers.

He nods his head, listening to whoever's on the other end for a few moments.

"Yes, as we discussed before. You're set to pick Emilia up tomorrow, my sister too. Take them wherever you would like... I'm done with them." I shudder at his words.

"Why?" He repeats the question. My heart thunders in my chest, threatening to break. "Well, because they both enjoy eavesdropping on conversations."

His eyes pan up to the balcony, a devilish smirk on his face. He never dialed anyone, and it was a joke. Not funny but deserved. "I know you guys are up there." He laughs, tossing his spent cigarette into the tray. We giggle, like schoolgirls as we dart back into the house, my relief palpable.

When I find him, he gets a well-deserved scolding from me. But I don't mind watching the way he doubles over in laughter from tricking us. His dimples prominent and his laughter filling my heart.

That night, we lay in bed together. With everyone

that we love inside the cabin. Mom and Howard really hit it off, Aiden filled me in. Howard's been going to see her regularly and he brings her tulips every time. They were still sitting by the outdoor fireplace when we went upstairs, she spoke to me briefly about him. She was so worried what I would think, I told her to follow her heart.

She said it best. Life is too short, don't hold back someone from love.

Everything is calm, as it should be. We're happy. It's normal.

"Tomorrow we start a new chapter of our lives." Aiden purrs, brushing the hair from my shoulders. "I hope you're ready."

Twenty-Four

I twirl my hair with a nervous finger. "I was kind of worried you were going to send me off somewhere without you."

Aiden and I are cuddled in the back seat of the suburban as Howard drives us to our new home.

As the cabin disappears, I take a deep breath. Closing that chapter of our lives with a small wave.

The next time we come here, it will be for a vacation, not a safe place to land.

"I'm too damned selfish to let you go anywhere without me." He caresses my thigh.

I sigh, melting into his chest.

I take my time on the ride to mentally

prepare. At nineteen, I'll be moving in with my boyfriend. The feeling is surreal. I couldn't be happier than to take this step with him.

I wonder what our home looks like, it seems like everyone has already seen it. I wouldn't care if we lived in a shoebox as long as we're together.

Before I know it, we drive through the familiar territory near the town I grew up in.

Turning down a long and winding road, we stop in front of an intricate iron gate, equipped with a keyboard that Howard uses to enter the street.

After passing a guard station at the tip of the neighborhood, we travel further in. Old-fashioned lanterns sit high on black iron poles as streetlights. Mansion, after mansion passes us by. Broad, lush lawns sprawl on for miles between each one.

Aiden tucks a stray piece of hair behind my ear, gesturing towards a Spanish Villa at the end of the winding road. "We're home."

I raise my head from his chest to get a better view. Oregon White Oaks line the stone driveway, threatening to spill over as their colossal limbs stretch across the lawn.

The Spanish Villa sits tucked away at the end of the drive, hugged by traveling vines and moss.

It's magical.

I'm speechless as we pull into the roundabout, tears threaten to spill.

I step out, turning in a circle as I take in my surroundings. Quiet and serene.

"Welcome to your new home, Emilia." Howard rounds the back of the car to get our things.

Aiden whispers to Howard, who then leaves our things by the front door and drives off with a grin.

"Where is he going?"

Aiden guides me to the front door. "We're alone for the night."

I wonder where Ash and Ricky will stay. I assumed they would be here, maybe they're just staying somewhere else for the night.

"Is it safe?" I ask quietly, curious about the lack of guards and Howard.

"Armed guard at the post, completely gated community, a top-notch security system." He smiles. "And you have me."

A wide grin creeps onto my face. "Aiden, this is insane."

He slides the intricate key into the lock. "I don't do anything that is *not* insane, Em. You should know that by now."

I reach up for a kiss. "It's absolutely beautiful. You know I don't need all of this, right? I don't care for your money. I only care about you."

EMILIA

He smirks, pushing the door open. "I know, babe. And that's exactly why you deserve it."

I gasp.

I move to take a step forward, only to squeal when Aiden sweeps me off my feet, bridal style, and walks inside.

"Oh my gosh."

My wide eyes drink in the room when he sets me down gently. White and gray marble flooring covers the open foyer where a massive, chestnut staircase winds up either side of the entryway.

"Oh my gosh." I repeat, unable to think of anything more to say.

Aiden laughs with a cocky grin, grabbing our bags and setting them down in the foyer. "I know."

Hand in hand, we pass a vast hallway and step into the living room. It is void of everything. No furniture, curtains, or lamps.

I have to crane my neck to look to the ceiling, everything is so… big.

"This is my favorite part!" I exclaim. Pointing to the intricate fireplace where a familiar white rug sits.

Aiden laughs, pulling me in for a kiss. "This is the first room you've seen. How can it be your favorite part?" He teases, shooting the rug a nostalgic smirk.

I glance out of the floor to ceiling windows, spotting a car pulling in. I bounce lightly on my toes when I see Ash and Ricky step out. Aiden sighs as they make their way towards the front door. I grin when she runs inside, jumping up and down.

"I love it!" She announces, her eyes panning around the room.

"Me too! Oh my God, can you believe it?"

She's practically dancing out of her shoes. "It's unreal, beautiful! But why isn't it furnished?"

I crane my neck to meet Aiden's emerald gaze as he pulls me into a warm embrace. "Because Emilia will be the one choosing everything."

"I will?" I raise a brow.

"Yes."

Ash sighs. "But where will we sleep tonight?"

Aiden smirks. "I'm not sure where you and Ricky will be sleeping." Laughing, he gestures to the only thing in the room, the white plush rug from the cabin. "But Emilia and I will be sleeping right there tonight."

"Okay, eww."

Ricky whispers something into her ear.

"You're joking!" She yells, her voice bouncing off the empty walls.

I turn to Aiden. "What's that about?"

Shrugging, he pulls me in for a kiss before

announcing, "They're our neighbors."

A dance breaks out between Ash and I. The guys laugh at our excitement and joy over being so close together.

"Ahh! I'm leaving. I *have* to see this! I'll come over tomorrow?" She rushes out after tackling me with a hug.

Aiden pulls me down onto the rug once we're alone.

"I want to explore!" I playfully swat him away.

He flicks a button, causing fire to crackle in the marble fireplace, casting a golden glow around us.

"We have our whole lives to explore. Let the rest be a mystery until tomorrow morning." He pulls me tighter against him.

"So, what do you mean by me choosing everything?" I inquire while slurping the noodles from our take-out.

"After we get up in the morning and I show you around, a designer is coming to meet with you. If you don't mind, I'd like for every room to have exactly what you want." He shrugs. "That's why nothing is decorated."

A tear rolls down my cheek, my heart overflowing with love. "You didn't have to do that."

Aiden pulls me onto his lap. "I love you, Emilia."

I show him how much I love him, all night long. In front of the blazing fire, on our white rug. In our new home.

Twenty-Five

Impatiently, I wait for Aiden to get up, gently shaking his arms.

"Why does it feel like Christmas morning?" I wonder out loud as I pull on his arm to lift him.

"Give me five minutes. Come, snuggle." Aiden murmurs sleepily, attempting to pull me down.

I huff.

He sighs. "Fine."

I don't miss the smirk playing on his face.

I dart, dashing through our home as he pushes off the ground and gives chase, cherishing the sound of his carefree laughter filling in the empty halls. I've decided the top floor is where I want to explore first.

"What's that?" I point to a closed-door to my right. I open it, thinking it must be our room. It's gorgeous, tall ceilings and a large floor area.

He clasps his hands together. "Guest room."

"This is the guest room?"

He nods and we head down the hallway.

"And this?" I gesture to another massive empty room.

"Another guest room."

I place my hands on my hips. "Just how many guestrooms does this house have?"

He chuckles, placing a finger on his chin in thought. "I'm not sure."

I narrow my eyes.

He laughs. "Fine. Ten."

I gasp. "Ten!" My head spins a little. "What are we going to do with ten freaking rooms?"

Aiden places his hands on my shoulders, calming me. "I know it's overwhelming, and you'd rather have a smaller home. But I promise you, once you have every room how you want it, it will feel more…quaint."

"This place… quaint?" I can't help the giggles that follow as I slide across the polished hardwoods in my socks. "For the record, I wouldn't pick any other home but this one. It's what you chose for us."

He smiles.

"So, we have to get ten beds?"

He laughs. "No, baby. Maybe six bedrooms, including ours. The others can be for things like offices, libraries, a gym." His eyes bore into mine. "Whatever you can imagine, I will deliver for you. No request is too grand. This is our home. I want you to make it yours."

"Why are you so good to me? Why do all this for me?"

"That's a loaded question. But to simplify, it takes an actual angel to love someone like me. I don't know how you do it, Emilia, but I'm so fucking thankful you do."

I don't hide my blush at his sweet words.

"Where is our bedroom?"

Aiden points downstairs and I take off on a race, skidding to a stop when I come across the most glorious kitchen I've ever seen. White marble countertops with light gray cabinets line the walls.

While there is no furniture, no expense was spared on appliances. Double ovens, an industrial size stovetop, and a fridge triple the size of an ordinary fridge tucked inside of a hidden door made to look like a pantry cabinet.

"Beautiful."

Aiden wraps his arms around my waist and kisses my cheek. "I thought you wanted to see the bedroom." His tone is seductive as he playfully smacks my ass.

I throw my arms around his neck. "Show me." I avoid looking out at the backyard, trying to soak up all the surprises one at a time.

Aiden throws open a set of intricate, white French doors.

My jaw drops.

A reading nook sits flush against one wall, while a king bed adorns the other, with floor-to-ceiling windows letting in natural light.

I twirl into the expansive grand bathroom. A large tub sits on old-fashioned claws, adding a luxurious feel to the already glorious space.

"It's perfect," I whisper in awe.

He gestures towards the windows.

I turn slowly and step towards them, realizing it's an entryway to the backyard. Hedges and shrubs are trimmed to match the rich décor. A pool and hot tub sit to the left of a circular courtyard. The vibrancy of the lush grass brightens up the drab winter. I take in the marble fountain in the middle of the courtyard.

My breath hitches. "Is that a greenhouse?"

My eyes fixate on the only pop of color in the backyard, bright yellow shining through the glass. I yank off my socks and step out onto the cool grass barefooted as Aiden takes my hand.

"Why is the grass not…dead?" I wiggle my toes in the thick, soft turf. Hues of red, yellow, and orange are scattered across the lawn.

"It's sod. It will be like this for a while." He seems pleased with himself.

I open the doors to the greenhouse and step into the heated room. He squeezes my hand lightly at my silence.

A smile grows on my face when I notice no other plants or flowers in sight, except for one.

Yellow roses.

They adorn every inch of space.

I trail my fingers along the soft petals, tears brimming in my eyes at the sweet gesture. We walk in happy silence, hand in hand. At the very back sits a bed in a separate area from the flowers. I'm met with more comfortable air when I open the door.

"I didn't want us to miss our rooftop bed, so this will be our new rooftop," He announces with a dimpled smile.

Pristine, crystal clear walls showcase the backyard. The bed sits in the middle of the space with a perfect view of the roses. Tall trees fence the perimeter, providing us with privacy.

"I'm sorry. I'm just so blown away by everything." I grin shyly, overwhelmed by the love and beauty from him.

I notice a chimney puffing out smoke nearby as we step out from the room. "What's that?"

A smaller, though beautiful home comes

into view.

"That's Howard's guest house."

I frown. "Wouldn't his family want him home?"

"We're his family."

I snicker. "Couldn't he live in our house with the five hundred rooms?"

Shrugging, he pulls me close as we head back inside. "I need my privacy with you. I'm tired of sharing you." He winks. "Plus, do you really want your mom staying here when she stays the night with him?"

I shiver. "Okay, eww. Point taken."

I love Howard and Mom, but I definitely don't want to think about them staying the night together.

Aiden picks me up and strides to our bedroom where he tosses me gently on the California king size bed.

I sink into the soft cotton sheets with a sigh. "There were two beds here and you chose for us to sleep on the rug?"

Not that I was complaining. Last night by the fire was…perfect.

A laugh escapes his lips as he climbs in beside me. "The greenhouse surprise would be ruined if we came here. The gardener only left about an hour ago. It wasn't quite finished when we got here yesterday."

I squeal. "Everything is so perfect. I don't

know how to explain it." I look around our empty bedroom, thinking of all the decorations I'm going to get to make it ours. "This is our home."

"Our home," He agrees.

The next few days are spent with our designer, Mrs. Nowak. A sweet old polish lady who jots down every idea I have. With Aiden busy with work and trying to ensure our safety, I've had plenty of time to think of each room.

Ashley and Ricky still haven't left their house. We went to visit, but they just keep hitting the intercom and giggling. They're in their own little world, just like A and I.

Mom has been extremely busy with her shop, but she's coming to visit soon. Christmas is in a couple of weeks and our home should be fully decorated by then.

I rush to the door excitedly when I hear the familiar hum of Aiden's challenger. I greet him with a kiss as he walks in, placing his jacket on the rack. He seems at peace.

"What's with the excitement?"

I didn't realize I was bouncing on my heels. "I finished a room!"

"Oh." He smiles, peeking around. "Where are the workers?"

"I wanted to do this one on my own."

He winks. "Is it a fun room?"

"A fun room?" I hurry him along, wanting to show off what I've been working on all day. Everything has been delivered over the past couple of days. Today was all about painting, which I didn't need help with.

"Like a room for us to..." He runs a finger down my arm. "have fun in."

I shake my head as we make our way upstairs. "I don't understand."

"A room for me to fuck you in, Emilia."

I laugh, rolling my eyes playfully. "Get your mind out of the gutter."

He takes a step back, taking in my appearance. "Why are you covered in paint?"

I point to the door at the end of the hallway. "Follow me to find out."

"You know I have painters, right? When you said you did this one yourself, I didn't think you meant all by yourself. I would have helped."

"I wanted to surprise you."

I go up on my tippy-toes once we reach the door and try to cover his eyes with my hands, despite his height. When I fail, he covers them for me as I guide him inside.

"Surprise!" I exclaim. He removes his hand from his eyes and brings it to his mouth. Silence spreads through the room.

Does he hate it?

"Emilia. It's beautiful."

I grin. I thought building him an art studio

would let him explore his creative side more. "I put your easel there to look over my rose garden."

"It's just…wow."

"I'm happy you like it," I'm practically squealing, before gesturing to the tarp covering the floor. "You got home earlier than I thought."

He pulls me tightly against his chest. "You're unlike any woman I've ever met."

I peer up at him through batted lashes. "Why?"

He laughs. "I hired a designer to turn these rooms into anything you want, with all the money in the world at your disposal." His fingers trail across the paintbrushes I bought at the store today. "You could have made it into an extra closet, a spa room…anything." He cups my face. "But no, my girl is so incredibly selfless that she designs an entire room for me and spends her free day painting it and getting it ready… just for me."

"You deserve it." I slide closer to him, his lips a feather away.

"I don't deserve you, baby." He smirks against my lips. "But I'm so happy you're mine."

Weeks pass by in a blissful blur.

All the rooms are finally finished. The hardest thing to decide on was the color schemes. Knowing how much Aiden loves black, I opted on gray tones with pops of yellows and blues ringing throughout our home.

Ashley is back in school, but I have a proposition for Aiden that I'm going to talk to him about soon. I broke in my new kitchen by spending most of December running a little business of selling baked goods to get some money for Christmas. It changed my thoughts on culinary school slightly. Our home smelt like gingerbread and cakes all month long.

"Wake up, baby. It's Christmas." Aiden kisses my shoulder.

I blink sleepily, reaching up to pull him down into a passionate kiss. "Our first Christmas!" I squeal, jumping out of bed and running towards the tree that Aiden chopped down himself at the tree farm last week. I remember my awe as I watched his muscles work, his veins bulging.

Aiden strolls after me, calm and collected as always.

I don't care how excited I look, Christmas is my favorite holiday. I'm horrible at keeping secrets, but Aiden still has no idea what I got him.

Our home is decorated in a winter wonderland theme, a mixture of white and silver, with the tree being the only pop of color. We'd haphazardly thrown ornaments on when decorating, like children creating a painting. It's my favorite part of our decorations.

"Good Morning." He grins.

"Good morning." I turn and reach up to give him his second kiss of the morning. "Okay, you first!" I hand him a box before tugging him to sit on the floor with me. I wipe the sleep from my eyes, watching him happily.

He gently shakes it once and listens to it rattle.

I wait in anticipation as he carefully peels back the wrapping paper.

He pulls out a glass vase filled to the brim with, "Sand?" He smiles, confused. "You got me sand? I love it!"

I giggle. "Not just any sand." A smile creeps up my face. "Sand that we'll be sitting on in a couple months! Just me and you, by the ocean, with no distractions."

"This is too much." He shakes his head with a Cheshire grin. "Where are we going?"

"Greece!"

Out of character, Aiden does a little dance, making my heart melt. He then hands me a large package with a wide grin. It's thin but wide.

I rip into the paper with a flourish. Tears brim my eyes when I catch sight of the painted canvas. "Aiden." My voice quiet as I take in the painting. Fine line work and oil painting collide.

It's a portrait of me.

"It's…gorgeous." Tears roll down my cheeks. I admire the painting for a few moments longer before Aiden hands me a second, smaller box. "What's this?"

"Open it."

I happily tear into the green wrapping paper, pulling out a mask with curiosity.

"We're hosting a charity ball," He announces.

I bite my lip, torn. "I know things have been calmer, but is it smart to invite a bunch of people into our home?"

He snickers. "That's why we'll be wearing a mask, baby."

"When?" I'm starting to warm up to the idea. It'll be a blast to have a ball with fancy dresses while raising awareness for a charity. I'm not sure which charity he chose, but I know it will be a good one.

"New Year's Eve, but we'll talk about that later." He pulls me into his arms. "Merry Christmas, Em."

That night, we were surrounded by those we love as we dove into a delicious Christmas feast. Howard and Mom are absolutely smitten with each other. She brought Rex with her -my childhood dog- and we played in the yard for hours.

I am so excited for the Charity Ball, everything is slowly getting back to normal.

Twenty-Six

Ash and I have spent the entire day getting ready for the masquerade ball, while workers in pressed black suits and dresses have been scrambling around the property all day.

White and gold is themed throughout the house. Floral arrangements of white roses in golden vases were provided by Mom. The Flower Patch is thriving because of Aiden's investment.

Erin, our hairstylist, pins my hair with another bobby pin while our make-up artist finishes Ashley's look.

"Now, you girls have to be extra careful getting into your dresses," Erin, warns. "You don't want to ruin all the work we've done."

Ashley looks like a princess with her hair down, long ringlets sweeping across her shoulders. I decided to have my hair curled and pinned up to go with my gown. Aiden requested for it, and I was happy to have my hair out of my face for the night. My promise ring, Aiden's locket necklace, and Mom and Dad's charm bracelet complete my look.

I squeal when Erin walks in with Ashley's gorgeous dress. It's off-white with the slightest hint of pink to compliment her skin tone.

"You are going to look so stunning tonight." I run my hands across the soft fabric before helping her into it.

She does a little twirl with the brightest smile I've ever seen. "Do you think it's too much?" Her smile fades as she looks in the mirror. "I mean it's a lot, right?"

I laugh. "No, it's perfect. I promise! I asked the same thing when Aiden brought my dress home. But from what he told me, this ball is extremely posh, and it only happens once a year. So, getting dressed up can be fun. Plus, we're donating our dresses to girls who need one for prom!"

She relaxes, smiling at her reflection. "That's so sweet! Okay, I feel better now because I've never worn anything like this. So, the charity is raising money for underprivileged kids?"

"Yup!" I say excitedly.

I thought it was perfect. The money raised will go towards housing, food, and extracurriculars for kids. I loved the idea as it helps parents and children, who want to be in extra programs like art classes and sports and now they have the opportunity.

I've been involved in the planning of the ball, mostly related to the food, but I'm extra excited about the endless waltz. Aiden spent days teaching me the dance he had learned from his mom. We switch partners every thirty seconds, and the dance lasts for an hour. If someone stops, they'll have to donate, which is a fun twist and will help raise more money for the cause.

I help tie on Ashley's black mask and take a step back. "I love the detail! It'll also keep us safe since we're still on semi-high alert, but security will be amped up for the event, especially with the high-profile guests."

Ashley clasps her hands together, looking past me. "Now it's your turn!"

I grin as Erin hands me my glittery blue dress. I step into it, running my hands across the material as Ashley zips me up. Hundreds of rhinestones sparkle under the light, the rich navy blue complimenting my skin tone. I let out a deep breath, looking at my reflection in astonishment.

I take the intricately detailed mask Aiden got me out of its box. Thin rose gold twists like vines, while diamonds encrust the front, shimmering against the vanity lights. It's cool against my skin.

I peek out of the window, watching as the cars roll in, before looping my arm through Ashley's. "Ready?"

She winks at me and we make our way out.

"Holy fuck," Ricky exclaims.

My eyes are trained on Aiden, greedily taking the sight of him in, as we walk down the grand staircase. His mouth is slightly agape as his eyes trail down my body. His hair is styled impeccably, his suit a pure black with a hint of blue in his suit pocket to match my dress.

Aiden takes my hand as I reach the bottom of the stairs, pulling me in for a kiss. "You. Are. Breathtaking," He whispers into my ear, as his fingers skim my exposed neck, sending chills down my spine.

I bite my lip, turning slightly to hide my pink cheeks. "You look amazing yourself."

I watch as guests file in. Women in formal gowns sweep the floors, while men in suits grab glasses of liquor from the bartender stationed at the entrance. My attention is captured by a woman walking in on Howard's arm, dressed in a floor-length red dress, her dark hair pinned back into a twist.

"Mom?" I say, my mouth open.

She waves. "Don't start." She warns, blushing slightly from our attention.

"You are breathtaking," I repeat Aiden's

words to her, which elicits a chuckle.

"Honey, you look like a star!"

I roll my eyes playfully as we head to the formal living room, which has been overhauled and turned into an elegant ballroom. Aiden pulls me in for our first dance of the night. I kick myself for deciding on such tall heels as he twirls me, but the way his eyes gaze at me as we dance makes me forget the pain.

Aiden guides me around after our dance, his hand on the small of my back, as we greet guests. He looks distracted. Perhaps it's the number of people around. He gets Howard to keep an eye on me before he excuses himself and leaves the room quickly.

I stay out of Howard's sight, so he can focus on Mom. Everything is fine and we're safe, if only for tonight. I sample the delicious food the caterers brought as I watch the donations roll in on the digital counter. It's such a success and the night isn't even over.

It's been an hour since Aiden left, and I step outside for a break after dancing with Mom, Howard, and Ashley. The sheer volume of people is overwhelming. I admire the thousands of twinkling lights that wrap around the trees, illuminating the backyard. I head for the greenhouse, pushing open the glass door, and stepping into the heated space. I inhale the heady floral scent as I roam the floor, my fingers trailing gently across the petals.

I hear a small chuckle and my cheeks flush.

Someone is here. Shit.

I tiptoe outside, suppressing my giggles. I peek through the glass doors out of curiosity, spotting two bodies tangled together, illuminated by the lamp. I turn away, realizing this is way more intimate of a moment than I had assumed, but not before seeing the man on top of a woman with chestnut brown hair.

I feel a stab in my heart as I watch Aiden's tall frame move from between her legs to hovering over her. My mouth opens to cry out, but the pain is so deep in my chest that nothing escapes.

Panicked and in pain, I rush back to the house, bursting through the French doors. A pair of strong arms wrap firmly around me, breaking me from my trance. I look around. The endless waltz is happening at the absolute worst moment. I twirl in almost a robotic fashion.

How could he?

Why would he?

I thought everything was going so well.

I can't wrap my mind around what I saw.

"Emilia."

The unfamiliar voice causes me to look up.

My dance partner looks down at me with

a serious expression.

"Hello," I greet, bowing my head slightly and trying to slow my aching heart. *Just one dance and I'll slip away.*

"I need you to listen to me."

I look into his unfamiliar smokey eyes, frowning. Do I know him? I don't know. Too much is happening right now.

I smile. "How is your evening."

With a shake of his head, he breathes in sharply. "You're not safe."

I try to pull away nonchalantly to not alert the guests, but he tightens his grip on me. My mind races as fear courses through me. "Please," I beg. "Don't hurt me." I keep my voice quiet, but my breathing grows erratic.

A small chuckle escapes his lips. "I would never. That's why I'm here." His expression turns grim.

I lift a hand to remove his mask, but he gently pulls my hand away.

"I wouldn't do that, if I were you."

"Is that a threat?" My body grows rigid as he twirls me.

He shakes his head with the hint of a smile. "Not at all, Emilia. I'm trying to help. I came here to warn you."

My breath whooshes out of my lungs. I thought this was over. "About? Who are you?" My breath grows shaky as my heart races.

The beat changes and everyone switches partners.

A new man grabs me. Tattoos peeking out from the bottoms of his sleeves make me nauseous, and I shoot daggers at Aiden as he smiles at me.

The soothing classical music Aiden and I are dancing to is a sharp contrast to how I'm screaming inside. I need to get him off this floor now. I would slap him, if it weren't for the press taking pictures of the event and the high-profile people taking up residency in our home.

I can't speak, my heart shattered.

Aiden looks at me with glossy eyes, a smirk playing on his lips. Does he not know he broke me? How can he not see it in my eyes? He pulls me close and my body grows stiff. I open my mouth to speak, but he cuts me off.

"You are the most stunning girl in the room." He leans down, so only I can hear him. "I can't wait to dip my cock inside of you tonight."

I can smell the whiskey on his breath. That's it. "Out of all the places, Aiden?" I choke back my tears as he cocks a brow at me. "In the greenhouse? On our bed?"

He sways a little, stumbling on his feet. "What are you talking about, baby?"

I look around, noticing our guests staring at us. "I saw you kissing her Aiden!" I keep my voice hushed while faking a bright smile.

He throws his head back with a laugh. My rage boils over as he grabs my mom for the next dance. I can't see past my jealousy to tell him about the warning.

What is going on?

"Wait!"

But he's already gone.

The stranger grabs me again for another dance but Aiden's too drunk to realize it's the same person I was dancing with when he took me away. I look around for Howard, but I don't see him. I tremble.

"I'm not trying to scare you."

I refrain from causing a scene. "Then tell me who you are."

He shakes his head. "It's not important. I just need you to understand it's not over. It's just begun."

I stand a little straighter. "You know nothing about me, and I don't trust you."

He nods his head towards everyone I love.

"That is your mother, Pamela Banks." Mom laughs as Aiden guides her through the dance, carefree and unaware of what her daughter is dealing with.

"That is your best friend, Ashley Walters." Ashley's blonde hair twirls as Ricky guides her in the dance. "That's her guard and boyfriend, Ricky Morris."

He looks right at me. "Your guard, Howard Nelson, went to the restroom."

His gaze sweeps dramatically to my right. "And finally, the one who got you into this mess, Aiden Scott."

My knees almost collapse as he twirls me out. "This isn't Aiden's fault."

Everyone changes dancing partners, except us.

He nods with a smile. "He's a good man. Lacks direction, certainly not worthy of you, but he does love you deeply."

"Are you trying to scare me?"

Because it's working.

He shakes his head, his dark hair moving with him. "No, I'm trying to show you. You're too comfortable. You need to be careful."

If this guy knows our names, and he seems to really know me, maybe he's right. "What do we do?"

"Lie low. And for the love of God, don't move again."

I laugh. That's exactly what we're going to do. The fact that he knows our whereabouts sends a shiver down my spine.

"I'm not playing around, the security here is top level. There isn't anywhere safer."

"You got in," I retort, narrowing my eyes as I try and look beyond his mask.

He laughs. "Not everything is so cut and

dry, Emilia. I got in because someone let me in."
So, we have a rat? "And no, you don't have a rat.
I'm close to someone in your circle. I'm not a
threat, or else I wouldn't be here."

"Then show me who you are."

He shakes his head at my request.

I need to extract as much information as I
can from him. "If you're not the bad guy, who
is?" I try to memorize every distinguishing feature
of the man.

"The man who took Aiden in Italy, he's
coming back." His expression is grim. "Not
tonight, but he's planning something."

My breath hitches. *It's just one man?* "Who
is it?"

"It's—"

Aiden grabs me once more. Musical chairs
with Emilia.

I turn towards the retreating man, raising
my voice. "How can I trust you?"

"Remember the yellow roses, Emmy."

My stomach drops. The only person
who's ever called me that was…Dad. But that
man definitely isn't him. *Who is he?*

I try to remove myself from Aiden's grip,
but his hands remain planted firmly around my
waist.

"Am I drunk, or did you just dance with
the same man three times?" His words slur
slightly. "And what did he say about roses?"

Our safety is more important than my seething disgust with him right now. "Something isn't right."

His eyes pan back to the man who'd vanished in the crowd.

"That man...he warned me that we're in danger, Aiden."

His body envelops me like a shield, his eyes scanning the dance floor. "Why didn't you start with that?" He straightens up, pulling me closer as we make our exit while he speaks into his cuff, where I spot a mic.

The crowd claps as we step off the floor.

Donation time.

Aiden's serious demeanor changes to a bright smile, calm and collected. I don't know how he does it. He writes a check and hands it to the woman at the counter.

I wave to the crowd as we retreat, trying to keep my emotions in check. I grab a glass of champagne from a server dressed in black to steel my nerves. From the way his muscles strain against the confines of his jacket, he's probably a guard. We hustle through the kitchen and past the caterers.

"Why are we going in the pantry?"

Aiden closes the door behind us. My question is answered when he reaches for the top shelf and pulls back a lever hidden inside a box of cereal. Like something out of a movie, the wall begins to move. He speaks in hushed tones as we descend the stairs.

I tug on his arm. "Wait. Mom!"

He gestures to the mic. "She's safe, I promise. Howard's with her."

We round a sharp corner and step into a room resembling a wine cellar with stone walls. It would be rather romantic if it not for the extremely bright lights overhead. I'm surprised to see a few people dotting the area.

"Meet my double." Aiden chuckles lowly.

I look over at the man who looks exactly like Aiden. My heart heals when I realize it wasn't Aiden I saw in the greenhouse. A red kiss mark marks his neck.

"Name's Will."

We exchange greetings as Aiden updates the men on what's going on.

"And Will, if you're going to have fun with a girl...for your sake, don't do it where my girlfriend can see you."

Upon closer inspection, I notice Will's jaw isn't as sculpted as my Aiden's and his eyes are more almond-shaped, having traced Aiden's features so many times.

Aiden pulls me close, wrapping me in a protective hug.

I can't help myself from asking, "Why didn't you tell me it was your double during the dance?"

"Why did you assume I would ever cheat on you?"

Point taken.

"We'll discuss your punishment later," He whispers into my ear.

Despite everything that's happening, my thighs clench at his words.

I look back at Will, who really does look frighteningly like Aiden. "Where is my double?" I'm curious if she really looks like me.

"Not here. We only needed mine tonight, just in case. You were always meant to come down here if anything were to happen."

I look around the brightly lit basement, stocked to the brim with monitors, showcasing every inch of the property.

"What did he look like?" Aiden takes a seat in front of one of the computers, his eyes sweeping frantically across the screens. "Was it fucking Leo?"

I shake my head. "No, he was older. American, tan skin, smokey eyes. Maybe in his forties, dark hair, a little grey peeking through."

Aiden nods, taking notes. "How did he get in?"

"Said he knows someone."

He runs a long hand down his face. "Fucking wonderful. This place is as secure as a maximum-security prison, but we obviously have someone we can't trust." He looks around the room. "Maybe it's time to switch locations."

The stranger's words run through my mind. "I think he was trying to help."

He scoffs. "Are you serious?"

"I think...I think he knew my dad."

Aiden stands, his hands clamping gently on my shoulders. "How?"

I tell him everything, hoping he can decipher anything I might have missed.

"You'll not speak to anyone of this, understand?"

I nod, agreeing that this needs to stay low.

Ricky walks down the stairs, his expression is serious. "Do I need to make arrangements for us to move?"

"No, we're done running. Fucking done."

"Follow me." Not waiting for me to move, Aiden captures my wrist and guides me down the hall and into another room.

He slams the heavy wooden door shut behind me, as warm light showers the room in golden tones. I don't have time to admire the stonework of the room or the peculiar box sitting in the middle of the floor.

"Where are we?"

He doesn't answer. Instead, he flips on a switch.

Nothing that I can see happens.

His emerald eyes bore into mine, anger swirls in his irises. "Control, Emilia. It's what I need right now." His head moves to my exposed neck and I shiver as he bites down. "May I do what I want with you tonight?"

Our lips collide. Fear, lust, and overpowering jealousy sends me into a frantic trance to have his hands on me.

The air heats up and I tug at my dress, wishing for it to be off. I'm thankful our masks were off the second we made it into the basement.

"Why is it so hot?"

Aiden pulls away. "We need to discuss why you think I would fucking cheat on you."

I bite my lip, wishing this conversation was never brought up again. I wipe the sweat from my forehead. "You could have warned me your double was here." My breathing is heavy, full of want.

He runs his hands over my curves, taking possession of my body with a simple touch, before snaking around the back of my neck. "I agree that was stupid. But Emilia, really, don't ever fucking accuse me of doing something so foolish ever again." His tone is clipped. "I would die before I betray you."

His words make my breathing halt.

How does he always know the exact right words to say?

He dips down, his teeth gently grazing my neck. "Understand?"

I nod, writhing underneath his feather-light touch, praying for his firm grip. "Please, Aiden. Take me."

Dazzling emerald eyes burn into mine. His rich whiskey breath is hot as it caresses my skin. "I'm going to take you, Emilia. To teach you a lesson. I'm going to fuck some sense into you."

His words are harsh but from his crooked smile , I know they're playful. The kind of playfulness I love in the bedroom, or on the hot stone slab I'm currently sitting on.

"What kind of lesson did you have in mind?" My mind protects itself from everything going on, my singular focus being Aiden.

He slowly lifts my dress, exposing my bare legs. "For starters, we're in a sauna."

My eyes dance around the room. *How did I not know about this?*

"And I turned the heat up to full blast." He smirks, stepping back to give me a full show. His suit jacket comes off, his muscles bulging against the thin material of his dress shirt. Agonizingly slow, he peels that off too, discarding everything on the floor.

I bite my lip at the sight.

He snakes his arm around my waist, pulling me flush against his body. "The way you spoke to me…" He shakes his head. "Raising your voice at me the way you did is unacceptable." He teases, gently biting my earlobe.

I admire the beads of sweat forming on his bare chest, trickling down his tattoos. The room is hot, not a suffocating heat but steamy and sensual.

He lifts my chin to look into his eyes. "I think those lips have better purpose wrapped around my cock, don't you think?"

I nod, biting my bottom lip in excitement.

He arranges his suit jacket on the floor before him. "Be a good girl, Em. Kneel for me."

I obey, my fingers graze the warm stone as I kneel, resting on his soft blazer. I unzip his pants and pull them down. I lick my lips as his erect cock bounces out of his tight boxers. Aiden moans, throwing his head back, as I lower my mouth over him.

I always love watching him come undone like this. He usually towers over me, but when I'm on my knees for him, it sends a different message to my brain seeing him so powerfully tall. It makes me feel safe, secure. As though when I submit to him, I don't lose power, but gain it, because he is the true definition of strength and when our bodies are tangled together, we are one.

His strong fingers grip my hair, still in its updo. His movements grow more powerful, his deep moans making my thighs clench.

"Look at me when I fuck your face, Emilia." His voice is uncontrolled, and husky.

My eyes pan up to his tan skin, accentuated by the golden heat of the sauna. The coals are glowing red in the peculiar box I saw when I walked in. The air is thick, with heat, with love.

I place my hands on his abdomen, my fingers trace his ink as he plunges deep into my throat. My gags only turn him on further, as his hands grope where he can reach. My tongue glides down his shaft as he unravels my hair, letting it cascade down my shoulders. The curls bounce as I move faster until he gently pulls me up by my hair and sets me down on the hot slab.

"You know you're the only person I would ever kneel for, right?" His tone is ragged, his hair falling to frame his sharp features.

"What do you mean?" I moan as he lowers to kneel on his jacket.

His head moves between my legs as he looks up at me through thick dark lashes. "It's a principle thing. I've never kneeled for anyone."

This admittance makes my skin flush.

"So I'm the first…" I don't finish my sentence, too shy to say it out loud. But the idea that I'm Aiden Scott's first for anything sends a heatwave through my already heated body.

His tongue glides through my folds. "Yes, Emilia. The only girl I've ever knelt for, the only woman I've ever swiped my tongue across their clit is you."

It surprises me because he does it so perfectly, one would think he's done it hundreds of times. The fact that I'm his first turns me on even more.

"I promise you."

"Why me?" I moan as he swipes his tongue back and forth against my clit. His low rumble makes me writhe.

"You deserve to be kneeled for, and selfishly, I craved your taste the first time I laid my eyes on you when you sauntered into the kitchen."

The memory flashes through my foggy mind, how different things were.

I tangle my fingers into his unruly hair, tugging him back down to taste me. The warmth from the sauna adds an extra level of sensuality to the already euphoric room.

Aiden

I move from between her legs, licking my lips as I chase the taste of her. She looks like a fucking movie star in that dress, but it needs to come off. Carefully, I peel her dress off and lay it to the side before moving between her legs. I nudge my throbbing cock against her. She's so wet, so fucking wet for me.

EMILIA

Her moans fill the sauna as I slide in and out of her. Sweat trickles down her skin, making her glisten under the light. I could stare at her all day. We're not close enough, I need more of her. Fuck everything else right now, we need and deserve to get utterly consumed by one another.

Her legs wrap tightly around my back as I lift her, bringing us closer to the hot coals. I would have brought her here sooner, but she didn't know about the monitors and I didn't want her worrying about how locked down our mansion is. I try to shield her from how hard I work to keep us safe. But now, she'll be comfortable knowing how tight I keep security.

Tight, so fucking tight.

I ram into her as she clenches around my cock.

"Aiden." She moans, encouraging me to bounce her harder onto my dick. Her curled hair showers us in its soft, watermelon scented beauty. I wish her body wasn't so delicate. I could fuck her here for hours, her exquisite frame suspended in the air as I force myself inside of her tight pussy.

"Do we need to go back?" Her eyes roll into the back of her head.

Always the one to worry about everything around her.

The point of all of this was to make her not think about anything but us.

I chuckle, pulling her back down onto my length. "There's no better place for you," I nibble on her silky skin, "than on my cock."

I need to cum.

Fuck, I wish I could take the chance of getting her pregnant, but it's too dangerous. I usually wear a condom, but on the rare occasions we don't, a primal urge seeps through me to cum inside of her. To not pull out and unload myself on her perfect face or tits, but in her.

I've never imagined that these thoughts would invade my mind. That's half the reason I wear a condom in the first place. I don't know if I would be able to stop from unloading inside of her out of instinct.

"Where do you want it?" I ask, letting her decide.

She wraps her arms around my neck, her moans so pure that I don't want to stop. "In me."

Did she just say that?

The words alone make my body twitch at our mutual need.

I pound into her, going as deeply as I can.

She wants it too. She wants me inside of her. My cum dripping down her legs would be a fucking perfect sight. Her legs tighten around my waist as her moans fill my ears.

At the last moment, I pull her up, stopping myself from unloading inside her. Now isn't the right time. Cum drips from my cock,

EMILIA

sizzling on the hot coals it lands on.
      We need to be more careful.
      I almost came inside her.

Twenty-Seven

Emilia

The ball went wonderfully besides the threat... or warning we received from the stranger, we raised well over our goal for the charity. Howard has been staying close to my mom, it's weird not having him around the house but I wouldn't want anyone else protecting her while we figure this out.

And to her, she doesn't suspect any danger. She's dating Howard, so it's normal for him to be around a lot.

"I just don't understand why we aren't making a move." Ashley says to Aiden, the sun set hours ago and they're still going at this.

Aiden stands, pacing the kitchen and grabbing sweets along the way. All of the counters are lined with various pastries and cupcakes, something I do when I get stressed. Bake.

"Because." He takes a swig of his beer after biting a cupcake, eww. "I don't give a fuck anymore; I'm done making you two run because of my shit. Before, when things like this happened, I didn't budge."

"Before what?" I ask, chiming in.

His features soften when they reach me, "Before I had Ashley back in my life and before I met you." He smiles, his emerald eyes dancing as they look at me. "My immediate reaction has been to move all of us somewhere safer every single time. Apparently, that doesn't work. Now we're playing the game my way and I'm letting them come for me."

I don't like the sound of that. "And by your way, what do you mean?"

"I'm staying put. Both of you are going to a safe house." His tone oozes finality.

Ashley laughs, "Okay, so you're saying you're done making us run but that's exactly what you're doing."

He shakes his head, taking another swig. "No, I'm saying that I'm staying and the best place for you guys will be close by in a safer location." he hesitates, "I just don't want to risk anything since the threat is supposedly coming here."

Ash slams her first onto the marble countertop, "You can't do that, Aiden!"

He's so cocky, and arrogant, and deliciously sexy. "I can, and I will." He states. Doesn't he realize that he can't get rid of me?

I laugh. "Hello." My voice is quiet compared to theirs and no one notices me.

Ashley stares daggers at her brother. "You do realize you can't tell me what to do, right?" Ash walks over to Ricky.

Ricky gives her a pleading look. "Babe, it's what's best."

"Hey." I say at a higher pitch, again no one hears me.

"Not you too!" her face collapses in her hands.

Aiden steps forward, talking to Ash. "It's only temporary, until whoever it is comes here... then we will fight, and I can't risk either of you being here." His words terrify me.

Ashley scoffs, "No, you have no idea if that threat was even credible, we have been totally fine and you're just going to lock us away when someone whom we don't even know says something like that?"

Aiden crosses his tattooed arms, examining the room and keeping his eyes away from me. "This isn't a discussion, it's an order."

"Hello!" I scream. They all turn to me, "We're not going anywhere. None of us." I state.

Aiden gives me a half-smile, "And what? You're going to fight off the mafia on your own?"

I nod, "If I have too. But none of us are separating, I won't have it. When we separate, that's when bad things happen."

Aiden runs a long hand down his face, "I'm just trying to do what's best."

I walk over to the fridge, grabbing a bottle of wine. "This is what we need right now." Ashley giggles, running over to me. She gives one angry look at Ricky before getting the cork opener.

While me and Ashley pour and sip our glasses, carelessly ignoring Aiden's insane orders, the guys talk in a separate room.

After thirty minutes, they make their way back. I can tell by both of their faces that they've caved. "It is true, this is the safest place, but you have to listen to me Emilia. I'm not playing around. If one threat is detected on this property, you and Ashley both have to go to the hidden compartment in the basement."

I nod, "Yes, completely understandable."

He continues, "I'm still going to work, Ricky's still going to run the club."

Ashley whines, "What about us? What do we get to do?"

Aiden smirks, "Online classes, both of you. You've both fallen behind because of me so you need to make up for it."

"Okay, dad," Ashley mumbles in a giggling tone. I nod in agreement; I had a business proposition for Aiden. I wanted to tell him about it before all of this happened, but it can wait. Online classes are more than welcome right now, a good distraction.

I bring the red liquid to my lips and watch as Aiden's eyes trail over me. "So why can you leave but we can't?"

His arrogant smirk makes me roll my eyes, "We can fight, we have guns, do you want me to continue?"

An idea pops into my head, "Teach me."

"About a gun?" Aiden raises his brow.

"No, my dad was a cop I know guns. I want to know how to fight."

He only ponders this for a split second, "That would require you possibly getting hurt so... absolutely not."

I glare at him, "A few bruises won't hurt me, I need to learn how to defend myself."

He walks over, placing a lock of hair behind my ear. "Sweetheart, you have me to defend you. I said no, that's final."

"Get up, Beautiful." Aiden's soothing fingers slide through my hair, but my head throbs from the two bottles of wine me and Ashley consumed last night.

"Five more minutes." I croak.

The covers get ripped off of me, "Nope, up." He tells me.

My eyes open slightly, catching sight of Aiden in his basketball shorts, no shirt and sweat glistening against his muscles. I recall his shimmering skin from the sauna a few nights ago.

Then I look at the alarm clock, six a.m. Nope.

He shakes his head, "I'm not playing around, Emilia. You wanted this." *Wanted what?*

I move the heavy comforter off my body. "Why don't you crawl into bed?"

His head dips, messy black hair flies in front of his face. "While I would love to ravage you in bed all day, I need to teach you a few things."

I wipe my eyes, to get a better view of him. "Like what?"

"How to fight."

After changing and eating breakfast, Aiden leads us to the basement through the secret passageway. I can't believe he's going to teach me how to fight after arguing about it last night.

This labyrinth in the walls that I wasn't aware of still confuses me, we have a regular basement with stairs leading from the living room, but I had no idea of the secret area. "Is there no other way down here?"

He covers my hand with his as we descend the stairs, "Yes, there's another way out."

I trail my fingers over the stone tunnel as we walk through, wall lanterns light everything in golden hues. "Can you show me?"

"Soon." His tone is clipped, but then he gives me a smile.

I bite my lip as we walk past the sauna, remembering the night we shared at the charity ball. Fear, love, want, so many emotions were experienced that night.

Finally, we reach an archway leading to a state-of-the-art gym. "Woah." I say, taking in all of the equipment around the room. It is surrounded by mirrors. Aiden immediately begins grabbing weights and placing them on a bar.

Winking, he gestures over to a rack with mats. "I want you to stretch, I'm going to warm up for a minute."

I begin stretching my stiff muscles.

With Aiden shirtless, and lifting the weight loaded bar above his head with ease, I have trouble concentrating. Eventually, I get into the rhythm of stretching and doing some yoga poses.

A loud clank hits the ground. "Did you really feel it necessary to wear yoga pants?" Aiden asks, his bottom lip tucked between his teeth.

I wiggle a bit while I bend down, "Am I distracting you?" I ask, trying to get out of stretching and into the fighting part.

His tongue darts from his mouth to lick his lips, "Every fucking day." He stalks towards me, then shakes his head holding up a finger and waving it in the air. "I know what you're doing, Emilia. It's not going to work." He smirks when I sigh.

I gesture around the room, feeling ready for anything. "So, what weights do I need?"

He wipes his hands, grabbing a bottle of water and taking a swig. "None of them, we're going outside."

"Why did we come to the gym then?"

He stretches his long arms above his head, his muscles contorting in a delicious way. "Because, darling. You don't need to lift weights; you need hand to hand combat. I needed to get warmed up and you needed to stretch."

He re-racks the weights while I fold up the mat and place it back on the shelf. Aiden surprises me with a slap on the ass. "And if I see you bending over in those pants anymore, I'm going to fuck you for the rest of the day, and we need to train."

I roll my eyes playfully at him, following his movements as we turn right out of the gym area instead of the original way that we came. He notices my confusion, "Showing you the other exit."

We reach a locked door and Aiden pulls a key ring from his basketball shorts, unlocking three bolts he opens the heavy door and ushers me out to a large clearing.

"This is beautiful!" I say, looking around at the space. The leaves have been gone for a while now and all that lays in the meadow is dead grass and bare trees, but it's still hauntingly breathtaking. During spring, this will be my oasis.

Aiden walks out a ways, getting into a fighting stance. Still shirtless and heart-wrenchingly beautiful, I feel my heart pound in my chest when he bends his knees and beckons me with a finger, "Come at me."

"How?" I ask nervously, a little worried I'm going to look like an idiot.

"Act like I'm about to attack you and come for me."

I shake my head, it's not that easy. "What if I hurt you?"

The laugh that forms from his lips is music to my ears, even at the expense of making fun of me. "You... hurt... me." He doubles over, "Emilia, just do it." I shake my head, I don't even see the point in this, what could I even do to someone who really was attacking me?

He smiles, "Pretend I kissed someone else."

I scoff, "That doesn't make me want to hit you, it makes me want to cry."

He thinks for a moment, "Okay, imagine I'm the bad guy. Now me, Aiden, is standing behind you, and someone's trying to kill him."

I lunge, trying my hardest to fight, but all I know to do is try and tackle this goliath of a man. My body slams into his, and I fall to the ground. He doesn't move an inch.

He crouches down, offering me a hand. "Are you okay baby?" Worry lines crease on his forehead, "Maybe this isn't a good idea I don't want you to get hurt."

I stand and shake off my nerves, "No, I'm not a flower. Bruises heal, we need this." I plead.

He presses his body against mine, the comforting heat from his bare chest radiates through the thin material of my tank top. He bends down to whisper in my ear, "I only like to push you around in the bedroom, are you sure this is okay?"

"Positive."

We spend the next hour with him teaching me how to dodge a punch, and how to properly throw one. Although, I feel like my punches won't do much as he didn't even flinch when I hit him. I sighed, about to raise the white flag and he graciously bent over in 'pain' on my last hit.

He nods approvingly after we finish, "Okay, I

think you've got the basics down. Now you need to disarm me."

I look at his hand, "Disarm you of what?"

He grabs a rock nearby and puts it to my temple. "Pretend this is a gun, what do you do Em?" He pauses, hesitating. "I hate this, I hate that you're having to fucking do this. You're too pure to be wrapped up in my bullshit."

I form a smile on my lips, trying to hold it together. "Aiden, all of this probably isn't necessary, just look at it as bonding."

He scoffs, "Bonding? I should be bonding with you with dates and dancing not teaching you how to protect yourself. This is all so fucked!"

I bring my voice to a calm tone, "It's okay, babe."

"Emilia! I was holding a fucking rock to your head pretending it was a gun because *that* is a possibility for you if you don't run the fuck away from me. Do you not get that?" He bellows, there are no leaves for his words to bounce off for an echo, they just disappear into the forest.

I walk towards him slowly, throwing my arms around his neck and staring deeply into his jade eyes. "You would never let me get that close to danger; this is for fun... okay?" I lie, trying to diffuse his freak out.

I grab his hand, bringing it to my head, he shakes off his fears as I think about what to do.

My line of sight goes from my shoe to his crotch, he notices. "Exactly, no need to do that to me." He laughs nervously, his body still rigid with worry. "But that's exactly what you need to do. Hit them in the balls and run away in a zig-zag motion or if you're able, bring your fist down on their wrist with as much force as you can."

I'm exhausted, and even though it's cold out I'm burning up. I collapse onto the dry grass, thinking about how nice my shower will be. Aiden sits down, studying me.

"We're doing this daily, breaks on weekends. I think you're onto something with this, it will make me feel better, you knowing how to fight."

Silence creeps through the meadow, I've been thinking about this non-stop, but I was too nervous to say anything, "You know the night of the charity ball?"

He smiles, remembering the good parts, the part I'm talking about. He slides up to me, his hair sits flush above his black eyebrows. "What about it? Wanna go again?"

"While we were..." I blush, "and I told you to, ya know-"

"You begged for me to cum inside of you." He deadpans, a smirk tilting on his face.

"Thank you for... not." His face falls. "Not because I don't want kids with you!" I assure him, kissing his cheek. "I just want us to not be in danger first, and... I always imagined I would be married but that's not to say you should propose right now… I'm not trying to force you into anything I'm just saying what I would prefer down the line whe-" He cuts off my rambling with a finger to my lips.

"And that's exactly why I didn't. I want those

things too, Em. When the time is right." He winks, causing chills throughout my body.

"We're going to be okay, babe. You know that right?" He pulls me into his lap and gently plays with my hair as we cool down from our work-out in the crisp January morning.

Twenty-Eight

A grin spreads across Aiden's face. "Let's go on a date," He suggests, gesturing to the guards behind us. His elevated mood makes my brow raise. "It will have to be a date with security, but I need to get out of here, besides just going to work."

I perk up. "What were you thinking of?"

I've been happily locked away in my castle, receiving every ounce of Aiden's attention when he's not in the office. Two weeks have passed, and my online courses are running smoothly. I'm, for once, not regretting my decision to major in business after finally deciding on the route I want to take in life.

Aiden thinks for a moment, tipping his

head down to look at me better. "Something spontaneous, at night definitely. That will be the safest way." His mischievous grin makes me melt.

I nod. "I like that. The city?"

"Definitely."

Hmm. "What should I wear?"

"Your yellow dress we got in Brazil," He decides immediately.

"Aiden, it's freezing! It's supposed to snow tomorrow."

With a dazzling smile, he wraps me in a hug. "Wear your big puffy jacket and tights. I'll keep you warm." He winks.

We leave the house at dark. If it weren't for the guards in our vehicle as well as the vehicle following us, it would feel as if we were sneaking out.

Aiden leans back to use his phone. The light illuminates his sharp features as he searches for a night market in the city. He looks like walking sex, dressed in a long-sleeve black T-shirt and jeans.

He grows tenser as we get closer to the city.

I pat his arm. "We'll be fine."

He chucks my chin, smiling down at me. We ignore the fear we feel. Being locked away with him in our home has been fun, but we're ready for this to be over. But what does that mean?

"The hat is cute."

I blush. He'd placed the soft, brown hat on my head that matches my yellow dress from Brazil as a disguise when we left.

We're dropped off at a vibrant street in Portland. Food trucks line the pathway, while colorful booths selling artwork dot the aisles. We stroll through the magnetic space hand in hand. Our guards trail around at various locations, grabbing clothing items while looking nonchalant and discreet.

I admire the thundering nightlife. The mouthwatering aroma of food wafting in the air makes my stomach growl.

"What do you want?"

I look at my options, unable to choose. They all look too good.

"A little of everything?"

I grin.

We sit at a blue table after ordering. A pink umbrella sits overhead, lit up by twinkling lights. Tacos, pizza, and brisket sandwiches sit on the table, along with freshly squeezed lemonade to wash everything down. Aiden wipes my lip with his thumb, bringing it to his lips to lick it. I shudder from his touch, as always.

"This. Is. Amazing." I declare through mouthfuls of food, not caring how ridiculous I look. I can always be myself in front of him.

He tilts his head, admiring me with a crooked grin. "I'm glad you're enjoying yourself. I'm sorry we've been trapped."

I roll my eyes at him.

"Again," He adds.

"Weeks, locked in our home together. How awful," I joke.

He knows just how much fun we've had together. And nothing has really changed. I see my mom, I go to school online, I live next-door to my best friend, and I have him.

We chat, flirting underneath the lights. Even though the thumping music provides an energetic feel, we're lost in each other, in our own world.

Midnight rolls around and we head home. I lean against his broad shoulder, tired and full from our date.

"I'm an idiot." He shakes his head.

I lift my head from his shoulder. "What?"

"I took the best baker in the world." I roll my eyes playfully at his words. "To Portland's famous night market, and I didn't even get her dessert."

I laugh. "No, tonight was perfect! I'm fine."

He rubs his chin. "Want some ice cream?"

"Aiden, it's one in the morning. I highly doubt we'll find anywhere that's open."

The guard looks in the rearview. "Want me to go somewhere else, Mr. Scott?"

Aiden gives him directions and we arrive on a dark street moments later.

I tug on his arm, trying to stop him as we step out of the suburban.

"We have six guards with us, and it's past midnight. No one's followed us." He reassures me with a kiss. "I don't like you being paranoid. You sound like me."

I let him guide us down the dark street. Guards in proximity until he tells them to back off a bit. He stops in front of a glass door, peeking his head around the side of the building.

"Bobby pin?"

I feel my hair for one. "For what?"

"To break in."

Is he serious?

I clamp a hand on my chest. "Umm, no freaking way!"

Aiden throws his head back. "Emilia, you said spontaneous sounded fun, right? Our trip to the night market was planned. This," He gestures to the door, "is the definition of spontaneity."

I look around the dark street. How embarrassing would it be if I were to be hauled off to jail in the city my dad worked in for decades. "What if we get arrested?"

"We won't. Hand me a bobby pin." He extends a hand, with a hopeful, boyish grin.

I cave. He seems too excited about this criminal activity. Maybe it'll be fun? My heart pounds as I slide the pin into his open hand.

"We'll leave five hundred dollars on the table," He reassures me.

A small light barely grazes the shop as we walk in. Aiden's lock picking skills are scary good.

"I really don't need something sweet this bad, Aiden."

"I was thinking. If you want…" Aiden walks to the side and flips on a switch, brightly illuminating our daring breaking and entering.

"Aiden! You're going to get us caught!" I squeal, about to book it back outside.

He takes one large step towards me, placing his hands on my shoulders. "How can we get caught if it's ours?"

My stomach drops. "Ours?"

He gestures behind me. "Turn around, babe."

I turn, gasping when I see the pink fluorescent sign above the glass display counter.

Emilia's Sweet Treats.

His arms wrap around me from behind. I can feel him smile against my neck.

"We can work on the name. I didn't know what you would like to call your bakery. I'm sorry if it's cheesy—"

I'm speechless as he rambles away, his hands tucked away in the pockets of his jeans as he rocks on the balls of his feet. He's nervous. Aiden Scott is nervous. He walks over to the counter and sits to stop fidgeting.

"It's perfect! Oh my God!" I giggle, tears welling up in happiness.

Everything is decorated like the fifties. I run to a candy red jukebox sitting against the wall, turning the pages before selecting a Beatles song, 'Blackbird'.

I drag Aiden over to the checkered floor. "Dance with me in my bakery." I demand with a wide grin. My tears fall as we dance with carefree movements. "I've been wanting to talk to you about this, but you went beyond what I was going to suggest."

He tilts his head in question.

"Well, I continued my business major and I wanted to start a legitimate bakery from our kitchen."

He nods, knowingly.

"Everything's been going so smoothly selling to the neighborhood, and word has traveled. I really think I could run a business but look at what you've done." I lift a hand from around his neck and gesture around us.

Having the attention span of a gnat, I dart over to a bare wall. Small circular tables decorate the area with matching white chairs. "Oh! Look, Aiden! We can display your art here! You could sell it!"

"No way." He scoffs, looking around to make sure no guards are inside.

I wish he wasn't so embarrassed by his art. "Anonymously, of course." I suggest.

He ponders on it. "This is for you, Em. Not me. I want you to decorate the space how you want it to be."

"Well, that's how I want it decorated," I state.

He smiles, but I can tell he's hesitant as he studies the empty space.

"I don't need the money."

"It can go to charity. You can sign it with a fake name, like Banksy." I snicker.

He wraps me in a hug.

This place will be covered in his amazing art as soon as I can open it. I ask what I'm dreading, knowing full well it isn't safe yet. "When can I start?"

"Well, that's the bad news. We won't be able to until this shit gets sorted out. I'm sorry, sweetheart. This has been in the plans for a while, and the timing's just off. I hate gifting you something that you can't use immediately."

"No! It's absolutely perfect. I have time to work out a business plan." I look into his emerald eyes, smiling as they twinkle for me. "I love you so much."

Twenty-Nine

He has to get up, now! "Aiden!" I straddle his warm, muscular body but he doesn't budge. I shake his arms, and he lets out a small grunt.

"We were up so late last night, baby. It's Saturday, let's sleep in." He pleads groggily. "Come back here."

He tries to pull me down, but I slip from his grip. I tug the heavy comforter off his body, admiring his inked skin against the black silk sheets.

"Hey!" His tone indignant.

I bounce on the bed, just out of reach so he can't stop me, before rushing over to the windows. "It's snowing!" I squeal.

EMILIA

"Get up! Ash and Ricky will be here for breakfast in thirty." I blow him a kiss as I rush out of the room, not missing his smile.

I miss Howard. I know he's keeping Mom safe, but I want everyone I love under this roof. But she has a life, and it would raise suspicion if I kidnapped her.

I twirl around the kitchen, still dressed in my robe, as I get breakfast ready, ignoring the bodyguards that roam the property. I lick the wooden spoon, making sure the pancake batter is perfect. I stiffen when strong arms grab my shoulders, twirling me around.

Aiden peers down at me, his hands planted on the countertop behind me. "Change. Now." He kisses my cheek.

I roll my eyes, playfully swatting him. "Aiden, no one's looking at me. They're our guards."

He rolls his lip between his teeth. "I'm looking at you." He breathes into my neck, his minty aftershave invading my senses. "You have five seconds before I lift you onto this counter and have a snack."

I blush before wiggling away to do as he asked. I look back when I hear sizzling. He's pouring the pancake batter into the pan, and looking wistfully sexy doing so. Ash and Ricky walk in just as I return.

"Guess what?" I'm unable to contain my

excitement.

They tilt their heads. Ricky grabs a piece of bacon while Ash looks at me in question.

"I have a bakery!" I squeal.

"Shut up!" Ashley looks to Aiden before rushing to give him a hug. "Celebration time!" She exclaims, running to the fridge and pulling out a bottle of chilled champagne.

Aiden takes it from her before she pops it. "Hey!"

"You were aiming it at Ricky's head. I didn't think you'd want to give him a black eye."

I pull out the orange juice along with some glasses. "Mimosa time."

"Girls against guys," I declare, drawing a line in the snow with a stick. "Losers have to serve winners drinks." My mimosa buzz is slowly fading. I want to get in the hot tub tonight and relax while snow drifts around us.

Hiding behind a rock wall near the empty fountain, Ashley and I form a game plan. The guys pummel snow in our direction as we struggle to make solid snowballs.

Realizing our situation, the guards sneakily prepare tightly packed snowballs for us from behind our barricade, which we happily throw at the guys. Usually straight-faced and serious, the guards sit on the wet ground in their suits, smiling as they stack them for us.

"They're quick!" Ricky growls to Aiden, as we pelt them with freshly rolled balls of snow. Not having to worry about making our own makes us unstoppable.

Aiden pauses, stroking his chin. "Yeah, too quick—"

I pelt him with a ball before he can complete his thought.

"That's it!" He lunges for me with a crooked grin.

With a war cry, I exit our barricade. I head straight for Aiden, tackling him into the snow and straddling him.

"Come here, babe." He grins.

I lean down for a kiss, shrieking when he bucks me off into the fluffy snow without warning. I sink into the soft cloud with a gasp.

Aiden grabs my hand, pulling me upright. "You're so short, you just…disappeared." He bends over, laughing.

I hop onto his back, outraged. "You tricked me!"

"I tricked you?" He places his hands under my thighs, holding me securely, before peeking behind our rock wall. His eyes widen as he takes in the security detail. "I think you tricked us with the guards bringing you guys extra artillery."

"Ash!" I yell as he tries to throw me off.

"Get him!"

I grin when I see her already ready, with a snowball in hand. It isn't long before we claim victory and begin our celebration with the guys bringing us drinks.

Aiden

Emilia is tipsy...more like shit faced. Mimosas since morning will do just that. But today has been perfect. The way her skin is flushed from the cold and running around all day is adorable.

Plus, everyone deserved a break so that was nice. We don't know what's coming for us, but we're prepared and ready.

"Babe." She slurs her words, biting her lip when I look her way. "Hot tub time." She says, twirling her hair. I know exactly what she really wants, too bad she's drunk.

I'm thankful Ash and Ricky went home, because she's very flirty when she's been drinking like this.

I shove a plate in front of her, "Eat this and then get changed." I disappear into the room, leaving her with a sandwich to hopefully sober her up.

EMILIA

Moonlight illuminates the snowy backyard.

"It's fucking freezing." I grumble as we make our quick entrance into the hot tub, steam covering us like a blanket.

I admire her white bikini cladded body as she slides her feet into the hot water. She visibly relaxes as she sits, rolling her shoulders as well as her head. Fuck, I wish she wasn't drunk right now. The sandwich I made her earlier didn't do a damn thing to sober her up, and the hot tub will only worsen her state.

She peers up at me. Her honey eyes are so fucking perfect, damnit.

"I've never been fucked in a hot tub." She deadpans, running her hands through her brown hair.

Just like that, my dick is throbbing.

"You've never been fucked anywhere but where I've taken you," I remind her. She scoots closer, and I get jealous of the way her teeth have trapped her bottom lip. *Shit.* I place my hand on the nape of her neck. "You're being awfully naughty tonight. I like it."

"Do something about it," She urges me on with sultry eyes.

I shake my head. "It's a shame that you're drunk."

She stands, slowly untying the strap of her bikini bottoms.

While I'm not going to do anything while she's drunk, I can still admire her. My eyes only. I've put all the guards on house duty and front yard duty, with some threats that if they looked at the backyard, that would be the last thing they see. I've been feeling extremely territorial lately.

Her eyes stay on mine as she steps closer. I love how exposed she is for me. I love her confidence when she drinks, and I also love her shyness when she's sober. Fuck, I love anything she does.

"Take me," She begs in an adorable, whiny tone.

I clench my fist. "You're drunk."

Silently, she unties her top, revealing her perfect tits, half-submerged in the bubbly tub. Those perky nipples are begging to be bitten by me, but I refrain. I stroke myself, trying to relieve some of my tension.

Realizing I'm not going to take advantage of her when she's drunk, she huffs and takes a confident stride only to trip over her own feet. Water splashes and drips down her soft skin. I would have caught her, but she held out a hand.

"Funny. You say you own me, but when I'm here, begging for you to take me…" She shrugs. "You deny me."

"Watch your tone." I warn, cocking a brow at her. "I do own you. Every fucking inch of your perfect body is mine." I growl, narrowing my eyes.

She heads for the stairs. "I'm a bit thirsty. Need anything?" She smiles.

I give her a knowing look. "Don't you fucking dare, Emilia." I grab her by her waist, yanking her into the water before she steps out. "You drive me crazy."

She giggles, wrapping her legs around my waist. She slides a hand down my chest to rub me through my swim trunks.

Fuck.

"Come here," She begs in a low musical voice.

I groan. Her hand feels so good. "Em…" She kisses my neck. "You're drunk." I lower us into the water, sitting on the bench seat where the jet hits my back. It takes everything in me not to ram my cock into her as she straddles me.

"It's okay. Please," She begs.

Fuck, I love when she begs for my cock.

"Tell me how much you want it, baby," I murmur, unable to stop myself.

She spreads her legs, guiding my hand to her slit. "Please, please fuck me."

"I don't want to take advantage of you." I slide my finger through her folds, desperately wishing she hadn't drank.

She leans towards my ear, her voice sultry and smooth. "Please, Aiden. Please. Do whatever you want to me. Take me. Take advantage of my body, it's yours. You own me and you can do as you please with me. Whenever your cock throbs for me, I will spread my legs for you."

Fuck me.

Fuck it.

I rub her clit faster. "More, Emilia. Tell me how much you crave for me to fill you." I'm hard as a rock. I can feel her slippery wetness. She feels like silk. I want to taste her.

She rocks against me, her naked body warm and heavenly as snow falls around us. I grip her thighs, admiring the contrast of her bare skin against my tattoos. Sinful, really.

"I do own you." I watch as she brings her lip in between her teeth.

"I know." She smiles, teasing my earlobe with her teeth.

"I would have fucked you, if you weren't drunk…but I can't stand it anymore. I need to feel my dick stretching your tight perfect pussy."

She moans from my words.

Her reaction to me is everything.

"Such a gentlemen," She jokes as she cups her breasts, fondling them.

I instantly get jealous. "I'm not going to fuck you like a gentleman tonight."

I lift her slightly to scoot my swimsuit off, gripping myself as I lean down to suck on her nipples. I pump myself before caressing her opening with my other hand, teasing her clit before pushing two fingers inside her. She whines when I return my hand to my cock.

"Be patient, darling. I need to get you wetter. Being submerged in water isn't always comfortable to fuck in, but you're so fucking wet for me already." I moan, stroking myself as she bucks her hips, inviting me in. "So impatient."

I'm amused at how she squirms for me. For my cock.

For me to be inside her.

I slide my cock up and down her clit, loving how her eyes roll back. "You like that?"

"Yes, sir." She moans.

I already know she does, but I love it when she speaks in that sexy soft voice that only I hear.

"Sir?"

"Mhmm." Her little body rocks against me.

I continue to stroke the thick head of my cock against her perfect clit.

"Calling someone sir is the respectful way to address a man of authority."

I love teasing her, there's nothing sexier than watching her body react to me. The way her cheeks flush and her pussy gets wet only for me. The way she bites her lip and moans my name.

Fuck.

As much as I would love to plunge my cock inside of her, I'm afraid I won't be able to last long with how fucking amazing she looks right now. Which isn't normal for me.

I watch as she squirms above me, gripping her delicate neck firmly. "You respect me, Emilia?"

She nods.

It's not enough.

"Speak." I move away.

She whines. "Yes sir, I respect you," She moans, thrusting her hips forward.

"Good girl." I slide inside her, gripping her hips to stop her from moving.

"Please," She begs, wiggling as she tries to move.

I fucking love the control.

I shoot her a warning glance and she stops, her pussy clenching around my cock as she waits.

"What are you doing?" She moans, breathlessly.

"I'm letting you warm my cock."

I tuck her hair behind her ear before sliding my hand down her body, greedily gripping her breasts and pinching her hard nipples. I take one between my teeth, gently biting as I move in and out of her, trying not to lose control with how fucking amazing she feels around my cock.

"You like me having power over you?" I ask through ragged breaths.

"Aiden," She moans.

EMILIA

I pull away. It takes so much fucking control, but I want to hear her answer. I don't like rushing my time with her.

She pants, collecting herself. "Yes, control me." She runs her hands over the ink on my chest as she looks down at me.

"Gladly."

I grip her waist, slamming her down onto my cock. Water splashes out of the tub as I fuck her. Her perfect, round tits bounce as I push into her and stretch her with my dick as she moans my name.

"I told you." I grip her neck, pushing her up. "I'm not going to fuck you like a gentleman tonight. You want to tease me like a bad girl, that's how you'll get fucked."

I nudge her to the side and she places her hands on the stone edge of the hot tub, her ass sticking out of the water. Holding her hip steady, I plunge into her tight pussy from behind. To better fuck her, I place one large hand wrapped around her throat and one on her shoulder, she loses control as I fuck her senseless. Thrusting, pounding, choking, and my favorite – pulling her hair – until her body physically can't handle anymore of me.

Tonight, I needed to fuck her rough.

Because tomorrow, with the surprise I have in store for her…

It's all romance.

Soft, and sweet. Out of my comfort zone.
Something that I would never do for anyone.
Except for her.

Emilia

Aiden's acting weird.

Like really weird.

"If you don't get out of this kitchen, I'm going to take you on the counter and then I'll never get dinner done."

That was *him*. He's kicking *me* out of the kitchen.

Candles are lit, while light music plays throughout our home, and Aiden is cooking.

He never cooks.

We're dressed formally. His request.

Me in a scarlet dress, and him in a black suit.

The guards are outside, even though it's freezing. I keep popping out to tell them to stay in the greenhouse or the guard post, but they keep telling me no. At least they're taking shifts, so they don't freeze to death.

"You know I can help you," I tease, jumping up to sit on the counter.

He gives me his best-crooked grin.

It's freeing with just us at home. We can do whatever we want.

I swirl the glass of red wine in my hands as he stirs…something.

I peek over. "What are you making?"

I can tell his concentration is faltering. I grin. My dress rode up slightly when I jumped up.

"I won't be making anything if I have to stare at those legs any longer," He grunts, pulling his bottom lip between his teeth. "Well, I'll be making you scream my name, but unfortunately we need to eat."

"Seriously, Aiden." I take a deep breath, "It smells lovely. But I can't figure out what you're trying to do."

He wipes his hands on a kitchen towel. "A family meal." He sets his wooden spoon down and refills my wine glass. "Before things went to shit with my dad." He looks around. "Or maybe it was always fucked, the lines blur easily." He waves a hand in the air.

He dips a slice of French bread into the pot before bringing it to my mouth. I hum as I taste the stew. It's delicious.

"It's the only tradition I ever kept. I eat it on my mom's birthday."

Then, it dawns on me. "Her birthday's today."

He nods. "She would have been 45."

I watch as he goes somewhere else, his mind transporting him to the past. I grip his large hands. "Thank you for sharing it with me. I didn't know you knew how to cook. That bite was delicious!"

He cracks a grin. "Don't get used to it. This is the only thing I know how to make. Go sit, my love."

My breath catches as I step into the dining room. I don't think tonight is simply about his mom's birthday tradition. From the looks of the dripping candles and dozens of red roses lining the room and tables, this seems like…

Is he going to…?

"Dinner's ready." Aiden walks in with two bowls.

I look down at my plated bowl. I grin. He even garnished the stew. Aiden returns seconds later with sliced French bread. I take a bite and moan. It's perfect. My mind races with possibilities of how tonight will go.

Aiden is quiet as we eat, his left leg is shaking.

Is he nervous?

"You did wonderful with dinner." I place my napkin on the table.

He shrugs, his fingers trailing down my cheek to my locket necklace. "You do so much for me, Emilia, yet I do so little for you. It's the least I could do…after everything I've put you through." He looks away.

I kiss his cheek. "Don't be silly. Look at our home, my bakery." I grin from ear to ear. "Everything will be okay, Aiden." My eyes burn into his and I put as much sincerity in my voice as I can. "Your mom would be so proud of you."

His eyes gloss over. "Thank y–"

My phone rings from the kitchen, halting our conversation.

Why didn't I put it on silent?

"Ignore it." I smile, taking a sip of wine.

We talk over the ringing, and I sigh as it goes away. Talking over each other on accident in an awkward dance.

The intensity of his stare causes my heart to thunder.

He covers my hand. "Emilia, listen–"

My phone cuts him off once again.

He throws his head back and stands.

"I'm sorry!" I call out.

He flashes me a reassuring smile before

heading to the kitchen.

I take in a deep breath once he's out of view. *I think he's going to propose.*

Aiden looks devilishly handsome, twirling my phone. "Your mom's called three times."

"I'll call her back later." I take my phone from him before gesturing for him to sit.

"Call her now. I have something I need to do anyways." He kisses me and heads towards the living room.

My phone rings once more just as I step into our bedroom for privacy. I grin. She really doesn't quit.

"Hey Mom." My voice is way too excited. I want to tell her so badly that I think Aiden is about to propose, maybe she knows?

"I hate that it's winter right now. I love roses during the summertime, don't you, Emilia?" The voice isn't familiar, but the accent is.

I pull the phone away, frowning when I see that it's Mom's number. "Who is this?"

A maniacal laugh sounds on the other end, as though the fear in my voice set him off. "I thought it was so brave how you saved your boyfriend."

I shiver in our warm room. Quietly, I pull the balcony handle and step into the frigid air. My thin dress barely providing any warmth. A lump forms in my throat as the man rambles.

"My men had him. I was so close, so

excited to get to him, and when I arrived in Campania, he was gone. Poof." He sighs. "I want to kill someone. She'll do." He laughs.

Tears streak down my face. "You have my mom?"

I decide that as soon as my shaking hands hang up the phone, I will run to Aiden and tell him...

"Come alone or I'll kill your mother."

I'm frozen, paralyzed with fear.

I look across the courtyard, spotting familiar salt and pepper hair. Howard. I remember Aiden telling me he was dropping by to grab some of his things.

We got too comfortable. This is it.

"Where do I go?" My voice at a steady tremble.

"Our location has been sent to you."

A beat of silence passes through the phone as I attempt to speak.

"And Emilia," He sneers. "I'm a man of my word. You come alone and I'll set your mother free. Your Aiden took something that was mine. Now, I will take something of his. You." His heavy Italian accent bleeds through the speakers and into my soul.

"Whatever you want. Just please...please don't hurt her." I beg, no other choice but to trust his words.

I hear him sucking his teeth on the other

end. "This won't be something you return from. You understand that, right?"

"Yes." I let out a breath. "Yes." I give in.

"Good girl." He laughs. "And if I think for even a moment that you told anyone or brought anyone with you, I will slit her throat and kill everyone you've ever loved."

He found it.

The one thing that will break us apart. That will make me back down.

My mom.

I plaster on a brave face when the line disconnects. I wipe away my tears and head back to our room. The classical music is louder now.

I take one last look at my phone before turning it off and sliding it into my bedside drawer. A picture of my mom, passed out, dried blood on her cheek. My heart races as I shakily jot down the address on a slip of paper before folding it and sliding it into my bra.

I can't tell him. I can't risk it.

He won't let me leave unless I do something drastic.

I'm going to have to break his heart to save her.

I know what I'm walking into.
I know what Aiden's about to do.
He's about to get down on one knee and

ask me to be his bride. I want nothing more in this world than to be his wife, to support and cherish him as long as we both shall live. But that isn't in the cards for me.

As long as we both shall live, ends tonight.

For me.

That's the exact reason why I need to break his heart. To make Aiden hate me enough to let me go. I need him to let me go, to let me leave.

I trace the walls with my fingertips as I head towards him. Trying to remember every smell and feel of our home before I never return. It's a suicide mission. I know this. But I can't and won't risk his or Howard's life.

I don't know what will happen, but I'm backed into a corner

My life for hers. I will gladly trade my soul for my mom. Aiden says he's damned and I'll go to Heaven. But I know him. The real him. And if anyone has a perfect spot in Heaven, it's him. We will meet again.

My heart clenches painfully as I step into the living room.

Aiden stands in the middle, the fireplace is roaring. Classical music sweeps through the space as he holds a comforting hand out.

My eyes take in the red roses around the room.

EMILIA

All they remind me of is blood.

Aiden's blood. On the rooftop.

I can't. I can't see anything happen to him again.

"Did I tell you how stunning you look tonight?" His baritone warms me.

I give a nervous chuckle as I take his hand.

We stare into each other's eyes. Him, admiring me. Me, memorizing the outline of his face and his bright emeralds.

"Emilia, I–"

I cut him off. *I can't let him do this.*

He doesn't let me.

I've never seen him look so intently, so purely at me before.

"I want to be with you, every day…like this." He gestures around the room. He pulls a black velvet box from his pocket and goes down on one knee.

I've been waiting for this moment my entire life. To be a wife, a wife to him. My entire life started with him, and it will end with him still owning my heart.

"Emilia Achelois Banks. Will you do me the honor of be–"

My heavy sobs stop him. I know he's going to propose, but knowing I'm about to deny him is ripping me apart.

He smiles, thinking I'm overwhelmed with

love.

I am, but the fear is overriding all emotions.

"I can't do this."

He shakes his head. "Because I'm proposing?" He stands, looking confused.

I nod. "I'm too young."

He places the box back in his pocket.

I didn't even get to see the ring he got for me. I bet it's perfect.

With his cool demeanor, he gives me a crooked smile. "No biggie, we can wait."

Always patient.

He pulls me in for a hug, but I quickly scoot back, shaking my head. "You misunderstood me. I can't do any of this. I can't be with you."

If you've never seen someone's heart shatter before you, then I can't fully describe what's happening in front of my tear-soaked eyes.

Realization dawns on his sharp features. "Emilia." He steps closer, towering over me as I try not to crumble. "Don't you fucking dare break what I just realized I have." His voice cracks. "My heart."

"I don't want this anymore," I deadpan, my face giving nothing away. My insides rip to shreds before his eyes, but he doesn't notice.

He shakes his head in disbelief. "I don't believe that. You're mine. I'm yours, Em. That's it." He sneers, his eyes darkening.

"I'm not yours!" I lie, my heart pounding in my chest.

His voice raises. "Stop fucking lying!"

I look around our fancy living room. "I wanted you for your money."

His laugh is almost animalistic. "That's fucking rich coming from you." He scoffs. "The girl who argues with me about buying her a two-dollar coffee. You're my assistant, you know I have millions in my bank account and that's just *one* business account. You're not a fucking gold digger."

He steps towards me menacingly. "Tell me the fucking truth, Em!"

If I don't do something, he's going to break my already crumbling resolve. I'll bow down at his feet to beg for his forgiveness and get us *all* killed, instead of just me. *How do I make him hate me enough to let me leave?*

My voice is small, and my lying words send bile up my throat. "That night in Italy… when…"

"Oh my God." He coughs, placing his hand out to halt my words. "Don't you fucking dare. Don't you tell me." He rakes a long rigid hand through his hair. "You wouldn't fucking do that to me."

Silence spreads through the room.

"Right, baby?" His hands are on his knees

as he tries to hold himself up.

I bite my lip, tears pouring. "I slept with Leo, Aiden."

His laugh actually scares me. "He touched you." With a shake of his head, he steps away from me. "Not only did he touch you. You *let* him fuck you."

He grows unhinged, pacing the large living room. "I've never let anyone in. You wouldn't…" He mumbles desperately.

"I did."

"I don't believe you." He's hesitant, but from the way his cold eyes look over my body, I can tell he believes me.

"I did," I lie.

"I'll rip his tiny cock from his body and kill him slowly for daring to touch you when you were vulnerable," He spits, his tone is venomous.

"Aiden, I'm not a victim. I wanted it." I'm about to throw up but I need to make this about me, not Leo.

He stares at me. His expression grim as he takes a step towards me.

I look away from his shattered heart. I have to get out of this house.

"Emilia, look at me!" He grips my chin as I look away, stealing my gaze. "You're fucking breaking me, sweetheart."

In one final attempt to make him loathe me, I grip my locket between my fingers and rip it from my neck. He looks at me with such sorrow as we watch the symbol of our love fall onto the soft carpeting. Maybe one day he'll understand why I did what I did.

His eyes are trained on the locket as a single tear rolls down his cheek.

It worked.

I broke him.

"I'm sorry. I have to go. I can't be here any longer."

He stiffens, his demeanor changing slightly. "Just…" His voice cracks as his eyes plead with me. "Stay here."

"I have to go. This is your home."

His chest stiffens, his anger flooding the room "The fuck it is! This house is *nothing* without you!" He grabs a vase, and with a quick sling, smashes it against the wall. Ceramic breaks and bounces off the marble walls, much like our relationship.

I clench my chest to keep my shattered heart from spilling out.

"I don't fucking want it, Emilia. I don't want any of it without you!"

I step away, and he calms.

"Don't be scared."

I fight back my tears. *I'm not scared of you, baby. I don't have much time. But I can't tell you that because you'll risk your life for me as you've always done. I'm sorry.*

His voice grows panicked. "Look, baby…" He places his hand on his head. "I can't call you baby anymore." Tears streak his perfect face.

I hate myself. I hate this.

"Aiden, please." The lump in my throat is too big for me to speak.

He paces. "You're safe here. Just stay here."

That won't work.

I stare at him, not knowing what to say.

"I'll go to Ricky's, okay? We'll figure this out, sweetheart."

"There's nothing to work out." If I give him the tiniest hope, he will stay to talk things through. "I slept with another man."

I thought all of this would make him throw me out with his own hands. But as he kneels before me looking hauntingly helpless, my heart shatters at his feet. He's never knelt for anyone. Getting on one knee to propose is different. This is him begging. The desperate action tears me up inside.

"It's okay." His voice panicked. "You love me, right?" He questions my adoration for him.

I hate this.

"We can make this work." He clenches my hand. "You thought I was dead, I don't blame you for seeking comfort." His eyes darken.

I don't say more. I can't. I've hurt him

enough.

"Do you want to be with him?"

I scoff, a natural reaction to the thought of being with anyone else. "No, no way."

"Then why are you doing this?"

"The guilt's eating me alive." I sigh. "And I can't be on the run anymore. I need a real life," I lie, digging into his insecurities. I would run with him across the Earth without a second thought and with no regrets.

"I love you, Emilia. I don't give a fuck what happened. We're bigger than that, we can work through anything. It's us against the world, baby. You know that, right?"

He collapses even though he's already on the ground.

Pleading with me. Begging me.

He looks up at me through thick lashes, and I down at him with falling tears. He stands, straighter than usual. He towers over me, as though he couldn't bear to be on the ground for one more second. To be below me for one more second. As if I would step on him.

But I did.

I took his heart, and I walked over it.

"Swear to me, Emilia. Don't fucking ruin us ba– I love you, you're not allowed to leave me. You understand that, right? I don't know how to let you go. I won't allow it."

I look at the door. I can't take this

anymore and I have to leave. "Just go, Aiden."

His eyes are bloodshot and his hair a wreck. "I'm sorry for raising my voice. I'm leaving. I'll send Howard to watch over you. Your mom has two guards at her house. I'll be more comfortable with him here for you."

Wrong, my mom's been kidnapped. But yes, please go. I can't hold on much longer.

He looks from me, to the locket, then to the door. "Do you need anything? I hate the thought of you sleeping alone."

I shake my head. "Maybe a hug? One last time?"

He wraps me in his arms before I get the sentence out, lifting me with natural ease. His head is buried in the crook of my neck while his hands caresses my body. The moment gets heated as he grabs the back of my neck possessively, forcefully.

"Let me fuck you, Emilia. To knock some fucking sense into you." He's so angry with me he's switching between anger, lust, and fear. "While you're still mine to take, let me take you," He pleads.

"I'm not yours anymore." I whisper.

Aiden sets me down immediately.

I watch as he steps out into the cold night alone, my heart is shattered as well as his. The door shuts quietly. In our empty home, I send him the only comfort I can. My words. I hope they will travel to his heart somehow, carried by the frigid wind outside.

'Aiden, you were always right. The words I love you were never meant for us. We're so much more than that. You're mine. You will always be. And I'm yours. Wholeheartedly, I am yours. I leave you with the heart I broke and my soul that belongs to you. I'm so sorry. There's just…you, Aiden. It will always be that way for my story. Just you.'

Then, I throw up the meal he spent all day cooking.

Howard steps in a few minutes later as I straighten, throwing his jacket on the rack.

"Bad fight?"

I keep my voice level. "Did you hear anything?"

"No, but Emilia, fights happen. Things will work out."

Good. He doesn't know anything.

"You're right." I straighten, pretending to believe him.

Only I know I won't ever see either of them again.

Now, for my escape. I can brush away my hysterics as the fight with Aiden, so Howard won't suspect anything.

I wrap him in a tight hug, just like Aiden but this is different, as though I'm hugging my bonus dad. "Thank you for everything, Howard."

"You okay, Emilia?"

I wipe my tears away. "Just worried about me and Aiden." I fake a small smile. "I'll be fine in the morning. I'm going to get in the sauna and relax."

He looks at me with concern. "Need me to walk you down there? You're so upset." He brushes a stray hair from my face. "You and Aiden will be just fine. That man loves you more than any person could possibly love another."

Whatever fragment of my heart was left…it's gone.

I shrug. "You're right. He'll come back tomorrow."

I try my hand at manipulation, and it works.

He touches my shoulder tenderly. "Of course. He'll stay at Ricky's tonight and come to you in the morning. Probably with roses and chocolate." He smiles. "Now, get in the Sauna and clear your head. I'll be here reading."

With that, I rush to my room and rip the red dress off, leaving it in a heap on the floor. I throw on a robe, tossing my things haphazardly into a black duffle bag. I snatch Aiden's key ring sitting on the nightstand.

Howard, comfortable and snoozing on the recliner, doesn't notice me slipping through the pantry door with a getaway bag in hand.

We've all gotten too comfortable.

I pass the sauna, having changed into all-black attire and headed straight for the secret exit door. The guards are in the greenhouse or around it, out of sight of this door.

I sweep around undetected and head into the garage, thankful that no one is guarding the front of the house. The garage door is already open, and I scope out which vehicle to take. Aiden's Challenger is gone. He must have gone for a drive.

I nod. Tesla, quiet and discreet.

Everything is going perfectly until I arrive at the front gate post.

"Where do you think you're going?" The guard lazily flips through a magazine.

"Umm…" I will my mind to think. "Following Aiden. He's letting me drive the Tesla!" I fake a squeal, hoping Aiden didn't talk to him on his way out.

He gives me a smile. "With no guard?" He cranes his neck to peek inside the car.

I bite my lip. "We're, umm…going to have some fun."

The guard nods in understanding. "No wonder Mr. Scott was in such a rush to get out of here." He laughs, pressing the button and opening the gate for me. "You two have a good time." He winks. I wave to him as I slip out into the night.

Thirty-One

Aiden

My lungs constrict as I stare into Emilia's tear-soaked eyes. My knees dig into the plush rug, holding me down when her words brought me to my knees. I need to stand for her, to show her my strength.

I look into her honey eyes, "Swear to me Emilia, don't fucking ruin us bab- I love you. You're not allowed to leave me. You understand that, right? I don't know how to let you go. I won't allow it." I plead, the heart I didn't realize I had is slowly beating, about to break.

Her eyes trail to the door, tears trickling down her rosy cheeks. "Just go Aiden." Hearing my name roll from her lips with such sorrow in her voice breaks me.

Guilt eats at me, why couldn't I have handled this better? But how was I supposed to handle it, I thought she would be my fiancée at this moment not... this. "I'm sorry for raising my voice. I'm leaving. Sending Howard inside to watch over you. Your mom has two guards at her house, and I'll be more comfortable with him here for you." Her jaw twitches but she can't fucking leave our home, it isn't safe, and I won't be able to handle her not being here.

My back to her, I look to her from the side. "I'm going to go. Do you need anything? I hate the thought of you sleeping alone."

She shakes her head, "Maybe a hug? One last time?"

I can't hide the broken sound that escapes my chest when I snatch her before she finishes the sentence, lifting her feet from the floor and wrapping my arms around her delicate frame.

Burying my face into her soft neck, I breathe her in. Touching and caressing her, pleading with her through my hands. I'm so fucking angry at her right now, before I know it my hand is clamped around the back of her neck, forcing her to look at me. "Let me fuck you, Emilia. To knock some fucking sense into you." It's what she needs, me. "While you're still mine to take, let me take you." I plead with her for her body, something I've never had to do. It takes every ounce in me to not wrap her legs around my back and drag her into the bedroom and have my way with her.

"I'm not yours anymore." She whispers, and I snap out of it. Setting her down and heading for the door, she doesn't want me anymore.

It's as if she just took my battered heart in her perfect hands and squeezed the life from it to save herself... I can't blame her. She always had my heart at her disposal, close to hers, even if she's never realized it.

I carefully shut the door behind me, not wanting to disrupt the quiet of our home anymore. She deserves peace.

My boots stomp against the driveway as I pace, cursing the ground beneath me for existing. The frigid wind whips, the bare trees swaying from its force.

For a few moments, I fight with myself to go back inside and make her love me again. Lost in my dark mind until Howard clears his throat, I didn't realize he was guarding the front of the house. "You okay?" He asks, fatherly concern plastered on his face.

No, I'm not. How can such a small, perfect girl crush a man like me?

I look to the black forest, "Yeah, fight with Emilia. Stay and watch her? She's upset." I don't want to get into any details. He nods coming towards me, undoubtedly going to comfort me, maybe give me the fatherly advice I was never worthy of hearing from my own dad. With a shake of my head, I effectively shut off the conversation by stepping into the garage, he retreats with a knowing look.

With shaky breaths, I slide into my challenger. Before her, the interior smelled of leather and smoke, but now her watermelon shampoo overpowers everything. I breathe in her calming scent, almost choking on what it entails when it will completely fade from my life.

Her hair whipping in the wind, my hand always gripping her thigh, her trying and failing to drive a stick shift. Too many memories, this is why I don't let anyone in. I never will again.

Once I hear the front door close after Howard steps inside, I break down. My palms and fist smashing against the wheel and dashboard. How could I have not seen how unhappy she was?

I'm a broken man, and the broken look on her face told me how much I've fucked her up. I always knew it would turn out this way, destruction follows me.

I turn the key, the roar of the classic engine drowns out any sound as I speed down the driveway. I rev the engine to alert the guard to open the gate. I'm in no mood to converse, I just need to get away... far away from the angel who tore me in two.

With the windows down, the frigid wind whips through the car. My mouth dry from screaming into the dark night. My stiff fingers are frozen to the steering wheel, but it's the only thing making me feel alive, the feeling of the cold to match my heart.

She still loves me, right? Fuck! Why would she? I've brought nothing but danger to her life. She always comforted me when I told her of my fears, scared she was unhappy living life in hiding. She would always tell me she wouldn't want to be anywhere else… with anyone else. It was all a fucking lie. My hands linger on the middle seat, where she loved to snuggle up next to me. The memory makes my stomach churn, was she cuddled with Leo that night?

Seeing her rip the necklace from her neck, no words.

Is she worth the pain? Absolutely. It's never been a question for me when it comes to her. I can't bear to think of her as anything but mine.

I don't give a fuck about the cliché storyline of letting her walk away and saying, "She'll find someone who will love her more."

I may not understand why she cares for me… or cared. But, she can't leave me. She can't. She just physically cannot find a single soul on this earth who will absolutely cherish her as much as I do. She's mine, my everything, my world spins on her axis. We are it. That's final.

There's nothing in this world more important to a man than the woman who made him feel loved for the first time in his life, nothing else compares.

Tomorrow, I'll walk into our home with flowers and chocolate and she'll look at me with her big doe eyes and forgive me for every error I've ever committed.

Or if she refuses to be with me, I'll lock her in that house until she changes her mind. Maybe I've gone crazy? It's big enough, she won't get bored. The prince locks the princess in the castle.

But this isn't a fairytale, and I'm no knight in shining armor. I'm more like the dark irredeemable prince who came into her life and destroyed her innocent mind.

My thoughts are everywhere, with Leo at the forefront.

The idea of him touching her. Being inside of her.

Fuck! My nightmares were real.

I'm going to fucking kill him.

My tires squeal as I skid to a halt in the parking lot of Leo's apartment complex. A sense of relief washes over me as I kick down his door.

"What the fuck?" Leo storms into the hallway in just his boxers.

I stand on his fallen door, burning with anger. He's shirtless, only in boxers.

Emilia saw him this way.

"Leo?" A woman's voice calls out.

Is he fucking someone else's girl?

The thought drives me to advance on him. He doesn't look surprised to see me, but annoyed. My hands encircle his throat and I slam his body into the wall. With a good view of his room now, I see a woman throwing on her clothes, shaking.

"Go!" I demand.

She looks to Leo, who nods slightly.

When the blonde exits the apartment, I nearly blackout. Punching him to the ground, my fist can't connect fast enough in my frenzy of emotions. He fights back but it feels like I'm punching him in a dream, distant and not hard enough.

A waking fucking nightmare.

"You took her from me!" I shout, the metallic taste of blood in my mouth. "She wasn't yours to take!"

Leo looks up at me through fluttering eyes. "Aiden."

I will not allow him to speak. It's making it worse.

His fist connects with my jaw, enticing my

rage further.

"She was upset because she thought I was dead! You took advantage of her. She's fucking innocent in this, you coward!" I throw my back against the wall, burying my face in my bloody hands. My body doesn't want to fight him. It simply wants to give up.

Leo wipes the blood from his lips with a smug smile. "Hello, Leo. How have you been Leo?" He mocks me, his Greek accent is replaced by a smooth American one.

I cut my eyes to him.

"If you missed me, you could've just called." He stands, stretching his limbs.

"Fuck you." I spit blood from my busted lip. Too many emotions are whirling through my head.

He pinches the bridge of his bloody nose, wincing at the pain. "Care to explain why you busted down my door and pummeled my face?"

I stand, snatching the glass of whiskey he poured from him and downing it. The burn from my open cut gives a good jolt.

My chest rises. "I know. I know about you and Emilia," I seethe.

Leo exhales deeply. "Please enlighten me, Aiden. What do you know?"

It takes everything in me to not beat him into a pulp and wipe that carefree smirk off his face. My eyes cut to his tousled sheets, my heart shattering at the thought of my Emilia tangled in the covers with him. I slump against the wall.

Leo refills my glass before dropping to sit beside me after throwing on some jeans.

"I don't know why I haven't killed you yet." I laugh, bringing the glass to my lips.

"Maybe because you just beat the fuck out of me for no reason, and you know it." He looks at me intently, his heavy accent slightly concerned. "What the fuck is going on?"

How did I go from murderous to wanting to confide in the one person I hate most in this world? Is this what heartbreak feels like? Just crazed emotions flipping back and forth.

"I proposed, and she told me no," I spit. "Because apparently, you two…" *I can't say it.* "In Italy."

He glances at me as he dabs his face with a towel. "I never did anything with her."

I laugh, remembering what happened to the last man who said Emilia lied to me. I wanted to kill him. Now, he sits in jail because Emilia's heart is too nice…too pure. Avery had harassed all his female employees. Thankfully, the police held him accountable. But she can't stop me from taking Leo's life.

"She told you I fucked her in Italy?" He smiles.

I growl.

"Aiden, listen. I don't know what the fuck

is going on. But I swear on her life, I've never touched her. Except the time I kissed her. That one time."

I lift my brow in doubt before narrowing my eyes. "Leo, I'm asking you man to man–"

He shakes his head, stopping me. "I never touched her. I promise you."

His words are sincere, but I can't trust him.

Emilia wouldn't hurt me. She wouldn't lie to me.

"Did anything happen before you proposed?"

I hate this guy, but I need to know what's going on. *Why she would want to not be mine anymore*? "We were eating dinner, she went to speak with her mom in our room. She came back a– Oh my fuck."

How could I be so stupid?

I stand, pulling Leo up.

Leo rushes around, grabbing his things before handing me guns from his drawers. "Did you leave her alone?" His voice is as frantic as mine.

I shake my head. "There are guards."

She fucking knew my jealousy would triumph over my sanity.

She knew!

"Does she know a way out? That they don't know of?"

The fucking sauna.

"Where is her locket?"

"She ripped it off in front of me." *My stupid, brave girl.*

Leo whistles, buttoning up his shirt. "Damn."

I pace the room. "Shut up. What do we do?"

He cocks his weapons. "Did she have her charm bracelet on?"

I feel a little guilty for beating the shit out of him when he touches his busted lip. He nods when I hand him an ice cube from the champagne bucket.

"Why does that matter?"

He laces his shoes. "Was she wearing it?"

The night flashes through my mind and I stomp down the heartache. I remember trailing my finger across her soft skin, to her locket, and down to her wrist where…

"Yes."

"Good." He stands, gesturing to his mangled door as he fumbles with his phone. "Let's go."

I tap his chest. "Why does that matter?"

He sighs. "I put a tracker in it." He shows me her location on his phone.

Relief floods through me as well as anger. I scoff. "You didn't put a tracker on my girl."

"Oh, but I did. For this very reason. She

never fucking listened to me."

I'm torn between hugging him and punching him in the face. I step on the broken wood, hurrying us out. "Because she knows better. Now, let's get the fuck out of here. We need to find her."

He opens the passenger door to my car. "How many times are you two going to make me save the other?"

He's joking, but I can tell he's nervous for her. It doesn't anger me, but instead empowers me. We're going to save my girl, together.

I turn on the ignition and peel down the road. "I'm sorry about the door… and your face."

He waves it off with nervous laughter.

I grip the wheel, heading to the love of my life in a frenzied rush.

"This ends tonight."

Thirty-Two

Emilia

I park the Tesla a few blocks away, wanting to arrive on my own terms and the headlights will probably get me killed quicker.

I've never been so frightened in my life, so terrified of what's to come. But this is better than the alternative. If I had told Aiden, he would've locked me in the house and gotten himself killed. I did what I had to. He'll understand when he finds my phone and my nervously scribbled note.

The place is near where Aiden took me to on our date night. Faint music and the chatter of people enjoying their night fill the air.

Darkness surrounds me as I creep down the tall abandoned buildings. I tiptoe through the alleyways, my heart beating out of my chest. Aiden's gun is heavy, tucked into my black leggings. I don't think I'll make it out of this alive. But if the man on the phone doesn't immediately let Mom leave, I'm taking matters into my own hands.

The building is so close yet so far.

A streetlight flickers overhead, making this seem like an actual nightmare.

I steel myself and push forward, my feet crunch against the jagged gravel on the pavement. My stomach drops when a hand covers my mouth firmly, muffling my scream, and an arm grabs my waist. Just like that, I find myself flying through an open door.

My back hits the cold concrete wall with a loud thud before I'm pressed up against it violently. The door slams shuts, and I can't see a thing. Darkness engulfs me. I can hear his ragged breathing. The hand remains plastered against my mouth, muffling my screams.

This is it.

I should have known they'd be waiting in dark corners.

"Be fucking quiet!" A voice growls.

My body stills before violent trembles rattle me. I hear a click before a swinging pendulum light illuminates the area just enough for me to see his face. I stare. There's no denying the midnight blue eyes glaring back at me.

Thomas Peters.

The man who killed my father.

I scream, in pain and horror.

He looks even more sinister with the dark hood pulled over his head. The dark shadows of his face are all I can see. I don't miss the shine of the pistol in his hand.

I recoil, my head banging against the wall, but I don't feel it with the terror coursing through me as he leans in close. Out of the corner of my eyes I see a figure emerge through the back, then another.

A gun cocks and I shut my eyes tightly.

"Let her go!"

Aiden.

His voice makes my body go numb in relief.

My eyes fly open.

How did he find me?

Oh, God. I'm going to get him killed.

Aiden steps closer, placing the gun against Thomas's temple.

I whimper at the sight of Aiden's busted lip. "I said let her go."

The other silhouette comes into view.

I was expecting Howard.

But... Leo?

His bloody face causes guilt to wash over

me.

Thomas lifts his hands, releasing me.

I suck in a deep breath and dive into Aiden's chest. Safe at last.

Leo keeps his gun trained on Thomas. "Turn around!"

Aiden's arms wrap around me so tightly I can't breathe. His large hand caresses my cheek as his emerald eyes track every inch of my body, making sure I'm okay.

"You found me," I whisper, taking a moment to breathe.

"I always will." Aiden cups my face.

I shake my head. A moment of relief isn't worth his life.

"You have to go!" I beg.

He simply laughs at my demand. The metal of his gun is cool against my cheek as his eyes bore into mine. "I'm not going anywhere. Tell me what the fuck is going on," He seethes, looking to the hooded figure facing the wall I was pinned to.

Leo's voice disrupts our conversation. "I said turn the fuck around. Show yourself!"

Thomas turns, dropping his hood.

Aiden's chest shudders as he sees his face. "Oh my God, Emilia, I'm so sorry," He whispers, his arms holding me protectively.

Why isn't he hating me for everything I did to him?

His hand brushes against the gun by my hip but he doesn't say anything.

"*Bampas?*" Leo frowns.

Aiden stiffens, his eyes darting between the men. "Get behind me, Emilia."

Leo lowers his gun just as Aiden points his at Leo.

"What did he say?" I tug on his sleeve desperately, to find out what caused the change.

Aiden shakes his head, his voice dripping with betrayal. "Who the fuck are you, Leo?"

"Aiden, what did he say?" I plead as Leo steps closer to Thomas.

Aiden turns to look at me, his expression a mixture of terror and realization. He flounders for words and after a long silence, he moves to speak just as Leo did.

"Dad?"

A sinister silence spreads through the room at Leo's words.

Thomas drops his weapon, the metal clanking against the hard concrete. He holds his empty hands up. "I'm not the bad guy. I need you to trust me." He looks at Aiden's raised gun. "Both of you."

I scoff. "No."

He speaks more lies, his pleading voice making me nauseous. "Your father wasn't who you think he was."

"Don't speak to me about my dad." My voice wavers. Aiden holds me behind him as I lurch forward.

"Don't go near him." Aiden orders me.

I look over at Leo, searching his face, trying to figure out why he came into my life.

"Your father was my friend," Thomas deadpans.

I laugh, terrified and hysterical. "Are you drunk?"

It's possible.

"He brought you a single yellow rose every week." I cover my ears, but he simply speaks louder. "Your mother and him went dancing every Thursday evening. You–"

I cut him off with a wave of my hand. "You stalked us."

I watch as he reaches into his back pocket.

"Stop," Aiden growls, aiming his gun between Thomas's eyes.

He doesn't flinch and, instead, retrieves a photo and a note.

Aiden takes them and hands them to me, never taking his eyes off Leo or Thomas.

In the photo is my dad, his arm slung around Thomas's shoulders. Next to them is a little boy, clutching onto a stuffed animal.

I recognize those grey eyes.

My hands shake as I bring the photo to

Aiden's eye level.

"How did you know my dad?"

"Your father wasn't a street cop, Emma. He was a detective."

The words rush through me. They don't make sense.

I frown.

Dad worked on the street. I saw his pins and medals.

"It was a charade. He was the best undercover detective in the city. The police chief hid things from the public to keep him safe."

I unfold the aged letter, taking in Dad's sloppy but perfect handwriting.

> Dean,
>
> I wish you could meet Emmy. She's so big now. She just won her first spelling bee. I'm so proud of her. Pamela is perfect, as always. I wish we could all get together. I think our kids would get along just fine. I can't wait for you to return from visiting Leo. How is he? Bring back something from Greece for me.
>
> Sending my best,
> Patrick Banks.

My heart sinks at the realization. "I don't

understand. Why didn't he tell us? Why did you go to jail for him?"

"We worked undercover on a lot of different cases. From sex trafficking to drug operations, and finally to the one that became his downfall. The Mafia. Helping the city was your father's life's work. We were both deep in an operation that night. The mafia in our city…they were doing unspeakable things."

"Someone found out about your dad, and they killed him. There were three of us. I'm the only one who made it out." He looks at me pointedly, "He would never have wanted my cover to be blown, and so I took the fall for his death. The only crime I committed was ending the low life who killed him. The operation trusted in me fully after they thought I was the one who killed the 'nark.' I was able to work from inside prison and sweep the city of the plague that was the operation, all because of your father's sacrifices."

Aiden isn't convinced. "That's a huge secret to bare, and five years you'll never get back."

He shrugs. "He was my best friend. Not only was he my partner, he saved my life on numerous occasions." His eyes grow distant and he grips Leo's shoulder. "He was family to us."

Aiden lowers his gun, his arm slinking around my waist to provide comfort.

"Why did Leo get to meet my dad, but I didn't get to meet you?"

"Leo lived in Greece with his mother. He was safe from the city," Dean explains. "He wanted me to meet you so badly, Emma. I feel like I've known you your entire life." He smiles.

Leo nods, stepping forward slowly. "I didn't lie to you about anything. I just never told you about my dad, and I'm sorry. It's true that I'm from Greece. I moved here five years ago, after Patrick was killed. My only job is to protect you. I knew what your father did for me and my dad. He was a good man, and a good man didn't deserve what happened to him."

He turns his attention to Aiden. "And I'm sorry I kissed her. The lines between us blurred. I'm so sorry I crossed the line."

I note a smile tilting on Dean's face as he shakes his head.

"Is that why your face is all," Dean gestures to Leo's face, "disheveled?"

Aiden and Leo shake their heads, not wanting to explain my lies.

"If the Mafia killed my dad…" I choke on my words. "Then why didn't they come for me and Mom?" I clutch the photograph, trying to hold onto my sanity.

"You and Pamela were always safe." His face contorts. "He's gone. They wouldn't seek vengeance on a ghost." He exhales, running a hand through his hair. "I waited, and called in Leo to watch over you. But no one came for either of you."

I bite my lip.

Five years. He's been watching over us all that time.

"Emmy. I'm sorry."

Realization dawns upon me. "It was you. At the party." I stare into his blue eyes. "But your eyes..."

"Contacts." He winks. "Leo got his gray eyes from his mother."

They exchange a long glance before smoothing out their expressions.

Aiden shakes his head. "Can someone tell me what the fuck is going on?" The anger in his voice doesn't match the gentle touch of his hands.

"They have Mom." My voice cracks.

Aiden's eyes widen and he steps closer to the men. "Is this about Emilia? Did they discover the truth about that night?"

"No. This is about you. Different Mafia, different operations."

He nods, caressing my back. "Figured as much. Who is it? Who took me? Why didn't they kill me?"

Dean shakes his head, pinching the bridge of his nose. "I don't know the answers, but I know who's behind all of this. The Matterazos."

Aiden scoffs, his gun lazily sitting in his

palm. "Impossible. I killed them."

"Yes, you killed Lucio and Vinny. But you forgot an important part of their equation. Their father, Stefano. And he's seeking revenge."

Aiden shakes his head. "Their father's been dead for years."

Dean shoots him a pointed expression. "No, he hasn't. That's who took you."

Aiden looks to Leo. "You knew all of this?"

Leo clinches his fist. "Yes, but before you get pissed, the information would have done nothing but get you killed."

Aiden shakes his head.

Dean speaks up. "He's right. It would have. When I got released, I dug into everything. We don't have much time. I need you to trust me. Is everyone ready to go?" He looks at me pointedly.

"Go where?" Aiden asks.

Leo and Dean check their weapons. "To save Pamela."

"We're ready." He gestures to me. "But she's not going anywhere."

"Emmy," Dean apologizes, but I don't mind hearing that name again.

I still can't believe that Dad was a detective and the man I loathed was his best friend.

"Emma needs to be there."

"I will not risk her life," Aiden disagrees.

Dean and Leo snap to attention. "You won't."

"Let me call in her double," Aiden pleads.

"No time. They're waiting for her. I was going to go in on my own until she stumbled down the street. Alone." Dean narrows his eyes at me.

My voice is small, confusion fogging my brain but also a sense of understanding. "I didn't know what else to do."

Dean waves his hand in the air. "We'll use it to our advantage."

Aiden's not having it. "No, we won't! The entire Mafia could be in that building!"

I check Aiden's watch. "Guys, they gave me three hours. I have less than an hour left before they kill her."

They nod, a silent symbol of uniting.

"I will lock you in this room. You're not coming, Emilia."

I pull the gun from my waistband. "Aiden, I don't know what's waiting for us in there. But Mom is. She's waiting to be saved." I cock the gun. "I saved you. I'm saving her. I know how to use this and I'm going. That's final. You'll have the element of surprise with me going in first. Alone."

"Where is my Pamela?" The familiar frantic voice sweeps through the room before I see a disheveled-looking Howard.

Aiden fills him in as we prepare for battle. I shoot Howard a broken look as Leo steps over to him.

"Where are Ricky and Ash?"

Aiden whirls me around to face him, his body flush against mine. "Home. They don't know anything." His broken eyes trail over my face.

I run a soft thumb over his busted lip. I feel as if he's going to hide me away somewhere.

Instead, he pulls me in close. "If anything happens to you, I'm going to let them kill me. You understand that, right?"

I breathe him in. "I'm sorry for earlier, Aiden. I'm so sorry. If we make it ou–"

He stops me with a deep, passionate kiss. "*When* we make it out, I'll make you my wife," He promises, placing a lingering kiss on my forehead. "Just please, please don't do this."

"Aiden, Emilia is family to me," Dean cuts in. "I will keep her safe. I wouldn't fathom asking her to come with us, if I didn't know she'd make it out unscathed."

Dean turns to me. "I know you don't know me, but I know everything about you. Your dad loved you and your mother unconditionally. I will protect you the way he protected me. You're my family. Whatever we have to do, no matter the outcome. It will be done."

EMILIA

I wiggle out of Aiden's arm and rush into Dean's arms. "Thank you." Tears roll down my cheek.

I tug on Leo's arm and pull him into a hug as well.

My eyes land on Aiden, who gives me a hesitant nod. He knows I won't back down.

They run through the plan.

"Ready?"

I nod.

Thirty-Three

I inhale deeply, trying to calm myself. "Hey fucker!" My voice echoes through the open industrial room.

A short, balding, and sweaty looking man turns his head. A smile creeps up his face at the sight of me.

He must be Stefano.

I scope the room and spot five men. Two of them on the top floor, their guns pointed at me. Stefano is standing beside Mom's unconscious body, two of his men behind him. She's tied to a large steel beam.

I place a shaky hand behind my back and hold my hand flush to showcase how many people we're against. Knowing my men are watching in the shadows gives me a boost of courage.

Stefano claps his hands with a smile. "Oh, how wonderful!"

His heavy accent is smothering me, even over the clanking industrial motors running throughout the building. I'm guessing to drown out any screams or gunshots.

"We've been waiting for you." He walks over to my mother.

She's so still it makes my heart stop…until I see her chest rising and falling. She's alive. I'm trying to be brave but seeing her so broken…

"I'm here. Now, let her go." My voice trembles.

He clicks his tongue, shaking his head. "I lied, darling. Your Aiden, he took my sons. In return, I will take both of you." He steps closer to me.

With four guns trained on me, I don't move an inch.

He fingers my hair, smoothing it out.

I cringe at his touch, my body vibrating with fear. I hope Aiden doesn't deviate from the plan. I'm our only hope to make it out of this. If I wasn't, he would have never agreed to let me in here.

"Revenge will be so sweet." He wields a blade in his left hand, showcasing it with a smirk.

Aiden's tall frame appears out of the

shadows on the second floor. I watch discreetly as he takes down one of the men silently, guiding the man's body to the floor with gentle ease. It's a good thing everyone's eyes are trained on me and the warehouse is so loud.

"Before I kill you…"

Another man falls, this time from Leo's doing, and the top floor is cleared.

"I think I'll have some fun with you." Stefano's hot breath makes me gag. His face too close to my neck as he sneers his foul words over the noise.

My ears ring. It feels as though I'm out of my body.

I need to be someone else, just like in Italy.

Emilia would never do something like this. Striding courageously into a building to fight grown men, or would she?

I stand a little straighter. I saved Aiden in Italy. I saved him from this monster, and I'll do it again for Mom. His disgusting lips touch my cheek, and I flinch.

"Like hell you will." In a matter of seconds, Aiden drops the last of Stefano's guards.

I reach for my gun, relief that we now have the upper hand.

Realizing it's an ambush, Stefano lunges for my mother and holds a knife to her throat. She stirs but doesn't wake. The tip of his knife pricks her skin, and I scream.

Howard snarls, stepping out from the shadows. "You lay one hand on her–"

"Or what?" Stefano laughs. "You'll kill my whole family?" He turns to Aiden. "You killed my sons. And I had you." He sighs. "I was coming in that night." His wild eyes dart to me. "The night you saved him."

He carelessly holds the blade to Mom's throat. "They say I went crazy, but it was justified. How could one little girl help you escape? And you!" He points to Leo, snarling. "You helped."

"I killed everyone who was there that night. The guards, workers, and guests who stayed behind. I had to hide all this time. At least I had a few loyal men left." He sneers. "But you killed all of them too."

He throws his head back in a fit of laughter. "All except one."

Cold, ruthless metal touches the back of my head.

I don't turn. I know what it is.

Instead, I look at Aiden, whose eyes are glistening and filled with fear.

"Drop your weapons, gentlemen." Stefano guides everyone's attention to me with the tip of his knife.

Stefano's greasy smile widens at the loud clanking of guns.

"No!" I scream.

But they don't listen. Too worried about me getting hurt, rather than saving themselves, or Mom.

This was my fear.

"Don't." Aiden orders. "Take me." He steps towards Stefano, unarmed and with open arms.

"Aiden! Please, no!" I protest, but he doesn't listen.

"Oh, I plan to." Stefano cackles. "You ruined my life." With that, he steps away from Mom, pointing his blade at Aiden.

The man behind me moves to my side to get a better view of the action.

I can't peel my eyes from Aiden as he allows Stefano to cut into his skin, right over the rose tattoo.

"Kill me. Cut me to shreds." Blood trickles down his skin. "Let her go."

Aiden's eyes lock on mine, he would fight if a barrel wasn't aimed at my temple. My worst fears are coming to life. Aiden is brave as usual. The beautiful, brilliant, selfless human he is tears me apart.

I have to figure out how to save him.

Stefano admires the shimmer of his knife before bringing it against Aiden's neck.

I would look away, but Aiden's eyes are boring into mine. Tears streak my face. He's telling me everything we will never get to say to each other with a brave crooked grin. Those dimples.

My eyes dart around the room, trying to figure out a way to help him. Howard remains still, tears in his eyes, while Dean is looking around the room, gears turning as he plans out his next move. I spot Leo creeping around the side while everyone is distracted.

I inch my hand towards the gunmen, remembering Aiden's lessons on how to disarm someone. But before I can do just that, Leo lunges for the man and they fall to the cold concrete and begin fighting for dominance.

A shot rings out and my head snaps in the direction.

Howard's gun is aimed straight while Stefano is on the ground, dead.

Aiden rushes towards me, generally unharmed, besides the deep cut on his side and the nick on his neck.

I can't take my eyes off Leo and the gunman as they tousle while Aiden drags me away. Another shot rings out so close to me I can't hear anything but a shrill.

What I see is so much worse.

Leo lays, bleeding out in front of me.

I drop to my knees by Leo's side, crimson red blood pouring out of the hole in his body. Frantically, I push my hand to his wound and apply pressure, trying to slow his bleeding as

Dean advances on the man who shot his son.

All I can see is Leo's paling face.

His hand reaches up to cup my cheek. "Em, it's okay."

"It's not okay!" I cry out. "You can't die, Leo! I'm so sorry." I weep.

Two more shots ring out, the sound deafening me.

I look to my left and my attention is drawn to the other horrific scene as Howard places his hands on Leo's wound. I hadn't noticed when Aiden joined the fight, thinking he was behind me.

I scream as I crawl over to his body. He's terrifyingly still, unmoving.

"Aiden!" I wail, a lump stops my breathing at the sight of blood dripping from his head. I lift his head gently onto my lap. "Oh my God!" I scream, tears blurring my vision. "He's been shot."

I rip off part of my shirt and press it to the wound. Howard is yelling at me, but I can't hear him past the ringing in my ears. "I'll fix you, A."

A warm hand cups my cheek, and I look down and gasp.

Aiden smiles at me, sitting up slowly.

The ringing subsides and I force him to stay still.

"Baby." His voice is distant, "I just got

knocked out." He peels my hand from his face, wiping the blood away to reveal a gash.

My heart starts beating again, until I remember Leo.

Aiden's eyes widen when he looks behind me. "Leo, you idiot." He moves in a flash, falling to his knees to stem his wound, letting Howard go to Mom. "I'm so fucking sorry."

Leo is calm as he looks between us with fluttering eyelids. "It's okay." He smiles. There's blood on his teeth. "Where's Dad?"

"I'm right here, Son."

I smile when I hear Dean's voice, but something is off. I look back, seeing the gunmen dead. To my horror, Dean's white shirt is soaked in blood and his breathing is labored. With his remaining strength, he stumbles over, reaching out to cup Leo's cheek.

Leo tries to move, but Aiden stops him. "Dad, you're shot."

With so much courage it makes my heart ache, Dean clutches Leo's hand. "I love you, my boy. You were always my greatest gift." He coughs, splattering blood onto Leo's neck.

It's heart wrenching.

"I love you too, Dad." Leo's accent is muffled by his agonizing cries.

"Get him out of here." Dean grips Aiden's hand firmly before turning to me. "I'm sorry we didn't get to know each other better,

Emmy. Take care of my boy. Both of you. Now, go before the backup I called gets here!" Dean orders.

With the last of his energy exhausted, he collapses to the ground.

"No!" Leo struggles as Aiden lifts him, tears falling. "Dad, I won't leave you!" His hand laces through Dean's.

It's devastating to see Aiden pulling Leo from his dying father's grip, but those were his final wishes. Leo doesn't have much time left.

Aiden's face is grim as he carries Leo away. "I have to save you, Leo."

I sit next to Dean, rubbing my fingers through his hair, trying to give him some comfort. This is where I need to be.

"Emmy."

I shake my head. "Shh, don't speak. I'm here. Please don't fight me about this."

His eyes flutter close, a small smile on his lips as he squeezes my hand weakly. "You're like your father." He whispers. "I did this with him, held him. He would have done it for me." I find solace knowing my father never died alone in the snow on that awful day.

"It's going to be okay," I whisper through my tears, calming my voice to a melodic pitch. "Leo will be okay. I'll protect him."

He smiles faintly as he slowly fades away. His grip on my hand grows weaker, until finally…he closes his eyes and lets go.

Then I break down, resting my head on his chest.

Aiden's strong arms envelop me, carrying me away from the bloody scene. I remain silent, even as my tears flow, unable to come up with any reasonable emotions or words.

A black suburban waits for us outside, a familiar guard from the house in the driver's seat. Howard is already inside with Mom leaned against him. Aiden slides me into the back, sitting me on his lap. I study his wound before holding a piece of my shirt firmly against it as he holds more fabric to his side.

He'll be okay.

"Where's Leo?" I crane my neck, looking for him.

Aiden gives me a small smile. "He's already at the hospital. Another guard took him. He's texting me every few minutes."

Mom looks at me, the dried blood on her face darkening.

Aiden dips his face into the crook of my neck and whispers, "I'm going to explain to her what happened."

Fear shoots through me. "She'll hate you," I whisper through my sobs.

"Dean told me a story to tell her earlier." He kisses my cheek. "It's going to be okay."

It's hard to breathe a sigh of relief as we

pull up to our home, knowing Dean is lying in that warehouse alone.

Aiden goes on the phone for a few minutes while Howard escorts my confused mom inside. I can't bear to talk to her right now. I would break down.

Aiden hangs up the phone and makes his way to me.

"How much longer will Dean have to be alone?" I hug myself, tears dripping down my face.

Aiden pulls me in. "They're already taking him away, baby. He's with his friends now. They'll take care of his…" He pauses. "His body."

I bury my face into his warm chest. "I feel so bad for Leo."

"I know, I know."

I look up at him. "Is it over?"

Aiden wraps me tightly in his arms. "The Mafia turned their backs on Stefano after I escaped and he killed all of those innocent people. He's nothing now. No one cares for him and no one will seek vengeance."

I sniffle. "How do you know?"

"I just spoke with a friend of Dean's." He coughs, his voice hoarse. "Stefano murdered thirteen high ranking guards and two high profile mafia leaders. There's a bounty out for his head. We killed him. We're being celebrated now, not hunted."

I cry into his chest, relief washing over me.

"It's over, baby."

Thirty-Four

'Take off your clothes and meet me in the water. Now.'

Aiden's order rings through the note.

With a smile, I rip off my robe and rush out of the condo's back door. My bare feet happily dig into the sand, still warm from the Grecian sun. The moon illuminates Aiden's floating silhouette in the ocean, his muscular back disappearing as he turns my way. A dimpled smile lights his face.

As I wade into the warm ocean water, I think about how different life was for us compared to four months ago. We've been blessed with four blissful months of no guards, no fear, and no distractions. We also mourned the death of Dean, someone I wished I would have known longer. His sacrifice will never be forgotten.

Mom is under the impression that Dad's job brought lingering danger to us. The thought didn't bother me. He wouldn't have wanted her to know the truth. Leo met her after he recovered, and she now knows that Dad was a detective. She adores Leo, and they talk regularly.

Aiden wraps me in his strong arms as my legs wrap around his waist. The ocean water laps gently against our skin. We are finally on our vacation that I gifted to him on Christmas. We've spent two weeks in Greece so far, experiencing things I never thought I would with him. Our private condo is in the outskirts of Greece, with no one around for miles.

Aiden's long fingers caresses my skin. "I'm glad you followed my orders," He purrs, nuzzling my neck as he kisses my damp skin while fondling my breast.

"Happy Birthday." I kiss his damp cheek.

He grins, his hands roaming my body.

My ache for him grows as his length hardens against me. In a frenzy of passion, we dive into each other. Our lips colliding and our bodies melting into one another.

"You're mine," I moan, tangling my fingers in his hair.

"As you're mine." He growls, pushing

himself inside me. We make love underneath the bright moon.

Aiden flicks his lighter to light his cigarette and the few candles he's set out by the blanket.

"Here."

I pull his shirt over my body while he slips on a pair of pants.

With a devilish smirk, he hands me a glass of champagne.

We gaze into each other's eyes.

I look away. Even after all this time, his intensity makes me blush.

"Emilia, sweetheart." Aiden cups my chin, making me look at him. His sharp edges are defined by the flickering candlelight. "I've never been able to look past the next investment, the next big deal, anything to make me the most successful man in the world."

His eyes bore into mine. "But I would give it all up, for you."

"Aww, Aiden." I smile, bringing my lips to his.

He cups my face gently. "Why? I don't understand, after all the danger I've put into your life, why do you still stay?"

I don't understand his insecurities. I never will.

I love him. It's as simple as that.

I place my hand on his cheek. "We were together, I forget the rest," I quote, nuzzling into his warm hand.

"Whitman." He nods approvingly.

The quote describes us perfectly.

"I'm about to say a bunch of really cheesy stuff," He warns with a grin. The water gently laps the shore and his warm baritone fills my ears. "You found me, baby. When I didn't want to be found, you found me and gave my life meaning. Before I saw you, I saw nothing."

Tears roll down my cheeks at his sweet words.

"Emilia Banks, when I look at you, I see forever." He pulls a familiar velvet box from his pocket.

My heart burst. I'll finally get to be his fiancée and see the ring he chose for me.

"I want…" He shakes his head. "No, I need you to officially be mine." He smiles widely, full dimples inviting me in for a kiss. He goes down on one knee. "Would you do me the absolute fucking honor of becoming my wife?"

"Yes!" I scream.

With a chuckle, he opens the velvet box.

I blink. All I see is a tiny, intricate key.

Aiden takes the key out and brings it to the bottom of the locket, to the keyhole.

I remember his words from when he first

gave me the locket necklace.

"I have the key and it will always stay locked. Always."

The lock clicks open, and the bottom falls out. I examine his palm as he takes the ring from the clasp it was set in. With a wink, he turns it to me, revealing the ring.

I gasp at the sight of its beauty.

It's the most beautiful and perfect ring. A solitary diamond sits atop a thin rose gold band, shimmering under the moonlight.

"How long?" I've had my locket around my neck for a year.

"That's my secret." He twirls the ring around his finger, showcasing the symbol of his love as he reaches for my hand. "I may not be a perfect man, but I will love you unconditionally every second of every single day."

Speechless from his loving words, all I can do is watch him in awe.

"Marry me, Emilia. Be mine, always, and make me the happiest fucking man on earth. You're my future. My solace at the end of every day." He slides the ring onto my finger, locking in our perfect destiny.

I cup his face. "Aiden, I don't see how you could ever be anything but mine." My lips press against his. "Forever."

Epilogue

One year later

Fresh spring air dove in through the open window, encasing me in its warmth. I looked to my mother's tear-soaked eyes, trying to hold back my own. "You look gorgeous Emma." She cried, wrapping me tightly in her open arms.

I memorized the smile lines on her face through the full-length vanity mirror as she buttoned the back of my dress. Taking her time, and carefully patting her cheeks with a tissue as she did so. Once finished, Ashley fluffed my train, taking a step back to admire her work.

They've spent hours getting me ready, and I can tell it's taking a toll on Ash. "That baby is going to pop out if you keep bending down like that!" I teased, looking at the tight fabric of her bridesmaid dress as she brushed her palm against the train of my dress once more.

"Oh stop." She clutched her perfect belly, lovingly. "It's my job to do all of this today."

I grabbed my mother's hands as Ashley fussed over my hair, my fingers grazed over her own wedding ring. Her and Howard eloped in Spain, a quick but perfect decision. They're so in love.

Ashley tugged a strand of hair out to frame my face. "You guys did great, I promise." I told her with a laugh, not caring what I looked like as long as I got to marry the man of my dreams.

Leo walked in the room, dressed in all black aside from the yellow rose that was tucked into his pocket to match the striking color of the bridesmaid's dresses. "Is this bad luck?" He asked, smirking at me. I rolled my eyes, bringing Zoe in for a hug.

"It's only bad luck for the groom, you idiot." I joked, taking Zoe's hand in mine to twirl her around. "You look stunning!"

"Me?" she croaked, "Look at you!" I didn't want to admit that I hadn't yet looked in the mirror. The entire morning, I was looking at Ash and mom through the vanity. I wasn't nervous, it was the exact opposite, I couldn't get everyone else to move fast enough.

EMILIA

Sweet Zoe. I've gotten so close to Leo's girlfriend in the past year. I had to warm her up to Aiden, as she was at Leo's apartment when he showed up on a war path. She quickly understood the situation and never judged any of us for anything.

"It's time baby." Mom squealed, straightening out her dress and rushing from the room. Light music played throughout the home, floating in the air around us.

My two bridesmaids linked their arms through mine as we descended the grand staircase. Howard waited for me at the bottom, looking dashing in a black tux. "Isn't she lovely?" Mom asked, kissing us both on the cheek before making her way out.

"You do look lovely, Emilia." Howard said, his eyes filled with tears. Mom's softened him up immensely, but he's always had a soft spot for me.

Classical music danced through the halls, signaling for us to come. Howard put his hand out for me, I grabbed it and his face fell to a somber frown. "I'm sorry you never got the chance to have your father walk you."

I looked to him, my eyes beaming with pride as tears threatened to spill. "I will always love my dad, but I love you too." I wished more than anything my father was alive, but I truly couldn't think of a better person to give me away than Howard. "You are my family. Now let's go!" I squealed.

We walked with linked arms over the marble flooring. Through the windows, I could see my bridesmaids making their way down. My eyes searched for Aiden, but I couldn't see him beyond our seated families and friends.

Howard's hand clamped over mine, firmly and carefully. "You ready for this?" He asked as two workers parted the doors.

I breathed in the familiar scent of our home; we didn't want to be married anywhere else. Then I stepped out towards my future. "I've been ready my whole life." I told him.

The music queued and we made our way down the rose petal path. My feet couldn't move fast enough, all I wanted was to see him. It was as if nothing would be real until I saw him waiting for me.

My heart fluttered the moment my eyes locked on his, as if time slowed to a standstill. His dimpled smile curled up when his eyes met mine. His tattooed hand covered his mouth as he watched me walk to him.

Our families sat in white chairs on either side of the aisle, while yellow roses draped the area. Overhead, hydrangeas cascaded, creating a fairytale. But I only knew the décor from the preparations. I hadn't noticed a single thing besides the man waiting for me at the altar.

Howard tried to slow my pace, but my heart was leaping to get to the end of the aisle. I couldn't wait another second. The crowd giggled as I took small but quick steps to my fiancé.

The preacher spoke as me and Howard stood before Aiden, his emerald eyes twinkled while he looked at me. "Who gives this woman to be married?"

"I do." Howard said proudly, my mother coughed from her seat. "And her mother." He grinned, placing my hand into Aiden's.

His strong hand encased mine as we stepped in front of the preacher. A photo of my father, and his mother sat on empty seats at the front of the aisle. Ricky, his best man, stood behind him. Behind Ricky, was Leo. I never would have imagined he would be a groomsman at our wedding, but the three of them are now inseparable.

Aiden couldn't take his eyes from mine; with a deep exhale I saw a tear form against his emerald irises. "Breathtaking." He stated, his voice low and powerful.

We repeated our traditional vows surrounded by everyone we loved.

But we saved our personal vows for after the ceremony, inside of our rose garden, before we headed to the reception. Aiden plucked a rose and handed it to me, I twirled it in my fingers.

There we stood. Me in my wedding gown,

the train traveling down the pathway in our greenhouse. Him, in his black suit.

It felt as if millions of butterflies fluttered their wings in my stomach, "Aiden Scott." I smiled, nodding my head to him. I didn't want to write down my vows to him, I just wanted to express the truth from my lips.

His crooked grin and empty hands told me he had decided on the same. "There's no way that anyone has ever loved another person, as much as I love you. I promise to always be patient with you. Even when you close my bakery down an hour early to drag me away for some fun." I giggled as he pulled me close, planting a kiss on my forehead.

"We can have some fun now?" He suggested with a wink, I playfully swatted at his wandering hands.

"And I promise to love you for the rest of my life."

His eyes bore into mine, all playfulness gone. "Emilia Scott." His shoulders rolled back as he let out a deep breath, relief of me finally being his poured through him. "I promise." He shook his head, "I swear that we will create a life made simply for us." I couldn't think of a better life to live. "I'll never change the way I am with you; I simply don't know how. You will always be mine, and I will always protect you with everything in me."

His finger lingered on my ring, "You took my soul and wiped it clean, my bride."

Two Years Later

"There she is." I smiled, watching as our little girl waddled to us.

Aiden scooped her in his strong arms. "How was your nap baby girl?"

"Good!" She squealed, her eyes widening with the pure happiness only a child can hold when she saw me. I'm her favorite, but don't tell Aiden that.

I had been Emilia Achelois Scott for two years, and I couldn't have been happier. Me, Aiden and our three-year-old little girl, Eliana. We called her Eli for short. Beautiful, spontaneous, and sassy.

I admired them as we stood in the kitchen, on a lazy Sunday afternoon. Eli's crimson hair was glistening from the sunlight beaming in through the windows.

"Mommy!" She wiggled from Aiden's grip, jumping into my arms. Full dimples and pigtails.

Her eyes roamed the countertops. "Cupcakes!" She exclaimed, gesturing to them.

Aiden smiled, grabbing one for her. "Lavender cupcakes to be exact." He told her, dipping his finger in the frosting and dotting her nose.

Eli licked the top of her cupcake. "Deeeelicious!"

I kissed her cheek. "New recipe for the bakery." I told her, and she nodded her little head in approval.

I finished my business degree that year, and I couldn't imagine anything I'd rather be doing than running my own bakery and being her mom. I hoped when Eli grew up that she would love to bake too.

She completed our family.

We wanted kids right away, but had trouble conceiving. It didn't matter the second our eyes landed on Eliana.

I didn't possibly think I could love someone more than Aiden, until we found Eli.

It doesn't matter how your children get to you, just that they do.

Two years later

Eli was five, going on thirty. I hovered over her in our kitchen, helping with her drawing.

Her father taught her everything she could know about painting, and she had been working on her masterpiece all morning.

"Okay, ready to show daddy?" I asked, running my hand along her strawberry hair.

"Dad!" She ran through the house searching for him, he was in his study reviewing paperwork. But as soon as she ran in, his eyes lit up and his work was put down for later.

Her little hands held the paper proudly as Aiden took it, "For me?" he gasped, and she giggled.

"Oh, I see." He examined it. "It's me, you, and mommy." His proud smile lit up the room. "It's beautiful! But your Mom isn't bigger than me." He laughed, turning the paper over to show her.

"She will be!" Eli's sassiness came out, her hands placed on her hips.

Aiden stood, towering over me as usual. "See, I'm much bigger than mommy."

I looked up at him with a smile while Eli pointed her finger at him. "She's going to grow! She told me!"

"Grow?" He muttered to himself. "Are you?" He wrapped me in his arms. "You're pregnant!"

I nodded, beaming. He lifted me carefully into the air, twirling me around. Eli got jealous and pulled at his jeans, he picked her up, holding us both closely to him. "You're going to be the best big sister!" He told her, kissing her cheek. Then he looked to me, "And you're already the best mom in the world."

Nine months later

"Sir! Please put her in the wheelchair."

Aiden shook his head to the nurse, refusing to set me down. "No. Where is the room? I'll carry her."

Nurses fluttered around us as Aiden refused to let me go, carrying me from the car to the delivery room. Mom and Howard had Eli for the night.

Aiden looked at me with wide eyes as the contractions got stronger, the epidural didn't work. "You've got this, baby." His hands rubbed my hair in a calming manner.

Tears streaked my face. "It hurts, A."

His eyes cut to the nurse, "Can you hurry the fuck up? She's in pain." He sneered. When he turned back to me, his demeanor softened.

The nurse gave Aiden a frightened smile, I placed my hand on his face. "It's okay."

The doctor got in between my legs, and then the room went into a frenzy. "Ready to push?" She asked, I nodded in confusion, everything was happening so quickly.

I began to push, for what felt like days. Squeezing Aiden's hand for strength and pushing with all my might.

"There we go." The doctor said, but me and Aiden were too afraid to look. We kept our eyes on each other.

Then, the most magical sound wrapped around the room, our baby's cry. "Our boy." I cried as the nurse placed him on my chest. His tiny fingers and toes wiggled about as he took in his first sights and sounds. I looked to Aiden, tears streaking his face. "He's beautiful." He said, running a gentle thumb along the tip of his nose.

We spent some time with our new baby, playing with his black hair and counting his toes. The next day, our families practically busted through the door when they allowed visitors.

Eli dragged my mother by her hand, she had been talking nonstop about her new little brother. The second her eyes landed on him, she sighed. "He is the cutest!" she squealed, calmly touching his cheek with her palm. The room was so crowded, but full of love. The doctors tried to only let a few in at a time, but Ashley wasn't having it.

Mom and Howard gushed over the new addition to the family. "What are you naming him?" Ashley asked, her slender arms wrapped around Ricky's waist as she looked at our baby.

Me and Aiden looked to Leo, "Patrick Dean Scott."

Leo whirled and picked baby Patrick up, Aiden grunted from the fast movement, but I patted his hair. "He won't break him, baby."

And so we lived, with our two beautiful children as the years passed.

Four years later

"We have one-night child free, Mrs. Scott. You better close this damn store before I do. It's already Eleven!" Aiden winked at me, flipping the sign on the bakery door to 'Closed'. No one had come in for hours, but I was busy preparing for Pat's Fourth birthday party that was the following day.

I bit my lip, "Okay, okay." I followed him out to the Challenger, it hummed to life as he turned the key. I looked to the midnight sky as we headed towards an unfamiliar, wooded area. "Where are you taking me?"

A devilish smile took up his whole face. "The backseat."

Little did we know, we were about to have a third child.

Eight Years Later

Aiden

I sat with my brides' hand tangled in mine, seventeen years of marriage. I was in my forties. Emilia, in her thirties. Raising three children… eight, twelve, and eighteen. But every time Emilia walked into a room, I couldn't help but admire her.

I didn't think it was possible but my love for her had grown deeper with each year. Emilia was always in her Bakery and Eliana helped her every day.

"Dad! I'm Eighteen and a senior!" she cried, "It's just Prom!"

I nodded, smiling at her dramatics. "Yes, a prom that your mother and I will be attending with you." I can't wait to embarrass her.

She threw her head back, "Justin won't dance with me if you're there! He's scared of you!" She planted her hands on her hips.

"I can't help that he's scared of me." I feigned innocence. "I haven't done anything wrong."

Emilia stifled a laugh beside me, "That poor boy came here to ask if he could take her on a date, and you threatened to murder him, Aiden.

He's harmless, babe."

Pat walked in, at only twelve he towered over his mother and sister. "I'll go dad."

Rose walked in, dancing through the living room. "Dad! If Eli gets to have a boyfriend, I want one too!" I buried my face in my hands.

I think I'm being tortured for all the horrible things I've done in my life. Two beautiful daughters, and a gorgeous wife.

Ten Years Later

Emilia

The sand burned my feet as we made our way towards the ocean.

Every few years we took a huge trip, surrounded by everyone we loved.

"Blake, you need sunscreen!" Ashley screamed at her youngest as he dove into the water. At nineteen, he had already broken multiple bones from his wild antics.

"Babe, it's cool." Ricky ran past her, diving in behind Blake.

I snickered at Ash as she slumped next to me, rolling her eyes. "They're going to be the death of me." The boys played rough, throwing each other into the waves. I looked to her granddaughter as she made sandcastles with Howard.

"It's a surprise he made such a calm child." I said, watching as Marissa gently patted the sand. Ashley nodded in agreement.

Aiden made his way towards us. His skin glistened in the sun, mesmerizing me. Even with his hair becoming more salt than pepper, I never could take my gaze away from him.

"Hey beautiful." He dipped down to kiss me before rushing towards Ricky and Blake.

Mom brought us fresh cut pineapple; her movements slowed with age. Her silver hair glistened from the bright Bahamian sun. "Where's Leo?"

I looked around the beach, trying to find him and Zoe. "There!" I pointed to where they stood at the edge of the water, their first grandchild was just learning how to walk. They held her hands as she dunked her tiny toes in the water.

I looked back to my family as they played in the gleaming ocean. Even though our children had grown, and some have started families of their own, we always spent time together.

"Babe! Get in!" Aiden yelled, I dipped into the water to join them. Laughing when Rose splashed me, and Pat yelled at her for doing so.

We made the most of our lives, enjoying every moment together.

Many, many blissful years later.

Soft music played throughout our kitchen, Aiden twirled me around the island, his smile lines prominent from years of crooked grins. With a final spin, he brought me close to his broad chest.

The music danced around us as I searched his emerald eyes. Even after all this time, I still get lost in them. His eyes that have experienced fifty years of marriage with me, and children, and all the highs and lows that come with sharing a life together.

But we persevered, even as the world was trying to rip us apart, we never strayed, and we never lost sight of what was important. Us.

Lost in our own world, we tried to zone out the excited screams of our seven beautiful grandchildren as they ran through our moving legs. We didn't mind, as their laughter was better than any song we could have chosen.

Aiden leaned in close, his lips brushed my cheek while his silver hair tickled my skin.

"We will always be slow dancing while they scream, my Emilia."

The End

Acknowledgements

We're here at the end of The Emden Series, and I have so many of you to Thank. I never imagined this story would touch so many people. Aiden and Emilia were a pleasure to write about and I give my endless gratitude to everyone who reads their story.

To my family, who supports me in everything I do. I love you.

My husband, for not sending me to an institution when I made people up in my head and began to write two books about them.

To Jessica Scott, at UniquelyTailored, for her always impressive cover design skills!

Thank you to my editor, Cheryl Lim, for helping with the series.

My Emden Family, Wattpaders, my ever-fabulous Group Chat, friends, and anyone else who made this happen, Thank you.

Printed in Great Britain
by Amazon